Splintered

AN UNLUCKY 13 NOVEL

ISABEL LUCERO

Cover Design: Rebel Ink Co.
Interior Formatting: Isabel Lucero
Editing: Cruel Ink Editing & Design

Blurb

Welcome to Black Diamond Resort and Spa—the best place to go when all you want to do is disappear and not have anyone expect anything of you.

Overwhelmed with work and feeling like I'm being pulled in multiple directions at once, I crave the serenity a private island holds for me. As a very recognizable figure in the adult film industry, I'm used to shelling out parts of myself for the sake of others. Everyone wants more pictures, videos, and more of my time and energy. Though I've created an empire that has made me lots of money in a business I enjoy, I still desire a break.

Sandy beaches, fruity drinks, and turquoise waters are all I expected from this trip. I definitely didn't anticipate running into my high school crush—the jock that never once looked at me the way I wanted him to.

Jarrod Bivens is now the star goalie of the San Jose Bobcats, and the person half the world is blaming for his team losing in the playoffs. Clearly here for his own escape, our chance encounter ignites an instant friendship. With each day on the island, I realize my crush is far from gone, but Jarrod's known for only dating Hollywood starlets, so he's obviously straight. Maybe those lingering gazes and small touches are all in my head.

But one day, something interesting arises between us—a moment I couldn't have prepared myself for. Our mounting tension finally snaps, but little did I know it was only the beginning of a rollercoaster ride of emotions. Our chemistry is undeniable, but the real world awaits, and life off the island is bound to be much different. How can two people from completely different worlds ever make it work?

To the other twelve authors in this shared world, I feel lucky to have been on this journey with you. Thanks for everything!

Playlist

"Island In The Sun" by Weezer

"Can I Be Him" by James Arthur

"Fuck Up The Friendship" by Leah Kate

"It's Yours" by J. Holiday

"F.U.C.K." by Victoria Monét

"I Knew I Loved You" by Savage Garden

"How Will I Know" by Sam Smith

"Angel Baby" by Troye Sivan

"Pillowtalk" by Zayn

"I Don't Want to Miss a Thing" by Aerosmith

"Used To Be" by Lucky Daye

"Dat Ass" by Jacob Latimore

"I Have Nothing" by Whitney Houston

"Someone You Loved" by Lewis Capaldi
"Love In The Dark" by Leroy Sanchez
"It'll Be Okay" by Shawn Mendes
"Talking to the Moon" by Bruno Mars
"Make You Feel My Love" by Adele
"F It Up" by Tank
"Die For You" by The Weeknd
"Say You Won't Go" by James Arthur
"Lovesong" by Adele
"Dirty" by Tank
"Let's Stay Together" by Al Green
"Lights Go Out" by J. Holiday
"Back At One" by Brian McKnight
"At Last" by Etta James

Authors Note

Writing Splintered was the best time I've had writing in a long time. The words poured out of me and these characters came to life with such ease. I'm in love with these two. Their journey is one of my favorites, and I hope you enjoy them as well. Happy reading!

xoxo

Isabel

Welcome To Black Diamond Resort and Spa

Since our founding in 2001 by the Diamond family, we've strived to provide a unique experience to those who live in the public eye. Privacy and discretion is of the utmost importance to us so you won't find paparazzi or journalists looking for a juicy story on our shores, only the relaxing lapping of waves and delicious drinks.

Enjoy the all inclusive, private, resort built exclusively for the elite. From luxury villas to gorgeous white sand beaches, there's something here for everyone on the island. Water sports, hiking, massages, and 5 star gourmet meals will have you never wanting to leave.

So take a deep breath and let us handle the rest.

One

DEVIN

"What the hell are you gonna do out there by yourself?" my agent, Steve Burham asks, his voice booming through the phone.

"Whatever I want, Steve. That's the whole point."

"When are you coming back?"

I sigh. "I don't know yet. I bought a one-way ticket."

"We got movies to make, Devin."

"We have other actors besides myself, Steve. It's why I started my own production company and hired a bunch of people to help run it. I don't want to have to be there twenty-four seven."

"There's a lot of guys trying to get hired after you said you'd pay them nearly twice as much as most of the other companies. Don't you wanna be here to help in the process?"

"I trust my casting directors. Plus, Cara is the production manager, and she knows her job better than anyone. She'll handle it."

"Did you get the email from Sword Savor? Your dildo

launch was exceptional. A ton of sites were out of stock within hours."

"Yeah, I saw it," I reply, handing my plane ticket to the woman at the gate. "I'm about to get on the plane, so I'll talk to you when I'm back."

"You're not gonna have your phone on you the whole time?" he questions.

"I want to disconnect from the world. I don't want anyone calling or texting. I will check in when I'm ready. Bye, Steve."

"Devin, wait—"

I end the call and turn off the phone prior to sitting in my first class passenger seat. Before everyone is on the plane, I already have my earbuds in and eyes closed. I'm beyond ready for a vacation. I don't remember the last time I went somewhere that wasn't in some way related to business.

My first five years in the sex industry basically consisted of taking any job I could so I was able to pay rent and eat dinner. After a while, and thanks to internet sites like Twitter and OnlyFans, I was able to grow my fanbase. Once companies started noticing how popular I was becoming, I started getting more job offers and was able to request a higher paycheck.

I've been working almost non-stop since then, needing to become more successful—seeking the title of the most popular and highest paid porn star in the industry. It started with simply wanting to get more than five hundred dollars for a scene, then I wanted to get scenes with popular actors, after that I wanted to produce and direct. Once I accomplished those things, I needed my own production company so I could treat actors the way I wish I had been treated in my first several years.

Now I'm creating a line of sex toys, can pick and choose my scenes with whoever I want, and have more money than I ever thought possible in this industry. However, I've recently started to feel like I've lost myself—like I'm splintered into different pieces to try to make everyone happy: my agent, my business partners, my clients, my viewers, and my parents.

Granted, my parents have not been happy with me for over a decade, but I feel like they were my sole motivation to get to where I am. They doubted I'd be able to be successful in such a *dirty and trashy* industry. They were embarrassed, and I wanted to prove to them I could be rich and famous in my own right.

As the son of Hollywood icons, Sofía De'León and William Davis, both of my parents wanted and expected me to take after them. They were huge advocates of nepotism, forcing me into commercials as a toddler and small roles in their films. As I got older, they wanted to introduce me to a friend of a friend for a modeling casting call, or promised I'd be a shoo-in for a role in a TV series.

It's not that I wasn't interested in being an actor, but when you have two people forcing you into it from a young age, it's no longer this lofty dream. It's work in an ugly, cutthroat business. It's spreading rumors about someone going against you for a role in order to secure it for yourself. It's not an easy industry to make friends in, and when you're young, all you want is for people to like you.

So, when I was eighteen, after a huge fight with my dad about not wanting to audition for a role in his film, I blurted out that I would rather do porn. That eventually turned into my reality, and when I moved out, I was cut off from their millions and forced to find a way on my own. That's what ultimately led to my workaholic personality and finding a business in which I could trick myself into thinking everyone I slept with actually liked me.

I'm successful now. The highest paid actor in porn sitting on an empire that will continue to make me money for years to come, and yet, I'm still not happy.

I'm taking this vacation for a sense of tranquility. I want to be completely selfish here and do what makes me happy without worrying about others.

I pull a blanket up to my chin and fall asleep, ready to be on a bright, sunny island where nobody should care about who I am or what I do.

"WELCOME to Black Diamond Resort and Spa," the man tells me as I approach the reception desk.

He's fairly young, his skin bronze from being out in this tropical weather all the time. His hair is sandy blond and his eyes are as blue as the ocean. I read his nametag.

"Thanks, Tyler."

Typing on his keyboard, he says, "I have you staying here for the rest of June, is that correct?"

"As of now."

He nods, a gracious smile on his lips. "Okay, we have you set up in bungalow six, and one of our employees will drive you out there." He hands me a folder. "This has everything you may need. There's a map of the island, a list of restaurants and activities available to you, and the phone numbers to the cleaning and butler staff if you need anything. Your room has a keyless entry. There's a bracelet that will unlock the door for you, as well as many facilities here at the resort like the gym and business center. Is this your first time, sir?"

I nod. "Yeah."

"Well, the Black Diamond Resort and Spa is split into two sections. You're here, on the resort side, but there is a rehab on the other side of the mountain. You should have no need to go over there, but if you're exploring the jungle, you may find yourself amongst new staff and guests. They have rules and curfews, so it's best to not go too far."

"I don't think I'll find myself in the jungle," I say with a laugh.

"There are some beautiful waterfalls, sir," he says with a smile. "Could be a nice place to relax."

I dip my chin. "I'll keep that in mind."

"I'm going to have Matteo drive you to your bungalow," he says, gesturing to a man in a white shirt and khaki pants who's standing near the door. "Please let us know if you need anything, and enjoy your stay."

"Thank you," I reply with a nod, hiking my backpack higher on my shoulder.

"Bungalow six, sir?" Matteo questions, though he obviously knows.

"Yes. Are my bags here yet?"

"We've already taken them to your room, sir."

"Oh. Thank you."

"Of course," he says, walking toward a golf cart.

I slip into the back as he drives us away from the main building, passing a large pool, other guests, and many, many trees. When he stops, we're in front of a long pier that travels out over the crystalline water where bungalows spread out on both sides, seemingly floating over the water.

When I look to my left and right, I notice there are a few more piers with the same setup.

"Are all of these occupied?" I ask as we begin our walk along the pier.

"No, sir. Out of the twelve on this pier, I believe only eight are currently occupied. That's not to say that won't change."

Even with my sunglasses on, I squint as I look out into the water, noticing some people on kayaks and others on paddle boards.

"Where do we go to rent a kayak?" I ask.

"You can call us and we can have one delivered to you, sir. Otherwise, the water sport equipment is farther down the beach."

"Okay."

We turn right, where the pier veers off to lead to a bungalow. "Here you are, sir," Matteo says, gesturing at the door. "The bracelet in the folder will open it up. Do you need anything else before I leave you?"

"Uh, no. I think I'm good. Thanks," I say, pulling the band from the folder.

"You're welcome. Enjoy your stay."

When I walk inside, I look through every room. It's even more beautiful than the photos online. I knew to expect opulence with the price tag that comes along with a private island stay in bungalows that sit over the Caribbean, but seeing it in person is incredible.

The king-sized bed looks out over the water and back

patio, and the kitchen is stocked with full-sized liquor bottles, juices, water, and other mixers. On the small dining table is a bowl of fruit and a basket full of bagged snacks like pretzels, muffins, and chips.

When I cross in front of the bed, I walk over a rectangular piece of glass floor, and find myself watching fish swim below me. My luggage is inside the walk-in closet where there's a robe, slippers, and extra towels and blankets.

The bathroom is incredible, with a large soaking tub standing right in front of sliding doors that will open up to the back veranda. From the inside shower, you can also step right outside to an outdoor shower. There's a small privacy wall, blocking anyone from being able to see me while I'm outside.

There's patio furniture, a private pool, a day bed under the palapa, and a few steps that descend to a lower platform with a couple of chairs.

Once I've taken it all in, I go back inside and flop onto the bed. I pull my phone out of my pocket, ready to power it on and see how many messages I have already.

As soon as it lights up, the notifications pour in. I've only been out of touch for eleven hours and Steve has left two voicemails and sent five texts. My business partner, Sayid, has sent an email about an upcoming movie we'll be producing. A handful of messages come from other actors I've been working with lately who are inquiring about job opportunities, and the company that made and sold the dildo created from a mold of my own cock is now interested in selling a mouth stroker.

I reply to what's necessary before shutting it down again and reaching for the remote on the nightstand. When I turn on the flatscreen that's hoisted on the wall to the left of the bed, it's already on a sports channel.

I'm not much of a sports guy. I know the names of some popular teams, but I don't regularly watch any of it. However, there's a familiar face on the screen, so I leave it on and turn the volume up.

"Bivens is definitely hanging his head after that crushing miss. The Bobcats, up the whole game with the finals in their sight, and all Bivens had to do was keep the Panthers from making a goal. And what did he do, Bob? He gave up two back-to-back! My god, that's gonna hurt for a while."

I watch as they replay the scene over and over, and then again in slow motion. I know we all have failures and make mistakes, but I couldn't imagine mine being broadcast over the TV like this, with commentators making you feel even worse.

It's been years since I've spoken to Jarrod Bivens. Last I saw him, we were in the uppity private school our parents put us in. High school was over ten years ago, and yet some of those memories are still so vivid.

Like the color of the convertible he was so happy about —cherry red.

The purple backpack he wore each year.

His eyes, the most unique set I've ever seen. He has Sectoral Heterochromia, so one of his eyes is this beautiful dark blue on the outer edge, melding into an aquamarine color, while his other eye is split down the middle, half brown while the other half has the same blue mix.

"I like your eyes," I remember telling him one day.

"Oh yeah? What else do you like about me?"

He was joking, but I always regretted never answering.

We were hardly friends, mostly associates. We didn't run in the same circles, but we had classes together. He was my first crush—first love, probably. Unrequited and mostly puppy love, but still. He blew open my world in a way he'll never know, and I was simply a guy who helped him pass his classes.

Now look at us. A porn star and a pro hockey player. We definitely don't run in the same circles now.

Two

JARROD

"Here you are, sir. Bungalow eight. Your belongings have been placed in your room already. Please let us know if you need anything. I hope you enjoy your stay."

I nod at the man who brought me to my temporary residence and close the door behind me when I step in.

After looking through the rooms, I grab a bottle of water from the fridge and immediately go out onto the veranda. I find a large outdoor storage container with snorkeling equipment inside, and a cooler sat next to a hammock made from what looks like a catamaran net.

This is exactly what I need. A tropical paradise on a private island away from any sort of ice, and hopefully away from anyone who knows anything about hockey.

My phone dings with a text notification, so I pull it out of the pocket of my shorts and stretch along the outdoor couch. It's from my older sister, Gina.

> Hey, just wanted to make sure you landed safely.

> I'm safe. Just hanging outside. You've got to see this view.

> Then FaceTime me.

She appears on the screen after a single ring. "How ya doing?"

"I'm good. Let me flip the camera."

I sit up on the couch and slowly pan the phone around.

"Is that an outdoor shower?"

"Yep. Also, there's a little floating thing attached to steps that take you to the water. So I can float in place," I say with a chuckle.

"The water looks amazing."

"Yeah. I can't wait to jump in later. Did you see the pool?"

"Why do you need a pool if you're surrounded by water?"

I shrug. "I don't know. Cleaner? No fish?"

She laughs. "Well, it looks really peaceful."

"That's what I'm looking for." I lie back down on the couch and switch the camera back to front-facing. "How's my niece and nephew?"

"They're fine. Crazy as ever. CeCe thinks she's a dinosaur and Connor is scared of her."

I bark out a laugh. "Gotta love toddlers."

"When are you gonna come visit?"

"Maybe after I leave here. I can catch a flight to Chicago before I go back to California."

"Well, we'd love to see you. You talk to Mom and Dad?"

"I spoke to them before I left."

She nods, chewing on her lip. I know she's wanting to say something, but she's doing her best to keep it inside.

"Just say it, G. I know you got some words fighting to get out."

"I don't want you blaming yourself, J. It's a team sport, and just because you're the goalie doesn't mean it's solely your fault. You had an amazing season, and you're still one of the best goaltenders in the NHL. Don't let this get to you too much, okay?"

I sigh. "Thank you. I just needed a getaway, you know?"

"I hope you have the best time. I'm jealous. I'll be in the office seeing patients tomorrow while you're skinny dipping in water that belongs on a postcard."

"Skinny dipping isn't a bad idea. It's pretty private over here."

She cringes. "Please. Have you heard of the penis fish? They can swim up the urethra and—"

"Okay, that's enough," I say, holding up my hand. "I'm pretty sure that's somewhere else, though."

"I'm just saying."

"Well, I'll do my skinny dipping in the pool."

"Good idea. I gotta go. I think Connor's crying."

"Okay. Love you."

"Love you more."

My stomach rumbles with hunger, so I push myself up and walk through the bungalow, exiting through the front door and walking down the pier.

I see a couple disappear into one of the bungalows, hand-in-hand and laughing. They're probably on their honeymoon. At another, there's a man pacing outside his door, looking completely stressed, and on the other side, I see a man wearing a black and white striped tank top and white shorts walk out of his place. I quicken my steps so we don't end up having to walk side-by-side all the way down the pier.

After about five minutes of strolling on a path that cuts through lush greenery and towering trees, I glance behind me and spot the guy in the tank top several yards back. He's got on a pair of sunglasses, his profile visible as he looks out to the left.

A spark of familiarity hits me, but I'm not sure why.

Another few minutes go by before I reach the main building. Inside, I wander around, avoiding what I think are curious gazes. I know a lot of people who come here are celebrities in their own right, or very wealthy, but that doesn't mean they can't be fans of other celebrities. Hell, I heard the drummer from Wicked Hearts was sent to the rehab side of this island last month, and if I saw him, I'd probably have a hard time not staring, too.

Doesn't help that my face has been plastered all over the TV the last couple of days, my failures on repeat for everyone to discuss and critique. So when I see a couple guys doing double takes in my direction, I make a sharp turn and exit the building.

I end up finding a restaurant that overlooks one of the resort's infinity pools. After being seated, I place my order and then get up to go to the salad bar. Once I've loaded up two plates with both salad and fruit, I head back to my table and wait for my burger to be brought out.

My eyes track the guests milling about below, wondering who all might be out here—actors, singers, other athletes.

After I polish off my salad, I push the plate to the other

side of the table and start on the fruit. The tank top guy strolls in, grabbing my attention. There's a handful of guests eating here, but there's something about this one that has everyone turning their heads.

A woman guides him to a seat several tables away and diagonally from my own, and I watch as he brings the menu up to his face. Something about him has me frozen in place, my gaze unable to look away. I know I know him from somewhere. Is he a model? Have I seen him on billboards or something?

Everything about him screams *model*. He's tall and lithe and moves with ease and comfortability.

Once the waitress brings me my food, I put all my focus on eating, not having had anything to eat on the trip over. When I'm done, I drink another glass of water and study the view. Movement gets my attention, so my eyes flicker over and spot the guy from earlier returning to his seat from the salad bar.

I watch as he pushes the glasses from his face to rest on his head, and almost like it's in slow motion, his eyes lift and meet mine. It doesn't happen instantly. I'm still trying to figure out where I know him from when his brows dip in the middle. His eyes widen and he cocks his head slightly, and I realize *he* recognizes *me*.

He mouths my name. I can't even hear it, but I know he says my name. Just my first name. Not both like people do with celebrities.

And all of a sudden, it hits me. I don't know him as a celebrity. I know him because we went to school together.

"Devin?"

Three

DEVIN

"Jarrod."

His name leaves my mouth in the faintest whisper. I just left my room and saw his face on my television and now he's here, staring at me like he's trying to remember who I am.

He's remained such a memorable figure in my life, and yet, I'm hardly recognizable to him.

When I realize my lips are parted, I close my mouth and shift in my seat, looking down at my food.

I hear his chair scrape along the floor, and without lifting my head, I know he's on his way over. It isn't until he's at my table that I allow my eyes to flicker up.

"Devin."

He declares my name like he's reminding me of who I am. It's not a question on his lips. He remembers, even if it took him a minute.

I smile at him. "Jarrod."

"Come on, man." His voice is boisterous as he outstretches his thick arms like he wants to hug me.

Standing up, I give him one of those weird hugs where you only wrap your arms around the tops of their shoulders without allowing the rest of your body to touch.

"Wow. I didn't expect to see you here," I say, taking my seat.

He sits in the chair across from me, his face alight with joy.

"Yeah, I bet. Holy crap. How long has it been?"

I pick up my fork and stab at some lettuce. "Well, high school was about eleven years ago."

"Damn. Don't make me feel old."

I laugh, my old teenage nerves coming back.

In school, anytime I was around Jarrod, my stomach was in knots. I knew I was gay then but nobody else did. Well, they might have guessed, but I never came out. I kept crushes a secret and didn't even think about having relationships. I went along with the crowd and avoided dating questions if possible. Jarrod was my first crush. I saw him and had never felt such attraction. It was him who really sealed the deal on my sexuality. I was questioning leading up to high school, and then there he was and I was done for.

He was the complete opposite of me. Where I was thin, he was wide with muscles. Though I had abs, simply for having almost no body fat and being a teenager, Jarrod, in my eyes, looked like a grown man. You could tell he'd been an athlete his whole life. His muscles were full and round. He's at least five inches taller than me, and where my hair is dark brown, his is very light with almost blond coloring naturally streaked throughout.

"You look good, man. What've you been up to?" he questions.

I don't allow the compliment to do anything to me, or at least, I only allow myself to focus on it for a couple seconds.

"Not much," I reply. "Just working all the time and now I'm finally trying to relax."

He nods and doesn't question what it is that I do. "I definitely understand."

"And you?" I ask, finally taking a bite of my salad.

I don't want to bring up the fact that I know he's a hockey player, especially since I'm sure he's not really wanting to talk about what just happened a few days ago.

"Just trying to live the life, you know?" he says after a few long seconds.

I nod along, chewing my food. "How long are you out here for?"

He looks to the side, checking out the view. "Well, it's gonna be hard to leave, that's for sure. I don't have anywhere to be until August."

I sputter out a laugh. "That's quite a while. Are you staying that long?"

Jarrod's eyes are back on me again, his grin widening. "I wish, but I don't know for sure. Just playing it by ear. A few weeks would be nice. What about you?"

"Hopefully the remainder of June if I can get away with it."

His brows raise slightly. We're both aware of the cost of this place, so he has to be wondering what I do to afford it. When we were teenagers we went to a school that most celebrities, politicians, and the extremely wealthy sent their kids. Maybe he assumes I'm here on Mom and Dad's dime. I know his dad owned a huge tech company, and I'm sure he still does.

"Where do you live now?" he asks.

"I'm still in the LA area, just a different part. You?

"San José."

"Ah. So, a good six or seven hours away."

"Something like that." He stares at me for a few seconds, his lips curled into a crooked grin. "And now we're here. What a small world."

I raise my brows, nodding my head as I dig around in my salad. "Indeed."

"So, catch me up. What's been going on? You married? Dating? Kids? Divorced?"

I put down my fork and bring a napkin to my lips. "If I was married and had kids and was spending a month out here, I'd say that wouldn't be the best look."

He chuckles. "Oh, right. I guess not."

"I'm not, nor have I ever been, married. No kids either."

"Same. Well, I date around, I guess. Nothing serious. Never even been close to thinking about marriage," he says, rubbing his knee.

The sun begins to go down, shining directly in my face, so I bring my glasses back over my eyes. "I'd like to get married one day, but..." I trail off, unwilling to say, *but I'll probably never find anyone who'd be okay with me doing porn.* "I don't know. We'll see."

He's quiet for a bit. "Did you get into modeling?"

My lips quirk. "You think I could be a model?"

"Well, I kind of remember you saying your parents wanted you to, and you look like...I mean, you know, models in LA are these pretty guys that are in shape but not very big..." His eyes go wide. "Wait, no. I don't mean that like... you know. I don't mean in a bad way. You just look like maybe you could be a model."

He's flustered, his cheeks turning pink, and it makes my smile grow wider until I'm laughing.

"It's fine. I get what you're saying."

Jarrod exhales, shaking his head. "I really didn't mean any offense."

"Offense?" I question. "You said I'm pretty and in shape. That's a compliment."

He has another crooked smile, his face still flushed. "I might be offended if someone called me small," he says with a shrug.

I bark out a laugh. "Nobody could mistake you for small." I'm thankful for the dark shades, because now he can't see my eyes perusing his wide shoulders and full biceps. "They'd be saying that simply to get a rise out of you."

Jarrod shrugs and looks away before focusing on my salad. "I'm sorry I interrupted your meal." He stands. "I can let you eat. Umm, I think we're staying near each other," he says, gesturing with his thumb. "The over-the-water bungalows?"

"Oh. Yeah," I say with a nod, looking up at him.

"I didn't realize it was you, but I saw you leave your place when I was walking down."

"So, I guess we'll see each other fairly often," I say with a smile.

"Yeah. I should give you my number. You can text if you want to get a drink or something. I know you probably came out here for peace, and I won't harass you too much, but it may be nice to have someone to talk to every once in a while."

"Well, if I remember anything about you, Jarrod, you were quite the friendly extrovert. I'm sure you'll make friends with two people before you even get back to your room," I say.

His grin falters just slightly before he forces it again. "That's true. I was always very talkative with everyone."

It's then that I realize his circumstances have changed. He's a celebrity now. He probably doesn't want to talk to just anybody.

"I left my phone in my room," I say. "Trying not to check it too much, you know? I can give you my number though."

He pulls his cell from his pocket and unlocks it. When I take it, it's already got a new message screen up. I type in my number and send a palm tree emoji as a text.

Jarrod looks at it and grins. "Cool. Thanks. I'll hit you up later or something. Maybe tomorrow? I don't know."

I chuckle. "Whenever is fine."

He puts his large hand on my shoulder. "It's really nice seeing you again, man."

With a smile and nod, I say, "You too."

I watch as he walks back to his table, tucks some cash beneath the plate, and saunters out of the restaurant, disappearing down the stairs that lead to the ground level.

For the rest of my meal, a small smile never fully leaves my lips.

Four

JARROD

I still can't believe I called him small and pretty. What kind of shit is that to say to someone you haven't seen in over a decade? Or at all?

Devin and I were hardly best friends, but we got along fine. We had some classes together, and I'm pretty sure I would've failed a couple of them if it wasn't for his help. But we didn't hang out outside of school, so anything I knew about the guy was fairly surface level. I always liked him, though. He was quiet, nice, and kind of kept to himself. He seems pretty much the same now.

I had a huge crush on his mom, and not even because I ever saw her, because I can't remember seeing either of his parents almost at all. But because when he told me who his parents were one day, I looked them both up. His mom was basically the Spanish version of Marilyn Monroe. A bombshell. An icon. She was *thee* name in the seventies and eighties. She was photographed all over the place, her olive skin and long, dark hair always flawless, her perfect teeth visible to every camera that ever captured a photo. And she was a phenomenal actress to boot. At the time I looked, she had countless awards.

Based on my nosy internet sleuthing as a teenager, I knew she had Devin in her early forties, because I read an article at the time that wondered if she'd still be considered a bombshell after having a kid. She definitely was.

Devin's father was just as well-known as Sofía, starring in serious dramas and action movies. Pretty sure he was voted *Sexiest Man Alive* at some point.

A lot of their stuff was before my time, but they have some films that remain classics that people always talk about. I think while Devin was in school, both parents were away filming movies, because I remember him mentioning having the house to himself for a while. His dad was nominated for an Oscar soon after, but I only ever found out through school gossip or my parents. Devin never really talked about their accomplishments.

My nosiness gets the best of me once more, and I look up his parents again. Apparently, his mom continued having big roles into her fifties and early sixties before she focused on TV roles. Her last movie was a couple of years ago, but she's seventy-one now, so I guess it makes sense to want to slow down.

His Dad is seventy-two, though, and just wrapped on some big movie set to come out next year. It's being directed by Richard Davies, whose success rivals Steven Spielberg and James Cameron. But, everything I see about them never really mentions their son. They've been on red carpets alone, and articles mention having a son together, but they never go into detail. And now I'm curious.

I type in Devin's name and wait for something to appear. Who knew there would be so many Devin De'Leóns. A journalist, a gamer, a business manager. Before I can go to click on the images, my phone rings.

"Hello?"

"Hey, what's up?" my teammate and best friend, Cory, asks me.

"Nothing. Internet stalking people."

He laughs. "Nice. Who are we stalking?"

"I ran into this guy I went to school with. His parents are Sofía De'León and William Davis."

"Oh damn. I just watched one of his dad's movies last night. This old one from the early nineties."

"Yeah. They're pretty popular."

"What's he do?"

"I don't know. That's why I was stalking."

He laughs. "Why didn't you ask?"

"I didn't want him to ask what I do."

"He didn't know?"

I sigh. "I don't think so, but I didn't wanna bring it up. What kind of asshole would I be? *Hey, so you know who I am, right? I'm in the NHL. I just lost the chance at winning the fucking championship.* Pft."

"Dude, stop worrying about it," Cory says with a sigh. "We don't blame you."

"*You* don't."

"We can try again next season."

"I'm just being a baby about it. Let me mope, get my vacation on, then I'll come back with a winning attitude, okay?"

"Fine," he says with a chuckle. "I'll text later."

"Cool."

When I end the call, I get up to take a shower, thinking I'll at least head to the bar for a drink before I come back and sleep for at least twelve hours.

Once I'm dressed in a pair of khaki slacks and a light blue Polo shirt, I let my fingers hover over the keyboard for a minute, trying to decide if I should invite Devin.

I don't want to be annoying, but it would be nice to have someone fairly familiar around to talk to.

Deciding against it last minute, I shove my phone in my pocket and head out. It takes several minutes to get to the Midnight Lounge bar. I walk up one of the two piers that lead to the circular bar surrounded by lights.

"Can I get a Jack and Coke?" I ask the bartender whose name tag reads *Holden*.

"Sure thing."

I spin around and look out over the water while I wait.

"Well, looks like you didn't want to have a drink with me after all."

I turn back and find Devin standing there looking...well, not what I'm used to.

He's got on a long-sleeved black shirt, but it's sheer and the V-cut is low. It's not tight, hanging sort of loose around his torso, but the hem is tucked into black slacks. It's definitely sort of beachy, but like he's going on a date at the beach.

"Wow. Hot date?" I say without thinking.

His brow arches, amusement flashing in his eyes. "Nope."

"I *was* going to text you."

"Uh-huh. Sure," he says with a grin, leaning against the

bar. "Tequila Sunrise, please," he tells the bartender as he places my drink down.

I watch Holden openly check Devin out. "What about Sex on the Beach?"

Devin's gaze slides to Holden, his eyes traveling up the bartender's tall frame before he gives him a smirk. "I prefer tequila over vodka."

"I can give it to you any way you like, doll," he says, leaning on the bar, his blond hair falling over his forehead.

My mouth drops and my gaze flitters between the two of them, wondering if I should step in. Is Devin uncomfortable with this? Isn't this unprofessional? He's an employee and he's hitting on a guest.

Devin leans closer, his arms folded on the bar top. "Oh, Holden." Holden gives him a smug grin, feeling entirely too sure of himself. "You have no idea what you're trying to get yourself into. You're not ready for me, okay? The Tequila Sunrise will do."

Holden looks surprised, slow to straighten up before getting to his job. Devin turns to me and shakes his head, a smile on his lips. Looks like he can handle himself.

Five

DEVIN

"That was pretty forward of him," Jarrod says when we get to our two-seater table.

"You don't get hit on by bartenders?"

He makes a face like he's thinking back to every time he's been to a bar. "I mean, I guess a few have been flirty, but I thought it was just part of the job. He was basically asking to sleep with you."

I laugh and grab my glass. "It's not the first time and probably won't be the last. He's innocent. There's some people that are pretty pushy and aggressive about things."

"But what about him assuming you're...gay or into guys at all?"

With the straw between my lips, I suck down some of my drink while maintaining eye contact with him.

After placing it back on the table, I sit back in my chair. "Well, I am gay."

He jolts just slightly, clearly surprised, but he quickly

relaxes his face. "Oh. Well..." he trails off, not sure what else to say.

"Yep, just another pretty gay boy in LA who is kind of in shape."

He gives me a look. "I didn't say *kind of*."

I laugh. "I'm teasing."

Jarrod shakes his head with a chuckle. "Anyway, guess I won't live that down."

"I'll try not to bring it up again."

He rolls his eyes and takes a drink. "So, I have a confession."

"Oh?" My pulse spikes slightly, but then I remember he couldn't have found out about the porn or he'd definitely know I was gay.

"I looked up your parents earlier. Just out of curiosity."

I laugh, probably a little nervously. "Oh yeah? What're Mom and Dad up to these days?"

He looks confused for a second. "Well, your dad's next movie is coming out next year."

I nod, taking another long sip. "Right."

"Do you talk to them regularly?"

"Not really. We had a falling out a long time ago."

"Oh." He tilts his head slightly. "I'm sorry. Is it because..." He doesn't finish, but he doesn't have to.

"Because I'm gay? No," I say with a shake of my head.

I don't offer any more information, so after a few seconds, he says, "I always wondered why you took your mom's last name and not your dad's."

With a laugh, I say, "Mom refused to take his name when they were married. I've heard her say many times that there's no reason a woman should have to give up her name and take her husband's. That she's not his property. So, since she never had his last name, when they had me, she wanted me to have hers. I don't think Dad fought her on it."

Jarrod nods. "I suppose it is very patriarchal." After a breath he says, "Okay, enough about family."

"Sounds good. Can I confess something to you?"

"Only if it's juicy."

I bite into my lip. "Now I'm not sure I want to. Your hopes are up."

"Come on. You have to."

"I take it back. I don't have a confession."

"Liar."

I suck down the rest of my drink. "I need a refill."

"I'm coming with you," he says, standing up and finishing his in one gulp.

"I'm still not saying anything."

"I'm just here to protect you from the overly flirty bartender."

"What if I want him to flirt with me?"

He looks at me. "Do you? Because I can be a great wingman."

"Really?"

"What? Is it different for gay men? I'm the best wingman. You can ask my buddies."

I laugh. "It's probably not any different, but I'll pass. He's not really my type."

"No? What's your type?"

I swallow, placing my empty glass on the bar. "Uh." I don't know what to say, because the truth of the matter is, Jarrod's my type. If I say masculine guys, athletic guys, tall guys, opposite of me guys, I'm going to be describing him. I don't want to make it awkward. "I'm not sure."

"Who knew you were such a liar?" he says with a wide grin.

Holden appears. "Back for more?" His brows wiggle suggestively.

Jarrod flattens his lips briefly. "We are. Can we get another Tequila Sunrise, Jack and Coke, and two shots of tequila."

I raise my brows at him and he shrugs.

"Sure, big guy."

When Holden wanders away to make the drinks, Jarrod sidles up to my side. "I'm glad he's not your type, because it would be hard not to judge you."

I chuckle. "He's not bad looking."

"Just annoying."

I shake my head. "So, we're taking shots?"

"I'm trying to loosen you up," he says with a nudge. "Get some confessions out of you."

"You're not prepared for my secrets, Jarrod."

"Ooh. You're only making me more interested."

I sigh. "My type is like...you know," I gesture with my hand, searching for some random guy in the bar that might fit the bill. "Guys..."

He laughs. "Oh, really? Okay, do you have a picture of your ex?"

"Who keeps pictures of their exes?"

"I probably have some. I never delete photos."

He pulls his phone out and starts scrolling through his album. He puts the phone in front of me. "I was with her for like...two days."

I give him a look. "That long?"

"Shut up. Okay, then this one for maybe a few hookups."

"You like brunettes."

He shrugs. "I guess."

With a sigh, I pull my phone from my pocket and start going through it. "I might be able to find something. I may have to search for him on social media."

Holden appears with our drinks. "Here you go, guys."

Jarrod grabs them and puts them closer to us before passing him a fifty from his pocket. "Thanks."

I find an old photo Mike posted of us on his Instagram and just never deleted. "This is us."

Jarrod takes my phone and studies the picture. "Hmm."

"What? Are you judging me?"

"No. He's fine. Normal looking."

I laugh. "I'm glad you approve."

"Well, I didn't say that. He's probably an asshole, right?"

"Why do you say that?"

"You're not with him anymore."

"Maybe I'm the asshole."

His lips twist. "I doubt it."

"Let's take these shots," I say, reaching for my glass. "Wait, I need a lime. Holden," I call out.

"Yeah, doll?"

"Can we get some lime wedges, please?"

"Of course."

He grabs a bowl out of a fridge and brings it over. "Take as many as you like."

I take one and give it to Jarrod and then take another for myself. "Just the two. Thanks."

"What are we toasting to?" Jarrod asks.

"Reunions?"

"Okay, to reunions on a tropical island."

We clink our glasses together, and I bring mine to my lips, swallowing down the liquid.

I go to bring the lime to my mouth, but it slips out of my fingers and careens to the ground.

"Here," Jarrod says, putting his wedge to my lips.

Time slows down as I bite down on the acidic fruit, sucking some of the juice into my mouth while his fingers touch the corners of my lips.

I pull away. "You get the rest."

He puts the same wedge to his mouth and sucks, and I quickly grab my Tequila Sunrise and take a sip.

"Ready to confess now?"

Yeah, about my undying attraction. "It's really not a fun confession, and I feel kind of bad about it."

Jarrod grabs his glass. "It can't be that bad. Here, I'll go first."

"You have another confession?"

"Well, after searching up your parents, I typed your name in."

My eyes are frozen on him, my fingers holding the straw between my lips. "Mmhmm."

"I didn't get far, because my friend called and interrupted my stalking, but I was *about* to stalk you."

After a few seconds, I say, "Come on." I jerk my head back toward the tables, and once we sit back down, I let out a sigh. "I know you're in the NHL."

Jarrod's eyes bulge slightly. "Oh."

"Yeah. I didn't want to mention it, because I'm sure you're

here to *not* be a celebrity, but it started to feel like I was lying."

"No, no, it's fine."

"I've seen you on TV a few times. I don't really watch sports, but yeah, I knew."

"Well, at least I can stop feeling weird about not saying anything," he says with a light chuckle. "To be honest, it was nice to not have it be the first thing someone knows about you. You knew me as the extroverted jock in high school. And my season didn't end the best, so I was hoping to get away from anyone who knows anything about hockey."

I give him a smile. "Well, I don't know anything about hockey, so you're in luck."

He pauses for a few seconds. "Nothing? Not even a little?"

I laugh. "Now you seem offended."

"I mean, hockey is one of the greatest sports ever."

"Some people would say the same thing about football or baseball."

"Yeah, but they're wrong."

Another laugh emerges from my throat. "I know you hit a puck into a net and that's how you score."

His eyes crinkle in the corners when he grins. "Good job," he says in a voice you'd use for a toddler. He picks up his glass for another drink and then stares into my eyes. "Okay, now what do you do?"

Six

JARROD

Devin looks like a deer in headlights at the question, taking his time sucking down the Tequila Sunrise. After it's almost gone, he finally puts the glass on the table but keeps his hands wrapped around it.

"Well, I'm doing a lot of different projects now. I've directed and produced some films, and have some entrepreneurial businesses."

My eyebrows shoot up. "Oh, so you did get into the movie business? Anything I'd have seen?"

He shakes his head. "No, they're smaller, more independent films."

"Oh okay. That's cool, though."

He nods his head. "Yeah." After a few seconds, he says, "Want another drink?"

"Are you trying to get me wasted?" I tease, holding up my half full glass.

He laughs as he stands up. "I'd be drunk before you. You probably have fifty pounds on me."

"What are you trying to say?" I ask after a dramatic gasp.

"Oh stop," he says with a chuckle, taking a step away.

I get up to follow him. "I compliment you and you mention how much heavier I am than you? Doesn't seem fair," I say, giving him a hard time.

"It's not an insult. I like—"

He cuts himself off.

"You like what?"

Devin remains quiet as he rests his elbows on the bar. I move in next to him, waiting for his response.

He tries to act like he doesn't notice me, but I see his lips twitching to keep from smiling. Finally, his eyes meet mine.

"It wasn't meant as a bad thing. I prefer bigger guys." His cheeks redden as he looks away. "Not that I prefer you, but just in general, if I'm with a guy, I go for the burlier ones."

I laugh and put my arm around his shoulders. "Look who's flustered now. I guess we're even. You're pretty and small, and I'm big and burly. Which, I *will* take as a compliment, by the way."

His eyes slide to mine, and he tries to look annoyed, but I can tell he wants to laugh. "This was your way of getting me to compliment you? Pretend to be offended?"

"It worked. I'm probably sixty pounds heavier than you. I don't care." I remove my arm from his shoulders and mimic his pose as we wait for the bartender to come over.

"Sixty? I'm not *that* small."

"Maybe I'm that big," I say with a wink.

He swallows. "How much do you weigh?"

"That's a personal question, Devin," I say in a playful tone.

His lips purse. "Please. I could find a more personal question."

My eyebrow quirks before I answer. "I'm probably around 235 pounds or so. Just depends if it's off-season or not."

"Two hundred and thirty five pounds?" he asks with wide eyes.

"Hey, don't give me a complex," I say with my hand on my stomach. "I'm also six foot four and a half."

"Oh, don't forget the half." He laughs.

"It's important. Now you go."

"I'm probably around 175 pounds or something. I don't know. I don't weigh myself often."

"Damn, I was right. That's sixty pounds. See, I'm good."

He rolls his eyes. "It was a lucky guess."

"Hey, don't argue with me on this, man. I could crush you."

"*I* could bring you to your knees," he retorts, and then almost immediately spins to face me with wide eyes. "Not... okay, that may have come off a little inappropriate, and I don't want you to feel uncomfortable."

"I'm not uncomfortable. Do you mean by pressure points or something?"

He chuckles and turns away. "Yes, that's what I meant."

I bump him with my shoulder. "Such a liar."

"Shut up."

"You guys are cute," Holden says with a grin as he approaches us. "I didn't realize you were together or I wouldn't have been so obvious with my flirting."

Devin opens his mouth to say something, but I beat him to it.

"But you would've still flirted? Just not so brazenly."

Holden shrugs. "I'm a flirty guy. So, same thing?"

"I'll just get a bottled water," Devin says. "Thanks."

"What about you?" Holden asks me.

"I'm good."

After he brings Devin his water and disappears down the bar, Devin faces me. "Why'd you let him think we were together?"

My brows knit in confusion. "I didn't really think about it. Why would I care?"

"Maybe because you're a famous NHL player."

I pause for just a second and then I shrug. "He doesn't know that. At least I don't think he does, and I'm not gay, so it's not like the story would go anywhere."

Devin nods before looking at his watch. "I guess I should get back to the room. I'm exhausted."

"Yeah, me too. I probably won't wake up until noon."

"Well, that's what vacation's for."

We start our journey, but our steps are slow and leisurely as we make our way across the beach, heading for the pier that leads to our bungalows.

"I'm really glad you're here," I tell him. "Doesn't really feel like ten years went by."

"Eleven," he corrects with a smile.

"Right. Eleven." After a few seconds, I say, "Did you come out here for solitude and now I'm ruining it by being around?"

He laughs. "I did come out here for some peace and to get clarity on a few things, but mostly to get away from people back home who all wanted something different. I felt like everyone had a piece of me and were just pulling. You know?" I nod but allow him to continue. "So it's nice to be away, but I don't mind the company. It's good to have someone to talk to. Even if they *are* into sports."

I laugh. "You're gonna be wearing a jersey before you know it."

He scoffs. "If you say so."

Halfway up the pier he veers off. "Well, this is me."

"I'm the next one up. We're neighbors."

Devin nods. "I guess I'll see you around then."

"Yes, definitely."

"Okay. Goodnight."

"Night," I say with a wave, heading up to my own bungalow.

Once I'm inside, I turn on the TV and make sure it's a channel that never talks about sports. I hate the silence, but for the time I'm here, I'm avoiding all sports related media.

After I use the bathroom and strip out of my clothes, I brush my teeth and crawl under the covers. I lie there just staring out at the water for a while before I reach for my phone on the nightstand.

> It's Jarrod. Now you have my number so reach out whenever.

> Hey. Send me a picture because I hate these gray circles with the letters. Everyone has to have a contact photo.

> What a weird pet peeve to have.

> Just send one.

> Maybe I want to be unique and stand out.

In my contacts, you definitely do.

Goodnight. See you tomorrow.

Send a picture!

I laugh and put the phone on my nightstand. Five minutes later, it dings. When I open it up, I see a few photos followed by multiple comments.

I didn't know you were a model. Look at these pictures I found. This one is from an article titled 18 Hunky Hockey Players.

This one is nice. You're pretty flexible for a big guy.

This is you and that one singer, but I can crop her out.

First of all, where did I land in the top 18? Number 1?

I look at the other photos and realize he found one taken during a hockey game where I'm in the butterfly position, one arm outstretched as I try to block a puck. My face looks insane. The third photo was taken on a red carpet with a pop singer I dated for two months.

You landed at number four.

Damn.

I like the action shot.

I hate that one. Use the first one.

Too sexy. People will think we're dating for real.

So you think I'm sexy.

Goodnight.

Okay, okay. I'm sorry. LOL.

You'll never know what I choose.

Okay, then send me one before I have to internet stalk you.

A photo comes through immediately. I can tell he took it just now. He's in bed, his arm slung over his head as he rests on a white pillow.

I find myself staring at it for longer than necessary. His lips are full, playfully contorted into a grimace. His eyes look like the color of the water outside, and a thin gold chain rests around his throat. With his face angled just slightly to the side, his sharp jawline is on display, and I really think he's doing himself a disservice not being a model. It makes no sense for a man to be this pretty. And with that, I close it out and send out a quick message.

Thanks.

Welcome. Now go to sleep.

Seven

DEVIN

Before falling asleep last night, I took and sent the quickest photo to keep Jarrod from Googling me. My Google images won't be as innocent as his. He'd end up finding me with a dick in my mouth, hand, or both at the same time. He probably doesn't want that as my contact photo.

When I started in the adult industry, I didn't use my real name. I used it for any official and legal documents, but I went by Dee Leo and eventually got the stage name Dickie Bangs. However, everyone finds out everything, so once I got popular, everything was revealed. I even have a Wikipedia page.

My parents hate that when you type in my name, the mini Wiki bio pops up on the right side and says, *Devin De'León, known professionally as Dee Leo or Dickie Bangs is a pornographic film actor,* etc. It also lists all the awards I've racked up over the years, but I suppose they're not as prestigious as an Oscar.

Eventually, Jarrod will find out. I know he will. He already admitted to almost stalking me, so he's going to look me up. I might as well prepare myself for the questions. I can only hope he isn't one of the people who likes to judge sex workers for their jobs.

Maybe I should just tell him and get it out of the way, otherwise I'll worry that the next time I see him, he'll have already found out and be weird about it.

> Hey. You up?

He doesn't reply immediately. I look at the clock. It's eleven, so maybe he's still asleep. He did say he'd probably sleep until noon, but maybe he ended up searching my name last night anyway and now he doesn't know how to talk to me.

I shower and get dressed, choosing to wear my swim trunks and a white tank top with a white button up over it. I leave it unbuttoned and casual, since I just want to get breakfast and then jump in the water.

It's not until I'm at the end of the pier that my phone goes off.

Yeah. Just got out of the shower.

It's hard to decipher tone over text, but I'd think it's a pretty normal response.

> Oh okay. I'm about to go get breakfast.

Wait for me!

I laugh and rest against the railing as I wait. It's only five minutes before he's running down the pier in a pair of black shorts and a sea green, short-sleeved button up.

"Slow down. I'm not going anywhere!" I yell.

"I'm starving," he says, coming to a stop next to me.

"I was thinking of going to Bamboo Terrace again. The place we were at yesterday? But there's another place that has Sunday brunch. It's a buffet."

"Sounds good to me." After a few minutes, he says, "It's hotter today. What's the policy on removing your shirt in a restaurant at a resort?"

I chuckle. "I really don't know. We're outside, so I don't see why there would be a problem."

Internally, I plead for him not to do that, because it's going to be hard to keep from staring. I'll be sure to keep my sunglasses on—just in case.

We approach the hostess stand and ask for a table for two. The woman is in a floral dress with a pink flower tucked behind her ear. She's pretty with long, dark hair and flawless umber skin, and she can't keep her eyes off Jarrod.

Same.

"Here you go," she says once we get to our umbrella-covered table. "Would you like anything to drink?"

"I'll have water."

"Same for me," Jarrod says with a smile.

"The show will start in thirty minutes."

"The show?" Jarrod questions.

She flashes her white teeth at him with a friendly smile. "We have locals who showcase their traditional dances for our guests. It's about an hour, and it'll be over here on this stage," she says, pointing to a spot about fifteen feet away.

"Okay, awesome. Thanks," Jarrod replies. "Can we just go to the buffet whenever?"

"Yes, sir. Help yourself."

Before she's even four steps away, Jarrod is up out of his chair.

"You really are hungry."

"I need my food."

I follow him to the buffet line and grab a plate. "Just make sure you leave enough for the rest of the guests."

"No promises," he says, lifting the stainless steel lid from one of the dishes and scooping out a whole lot of scrambled eggs.

"Hold on," I say, reaching back for another plate.

A guy behind me steps back to allow me to grab it, but when his gaze lands on me, something flashes in his eyes.

"Excuse me. Sorry," I tell him with a smile.

He quickly grins back. "No worries."

I give Jarrod the extra plate knowing he'll need the space and then take my time looking through each serving dish to see what I want.

"It's nice here, right?" the guy behind me says.

I glance over. "Yes. Very."

He sticks close to my back, making friendly conversation about the food and weather. He's cute. Probably a handful of years younger than me, but that's not a deal breaker. Maybe having a tropical hookup will be good for me. It's not gonna be Jarrod. I've come to terms with the fact that my attraction and feelings were, are, and will always be unrequited. Being friends will have to suffice.

"What's your name?" I ask him, stopping at the bacon dish.

He smiles. "Ethan."

"How long are you here, Ethan?"

"Another week."

I give him my hand. "I'm Devin."

His lips draw up even higher. "Nice to meet you."

"Hopefully I'll see you around."

"Yeah," he says, brushing hair from his forehead. "For sure."

I take my plate and head to the table where Jarrod is already digging into his food.

"Is it good?" I ask.

"Delicious."

"I'm surprised you can tell. You've inhaled half your plate."

"Are you one of those people who savor every bite?"

I dip my spoon in some whipped cream on my plate and bring it to my mouth. "Mm."

Jarrod's eyes are on me, and once again I'm lost in the uniqueness of his. His gaze flickers to my plate and then he clears his throat.

"What's that? I didn't see those," he grunts.

"It's a waffle roll cake. It's just waffles, whipped cream, and strawberries rolled up like giant sushi rolls."

"Hmm."

We eat in relative silence as Jarrod finishes his plates and goes back for another. Ethan sits a few tables away with a couple of guys and a girl. He looks over, making direct eye contact with me before ducking his chin like he's embarrassed. I chuckle to myself.

"Is that the guy you were talking to earlier?" Jarrod asks when he approaches the table.

"Yeah. His name is Ethan."

Jarrod looks over at him. "He doesn't look like your type." He takes a bite of a sausage. "He's not that big."

I study Ethan again. He's probably my size, if not an inch or so shorter. "Yeah, but he's cute. It's not like I always end up with people who are my exact type."

The show begins when a group of large, shirtless men appear on stage. They have thick decorative belts with what looks like shredded tree bark hanging from it, as well as tassels and beads. The same type of thing is wrapped right under their knees, hanging to their ankles.

"Talk about burly," I say, raising a brow when I look at Jarrod.

He snorts and shakes his head.

We finish our food and enjoy the show, and almost as soon as it's over, a couple of guys walk by our table. One does a double-take before stopping. Uh oh. He probably recognized Jarrod.

"Hey, do I know you?"

I immediately glance at Jarrod who looks up from his phone. When I turn back to the guy next to the table, I realize he's staring at me.

"Who? Me?" I question, my hand on my chest.

"Yeah. You look familiar."

I shake my head. "I don't think so."

He tilts his head and studies me for a few uncomfortable seconds. His eyes widen slightly and his lips part. He looks at his friend who's standing nearby appearing confused and annoyed that he's being held up. When color rushes to his cheeks, I understand what's happening.

"Do you know me?" I ask, taking off my sunglasses.

It's clear he does recognize me, but he's not about to say from what.

"Maybe not."

I smile. "Oh. Have a good day."

"That was weird," Jarrod says after the guys scurry off.

"I guess I just have one of those faces. I look like everyone."

Jarrod scoffs. "Nobody looks like you."

Our eyes meet briefly before he focuses back on his phone.

Eight

JARROD

I don't know why I keep saying stupid shit. He's looking at me like I'm crazy, but it's not like what I said was untrue. Nobody looks like Devin. I've never seen a guy like him before in my life, but maybe it's weird to say. I guess I should get my filter checked.

"What are your plans for the rest of the day?" I ask, then immediately regret it. He probably thinks I want to spend the day attached to his hip. I mean, I wouldn't mind hanging out with him, but I don't want to overstep my boundaries. "I may go relax in the water back at the bungalow."

"Yeah, that was basically my plan. It's why I have my swim trunks on," he says, gesturing to the dark blue and green shorts that have palm trees on them.

I laugh. "Uhh, the placement of the tree is kind of unfortunate."

He looks down at his lap and pulls at the material. The

trunk of one of the palm trees is right over his crotch, curving to the right.

"Mine doesn't even curve that way."

I bark out a laugh. "I'd hope it's not that thin, either."

He shoots me a look. "It's not." Standing up, he tugs the shorts down and studies the material. "And the palm fronds of this other tree are right here, spreading out on both sides like a big bush. This is terrible. I didn't even realize."

I stand up and laugh. "Sorry, man."

"Let's get out of here."

As we're leaving, Ethan stands up from his table and awkwardly steps in front of Devin. "Hey, sorry. Uhh. I'm gonna be at Midnight Lounge tonight around ten, if you want to have a drink."

"Oh. Yeah, maybe I'll see you then."

The guy smiles, finding my gaze and quickly turning his attention back to Devin. "Cool."

We walk in silence for a few minutes until he says, "So, my place or yours?"

"Buy me a drink first, Dev. Geez."

"Oh, please."

I laugh. "I don't care. I gotta change, so I guess you can come to my place."

"Okay."

Once we get to my door, I put my wrist up to the lock and it opens it up for me. Inside, I immediately kick off my shoes and unbutton my shirt.

"Did you see they gave us snorkel equipment?"

"Really? I must've missed it."

I remove my shirt completely and throw it on the bed. He averts his gaze like he's trying to give me privacy.

"You can throw your stuff wherever. I'm gonna change into my shorts in the bathroom."

"Okay."

When I get back into the bedroom, I don't see Devin anywhere. His shirts are folded neatly on the table and his shoes are by the door that leads to the deck.

I spot a dark head of hair emerging from the crystalline water, and I watch as his face breaches the surface. I've never seen someone come up from underwater so elegantly.

"How's it feel?" I ask, stepping outside.

"It's nice," he replies, shaking his head and running his fingers through the wet strands. "It's warm."

I head over to the container with the snorkeling equipment and grab one for each of us. "These are full face masks. I haven't seen these types before."

Devin makes his way to the steps where I'm descending, reaching for one. "Well, all I know is we're gonna look really cool with these on." His tone suggests the opposite.

"For sure," I say with a chuckle, getting into the water.

I struggle trying to get the mask on properly. "It feels loose," I say, tugging on the straps at the back of my head. "It'll probably fill up with water."

Devin watches me with an expression that tells me he's trying not to laugh. "Let me help. You look ridiculous."

"You're gonna struggle, too. Watch."

"I'm not, because you're gonna help me," he says, handing me his mask. He walks behind me, his fingers brushing my hair out of the way. "I'm gonna try not to pull your hair."

"Nobody died over a little hair pulling."

He snorts, and then his fingers graze the side of my neck

as he fixes the straps that rest under the ears. When he touches the base of my skull as he pulls them tight, my shoulder ticks up.

"These were twisted."

"Oh."

I shiver with another brush of his fingers against my neck.

"You cold?"

"Just ticklish," I say with a chuckle. "I was trying to play it cool."

"Oh," he replies with a small laugh. "Does it feel okay?"

"Yeah. Much better. Thanks."

"Okay. Do me now," he says, walking around in front of me.

He takes the mask and puts it against his face before turning around and giving me his back.

"You have tattoos."

"Just the one."

"Can I ask why a window, or is it personal?" I start adjusting the straps, but his hair is longer than mine. "Also, I'm almost definitely going to pull your hair."

"I don't mind." He clears his throat. "The window represents new opportunities and fresh starts. Looking through it, you see the possibilities of your future. When I got it I was feeling trapped, wanting something different but not knowing what. I got the window, showing a beautiful and peaceful landscape, hoping to find that serene feeling one day."

"Have you?"

"Not quite."

My hands drop from the straps, brushing against his shoulders. "Okay. I think you're good."

When he spins around and we look at each other with these masks, we both break into laughter.

"Whatever, let's look for fish," he says, immediately going to his stomach.

The two of us float and swim, watching as schools of small fish swim right in front of our faces. As we move a little farther away, larger fish swim by—these ones black, white, and yellow.

Devin taps my arm and points, showing me a few orange fish.

"Nemo?" I exaggerate the word, unsure how muffled my voice is in this mask.

He laughs.

After a while, we stand up, making sure to not step on any coral reef.

"Damn, my back is hot," Devin says, reaching over his shoulder to touch it, his muscles flexing.

"Oh fuck. We didn't use sunscreen. Let's go put some on. I'm sure they have some here somewhere."

We remove our masks and walk up the steps to the deck. I go inside and search the whole place, finding some sunscreen in a woven basket under the bathroom sink. I grab a couple of towels and head back outside.

"Got it. Here you go," I say, tossing Devin—who's squeezing water from his shorts—a towel.

"Thanks."

We both pat ourselves dry, and then I hand him the sunscreen. "Please."

He playfully rolls his eyes and takes it from me, squirting a glop into his palm. "What would you do if I wasn't here?"

I shrug. "Be miserable and sunburnt?"

Water droplets cling to his neck and shoulders, while more drip from his dark strands and streak down his face. His pink lips twist into a smirk, and I watch as they part.

"You're gonna have to turn around."

My eyes snap to his. "Oh. Right. Sorry."

What is wrong with me?

I gasp when the cold liquid touches my upper back.

Devin laughs. "Oops. Sorry."

His hands smear it into my skin, getting my shoulders and top of my back before he needs more. Once again the coolness of the sunscreen seeps into my flesh, this time lower as he focuses on my lats and down to my waist. He squeezes slightly, like he's massaging me, and my eyes flutter closed.

"Mmm."

His chuckle is low. "I'm gonna put a little on your neck and then you can take care of your front."

Delicate fingers rub the scented sunscreen into my neck, teasing my hairline. I twitch at the touch and wonder why I'm reacting this way. It would be inappropriate to ask him to cover the rest of my body when I'm capable, but I sort of want him to.

Maybe I'm just touch deprived. I haven't had a massage in weeks, when I usually get them fairly regularly. I also haven't been with a girl in several months, so any sort of touch seems pleasurable. I'm sure that's why.

"I'll get your back first," I tell him, taking the bottle.

"You don't have to. I'm sure I can reach most of it."

"Just turn around," I say, squeezing the liquid into my hand.

He listens and faces the water, so I begin to rub it into his skin. I start at the neck and spread it over the tops of his shoulders. My eyes remain focused on the tattoo staring back at me. The scenery is similar to what we have here, though maybe not as tropical. Green trees, blue water, and a clear sky with the sun beaming in the corner.

When I realize I've been focusing on just rubbing his upper back, I get some more sunscreen and massage into the lower part.

"There you go."

"Thanks."

I take the bottle and squeeze lines onto my chest and stomach before handing it to him. He watches me with his bottom lip between his teeth and my stomach tightens.

In relative silence, we both cover the rest of our bodies, but my eyes keep watching the way his taut body turns and bends with each movement. His eyes flicker toward me, catching me in the act, but there's nothing I can do. I don't even know why I'm so fascinated.

"Want a water?" I ask when he catches me another time.

"Please. That would be great."

I go inside and grab a couple of bottles, tossing him one when I'm close. "Want to sit on the chairs down there? The couch? Or in the shade?"

He eyes each spot. The chairs on the lower deck are so close they touch, and the couch is directly under the sun, but the shaded area is a rounded daybed where we'd be fairly close to each other.

"Probably the shade, if I'm being honest. At least for a little bit."

"That's cool."

We walk over to the bed and I shove some pillows away. I flop down on one side, my feet dangling off the cushion while Devin takes care to sit on the edge, not bothering to relax and lay back at all.

"If you want to lie down, I'll move. I mean, there's space, but I can move."

He angles his head over his shoulder and smiles. "If I lie down I might fall asleep."

"Well, I won't charge you for that," I joke.

"No? What do you charge for?"

"That water, my massage services, mask adjustments, you know, stuff like that."

He shifts slightly to face me, his knee bending to rest on the cushion. "I did those things, too. So we're even."

"Well, you didn't give me anything to drink."

Devin's lips lift. "I'll give you something to drink later."

It's an innocent remark, but once again, we're both locked onto each other, and if I'm not mistaken, there was a tone to his voice when he said it. Maybe it's the way he's used to joking with his friends, or maybe it's just my brain being used to all the sexual jokes my teammates make, but it sounded like an innuendo. *I'll give you something to drink later.*

"I'll hold you to that," I finally say. "Speaking of drinks. You have your date later. Are you nervous?"

He turns away and takes a sip of his water. "No. I don't get nervous. Well, not normally," he says with another glance in my direction.

"So, you're excited?"

"I don't know what I am. I just figure, why not? You know? I'm on vacation. It won't be anything serious."

I nod and then take a gulp of my water. "I guess that's how I've been treating all my relationships. They're never serious."

"Never?" He turns to face me. "What about that one model?"

I make a face. "Definitely not."

"The singer?"

"Nope. I mean, I liked them, but I always knew I was never gonna settle down."

"You don't want to get married?"

"At some point. What about you? You just doing the no strings attached thing?"

"Mm. It's complicated. It's hard finding someone who is okay with..." The sentence dies on his lips before he starts over. "You know how sometimes people just use you for sex?"

I nod. "Yeah. I've been on both sides, if I'm being honest."

"Yeah, well, I think we're all kind of like that at some point, but with me, I feel like *everyone* wants to be with me for sex. They don't want the other stuff. They don't want the normal dates and nights at home."

"What about your ex? The one you showed me."

"He was okay for a while. We worked together and uhhh...he just couldn't take the workday stress on top of everything else. I don't know."

"If you're wanting to be done with meaningless sex, why are you going out with this guy?"

He spins around and pins me with a look. "Who says I'm going to have sex with him?"

I shrug. "I guess I'm projecting, because it's probably what I'd do. Well, not with him, but you know."

He shakes his head, a smile tugging at his lips before he turns away. "I just want to choose someone to spend time with. I want to be with them for my own reasons—normal, regular reasons like they're hot or nice. And I don't want them to know who I am or be with me because of who I am."

"Because of your parents and their wealth and fame?" I ask.

His shoulders drop slightly and he nods, facing the water.

"I should tell you something," he says.

"Okay."

Before he can say anything, I hear my cell ringing from inside. "Oh, one sec. It might be my agent."

"It's fine. You go, I'm gonna grab my things and head back to my place for a while."

"I won't be long."

"I should shower and eat. Maybe take a nap before tonight."

"Right. Okay. I'll see ya later."

I rush in and pick up the phone, listening to my agent as I watch Devin slip on his shoes and forgo putting on his shirt. He waves before heading to the door and leaving, and I feel a small prick of loneliness as soon as he's gone.

Nine

DEVIN

After taking a shower, I slept for hours, forced myself to respond to emails and texts but only the important ones, went and got something to eat, then came back to my room to waste more time.

I haven't heard from Jarrod since I left his bungalow, and that's fine. I didn't come out here to spend every hour of the day with someone else. Though, it's been nice being around him. It's strange how you can go so many years without seeing or talking to someone and then immediately hit it off and feel as though you've been close for years.

I've noticed him watching me, but I think it's because I've been looking at him. I thought I was being discreet with quick glances, but he seems to notice.

What I don't need is him to think I'm checking him out every time we're together. I mean, it's hard not to when he's literal perfection. I think most people—gay, straight, bi, and everything in between—would find it hard to not stare at the person who embodies their perfect partner.

I know a lot of straight guys get uncomfortable around gay guys, because they assume we want them simply because they're men. That's ignorant thinking, but Jarrod may actually start to think that if I keep gawking at him in ways you don't look at friends. It's not that I'm falling into the stereotype, it's simply that Jarrod is absolutely gorgeous.

By nine-fifteen, I'm too bored to continue to stay in the room, so I freshen up and pick out a nice outfit. It's a short-sleeved, white button up with black line art print, and I leave the first few buttons undone. After I put on my black pants, I slide into my Oxfords and head out.

The walk along the pier is quiet, the sound of water lapping at the beach is the only noise until I get closer to Midnight Lounge.

Once I arrive at the bar, I stand in the corner and wait for Holden to spot me.

He grins and holds up a finger as he fixes another drink. I watch as he shamelessly flirts with that customer before walking over.

"Hey. Where's the boyfriend?"

"He's not my boyfriend."

"Really? Wow. So, you're single?"

"I just watched you ask that guy over there the same question," I say with a grin.

"Yeah, but—"

"I'll take a Tequila Sunrise."

He winks at me before starting to make it. I glance around and notice how busy it is. Almost all the tables are full along both piers and several people are mingling under the cover of the hut. Once my drink is done, I take it and drop a twenty on the bar before I walk over to the outer edge. I rest an arm on the railing and look out at the water.

To the left I can see the collection of bungalows where I'm staying. It's too dark and a bit too far to make out any details, but I wonder if Jarrod is on his deck looking this way.

Twenty minutes later, when I'm back at the bar for another drink, I watch Ethan walk up the pier. He's got on blue shorts and a floral print shirt that he probably bought while here. His dirty blond hair is windswept, and when he meets my gaze, a smile stretches across his face.

"Hey," he says, coming up next to me.

"Hey. You're early."

"I was nervous I was going to be late. You were even earlier, I see," he says, glancing down at the empty glass in my hand.

"I was bored," I say with a chuckle.

Holden comes back and brings me another drink before looking over at Ethan and asking what he wants. Once Ethan has his beer, the two of us walk back over to where I was standing earlier.

"So, are you with your family?" I ask.

"Yeah. Every year we come here for a family reunion. My brother and sister live on opposite sides of the country, and I'm usually traveling, so my mom makes sure we all schedule time to come together."

"That's nice."

He shrugs. "Sometimes. Family, you know?"

I laugh. "Yes, I know.

The next two hours go by quickly, and I find Ethan more likable than I expected. He tells me he has a loft in New York, but does a lot of overseas traveling. Based on some comments, I'm pretty sure his dad is an investment banker. He hasn't mentioned what he does, so I'm wondering if his parents just give him money.

He drinks another two beers, and I have one more drink before he asks if I want to go for a walk.

As we're strolling along the beach, we notice some picnic tables nestled between trees to our left.

"Want to sit over here?" he asks.

"Sure."

There's nobody else around, but on the other side of the trees, you can hear the voices of people walking on the path that leads to the resort pool.

I have my ass resting against the end of the table when Ethan walks toward me. His fingers brush against the back of my hand before he looks me in the eye.

"Can I kiss you?"

I smile and dip my head in a nod.

He comes in fast, his lips pressing against mine briefly before his tongue forces its way into my mouth. His hands roam, touching my hips, thighs, and crotch as he moans. It's too fast. Too aggressive for a first kiss.

I try to pull away, but he comes in closer, attempting to get me to lean back over the table.

"Ethan," I say, turning my head to the side and putting my hands on his chest.

"I'm sorry," he says, still not giving me space. "I've been wanting to do this for so long."

"So long? Since breakfast?"

His smile is mischievous. "I know who you are. I've watched your videos."

I stand up straight and push him away, my face hardening. "Excuse me?"

"Dickie Bangs," he says with a chuckle. "Of course I recognized you. I never thought I'd have a chance to sleep with the porn star I jack off to. I've been dying to know how you feel and if you're as good as—"

"I am *not* sleeping with you," I snip, stepping away from the table.

"But that's what you do."

I debate arguing with him, but there's no point. I'm just disappointed he had me fooled.

"Good luck in life, Ethan. I have a feeling you're gonna need it."

As I'm walking off, he says, "What the hell, man?"

I keep going and don't look back, wanting nothing but to be in the confines of my bungalow.

Away from everyone.

Ten

JARROD

When I wake up in the morning, I throw on some gym pants and a loose tank top, knowing I'm gonna go to the fitness center after breakfast.

I think about texting Devin, but I know he had his date last night, and I don't know what happened by the end of it, so I don't want to interrupt anything. However, a weird feeling sits in my gut, hoping that random dude isn't in his room with him right now. I'm not sure why. I didn't even speak to him, so he might be a nice guy.

Screw it. I'm just his friend. It's normal to text.

Hey. You want breakfast?

Nah. I'm not feeling too good. I'll probably just stay in today. Thanks, though.

What's wrong? Need anything?

Probably just sleep. I'll see if they can bring some food out here.

I'll bring some back. I'll be faster. They're probably swamped with room service requests in the hotels on land. Plus, you don't want them shaking your food all up on their little golf carts.

It's fine. I'm not starving anyway. I have some snacks here.

I don't reply back because he's obviously going to be stubborn, so I head to the restaurant where I first saw Devin, bypassing Gardenias since it's busy.

Bamboo Terrace has a handful of guests, but it's a little more low-key and quiet. When the hostess approaches me, I give her a smile.

"Hi. I was going to dine in, but I need to take some food to a friend of mine. Can I place an order to go?"

"Sure. Give me one second."

She grabs a waiter and he comes over with a tablet to take my order. While I wait, I wander over to the edge, looking out at the two infinity pools that are below the restaurant. I read in the pamphlet that one of them is sand-bottomed and there's a swim-up bar at the other.

"Here you go, sir," the waiter says, bringing me two big bags of food.

"Thank you so much." I hand him some cash.

"Have a good day."

I walk back to the bungalows as quickly as I can, getting there in less than ten minutes. I go to his and knock on the door.

When he opens it up, he doesn't look sick at all. Maybe tired, but that's about it.

"You're the best looking sick person I've ever seen."

He eyes the bags. "What did you do?"

"I got food," I say, lifting them up. "Now let me in because I haven't eaten, and I'll get grumpy soon."

With a laugh, he steps back, and I walk in and place the bags in the kitchen. As I tear into the plastic, I look over my shoulder and watch as he closes his laptop and puts it on his nightstand.

"If you said you were sick so you didn't have to come have breakfast with me, I'd say it backfired."

Devin looks up from fixing his bed. "I wasn't trying to avoid you."

"Good."

"I tried to remember what I've seen you eating before, but I also thought you were sick and didn't know what kind of sick, so I got soup and crackers as well as fruit and then typical breakfast food."

"I never said I was sick," he says, coming up to look through the food. "I said I wasn't feeling good."

"I think that means sick. Why don't you feel good, then?"

"Maybe I drank too much last night."

"Ah," I say with a grin. "It was a drunken date. I got you."

"No," he says quickly. "Not a date. That won't happen again."

Weirdly, a sense of relief washes over me, but that makes me feel like a bad friend.

"What happened?"

He shakes his head and I can see the frustration on his face. "He was...typical."

"What's that mean?"

"Just a little aggressive."

I put down the food and face him, my jaw ticking. "What do you mean aggressive?"

Devin's green eyes stare at me through dark lashes. "Maybe that's the wrong word. He was just looking for sex, and I wasn't interested. I put a stop to it, so it's okay."

"It's not okay if he made you feel uncomfortable."

He gives me a forced smile. "It's really fine. Let's eat. You're getting grumpy."

I *harrumph* but start opening up the boxes and setting them on the table. After we clear away the mess, we sit across from each other and start eating.

My leg keeps bumping into his because of the small quarters. The first two times, I apologized and moved it, but when I do it again, I leave it resting against his.

"You went to the gym?" he asks, eyes dancing over my exposed shoulders.

"Not yet. I was gonna go after breakfast."

"Oh okay."

"Wanna come?"

He tilts his head from side to side, scrunching his face. "Mmm."

"What? You think you'll run into that asshole?"

"It's not that. I don't know. Just feeling kinda blah. That's not the best way to explain it, but..." He trails off with a shrug.

"No, I get it."

I take another bite of my omelet as he sits back in his chair, running a hand through his hair. I find myself staring at him again, so I quickly focus on my food. When my traitorous eyes flicker up one last time, he's watching me with a small grin.

"What?" I question, even though he's the one who should be asking me that.

He shakes his head. "Nothing. I just never thought we'd be here."

"What do you mean?"

"You were just this guy I knew in school. Eleven years go by and you're in the NHL and in my bungalow on a private island, eating breakfast with me. It's strange."

I chuckle. "I guess so."

He rests his cheek in his palm as he studies me, and now I feel flustered. My cheeks redden and I sputter out a laugh. "Do I have food on my face?"

"No," he says with a shake of his head. "Just looking at your eyes."

"Oh." I stare back at my food. "I've always been self-conscious about them."

"What?" he exclaims, almost offended. "They're beautiful. And unique. It was one of the main things I remembered about you."

I put my fork down and sit back a little. "You remembered me? I mean, over the years, you thought about me?"

He looks embarrassed. "Don't make me sound like a psycho."

I chuckle. "I'm not. You said it was one of the main things you remembered. I guess I'm just wondering what else there was."

Devin looks out the window, his chin sitting in his palm. When he looks back at me, his eyes twinkle in the sunlight.

He puts his hands down on the table and starts spinning the bottle of water. "Sometimes there's just memorable people from school, you know?"

I don't let him try to skate by it. "You remembered my eyes. What else did you remember?"

He sighs, digging his teeth into his bottom lip. "If I say it, you're going to feel weird, and I don't want things to be weird. We're here together for a few weeks, and I like hanging out with you, so I just don't want to mess it up."

"Well, now I'm very curious," I reply, folding my arms on the table and leaning in.

He rolls his eyes and stands up, busying himself by gathering the trash. "I might have *maybe* had a little crush on you. It's not a big deal, but yeah, I just remember telling you that I liked your eyes once."

My heart slams against my ribs. Devin had a crush on me, and I had no idea. I feel bad for basically blocking out almost all of high school. I think back, wishing I could remember more. I never caught on that he was into me like that, so he must've done a good job playing it off.

After several seconds, I say, "What else do you like about me?"

Devin's eyes snap to mine. "What?"

"That's what I said that day. I remember."

His cheeks redden and he ties the plastic bag. "Right. Yeah, that's what you said."

"Okay, so you had a crush, but that doesn't tell me what else you remembered."

I don't know why I'm pushing it, but I need to know. I want to know what was on his mind when he thought of me.

"When you smile, it's almost always crooked. The right side is raised more than the left, and you were always running everywhere. It's like you were incapable of walking.

Oh, and the way your hair blew back in the wind when you'd speed off in that convertible."

When the last words leave his lips, he freezes, looking at me. "Okay, that made me sound like a psycho."

He turns to spin away, but I reach out and catch his arm. "Hey." His eyes find my fingers wrapped around his forearm before they land on my face. "Thanks for telling me. I didn't mean to make you feel uncomfortable."

With a laugh, he pulls away and puts the trash in a bin by the door. "If anything, you probably feel uncomfortable. I'm sorry. It was eleven years ago, you know? We were kids."

"Right. I don't feel uncomfortable."

"Good," he says, but he doesn't look at me. He just continues cleaning up.

"Did anyone in school know you were gay?" I ask.

"No. I didn't come out officially until I graduated, but I always felt like people knew or at least questioned it."

"So you never dated anyone?"

He finally looks at me, leaning against the fridge. "No," he says, drawing out the word. "I mean, I didn't really even admit it to myself until high school. There was a moment when I was like, *Ah. Yes, I'm definitely gay.*" He laughs. "Then I kept it a secret."

"What was the moment?"

Devin laughs. "Oh, no. You're not getting that out of me. You've gotten enough juicy secrets for the day."

"That was like...one secret."

"That's one more than you've given me."

"You want a secret?"

"I mean, it's only fair," he teases.

I think over some things and then say, "Okay, this is

pretty bad, and if you ever meet any of my teammates, please never bring this up."

"Oh. I do have a date with your entire team next week, so I'll try to keep my mouth closed."

I twist my mouth at him. "Anyway, about a year ago, one of the left wingers went through a breakup. He was pretty broken up about it, because *she* dumped *him*. Anyway, fast forward to like two weeks later, and I got drunk and slept with her."

Devin's eyes widen. "Jarrod!"

"He never found out."

"Until I tell him."

"Shut up," I say with a laugh. "He ended up finding another girl months later, so I'd like to say he'd probably be okay, but who knows."

Devin shakes his head. "What a naughty boy you are."

"Now we're even," I say with a grin. "A secret for a secret."

"You better think of a really good one, because I still have one that may blow you away."

He walks away, leaving me desperate to know what could be more mind-blowing than him having had a crush on me.

Eleven

DEVIN

I ended up having to basically push Jarrod out the door so he'd go to the gym, but he kept harassing me over the other secret I have.

Nearly four hours later, at around one o'clock, there's a rapid knock on my door.

I yank it open and find Jarrod there with more food in his arms, dressed in a pair of basketball shorts and a plain white tee.

"Do you have plans?"

"No," I reply, stepping back to let him in. "Why? What's going on?"

"We're gonna eat and watch a movie."

"We are?"

"Yes, I'll tell you why later."

"There's a reason for watching a movie?"

"Yep. Here," he says, shoving a box at me. "The resort had these flatbread pizzas so I got that. We can share."

"Okay," I say, taking the food to the kitchen while he

grabs the remote for the TV. "Didn't you just spend hours at the gym?"

"Yeah, but that's why I get to eat like this. I'll clean up closer to the season starting. I'm on vacation, don't judge me."

I laugh. "I'm not. Sorry. I should probably hit up the gym while I'm here too, though."

"Just come with me."

"Maybe."

"Okay, I'm logged into my Netflix account. Come sit down."

"I'm getting plates and napkins. Calm down."

When I walk back in, he's moving the chairs and tables, spinning them to face the TV on the wall instead of the view out back.

"I understand the view is beautiful, but the TV is really in a weird spot and none of the furniture is facing it. I'll move it back."

I laugh. "You don't have to explain."

"Okay, you can put the pizza on the table between us."

I put a couple slices on my plate as he scrolls through movies. He gets up and turns the lights down and then drops to the chair and kicks his feet up on the ottoman.

"Have you seen this?"

"I don't even know what *this* is."

He grins, but doesn't say anything else. The movie starts and a really good-looking guy appears on the screen. Almost two hours later, the pizza is gone and the movie is over.

"What'd you think?"

"It was good. I don't watch many action movies, but I liked it."

"That guy, Elijah Hunt, he played the main character... he's on the island. I saw him."

"Really?"

"Yep. I saw him in passing, but I recognized him immediately."

"Wow, that's awesome."

"Yeah, so it made me want to watch this movie. Thought I'd share the experience."

"Thanks," I say with a laugh, standing up to stretch.

Jarrod's eyes track my movements from his seat. There's something interesting in the way he looks at me, but I'm trying not to think too much into it.

"What do you wanna do now?" I ask.

He hesitates to answer, and when he does, it's like he had to shake himself out of a trance. "Umm. I don't know. Have you seen the swim-up bar in the infinity pool?"

"It's a real bar?"

"Yeah, there's chairs in the water, so your ass will be just barely under the water, but the rest of you is above it. Some people come up to get a drink and wade back to wherever they came from. It's under this huge hut, so it's shaded, but we can wait an hour or so until the sun goes down."

"That sounds good. We can go whenever. I just need to change."

"Me too. I'll meet you out front in a few."

"Okay."

Thirty minutes later, we're sitting at the bar, half in the water, half out. When the bartender comes over, Jarrod orders first.

"Can I get a Sex on the Beach? Wait, you have it in slushie form?" Jarrod asks, looking at a menu trapped under the glass bar top.

"Yes, sir."

"I'll take that."

"Ooh. Holden will be so disappointed you didn't order that from him," I say with a laugh.

"I'll get one too," I tell the bartender. "But with tequila please."

"I think Holden wants that from you, not me," he says with a chuckle.

"I think Holden wants everyone."

I watch as the bartender mixes the orange juice, frozen peaches, ice, and liquor into the blender, making Jarrod's first before starting on mine. A couple minutes later, he's topping them with orange slices and cherries and placing them in front of us.

"This is nice," Jarrod says, spinning in his seat to face me.

"It is," I reply after taking a drink.

He smiles. "I mean *this*, being here, drinking frozen cocktails on a tropical island, in a pool...with you. We should make this an annual thing."

I try to keep my eyes from giving away my surprise, but it *is* surprising. Jarrod wants to vacation with me every year? The thought of it does give me butterflies, but that's probably why we shouldn't.

I laugh and nod, and then try to distract him from that thought. "Do you usually take vacations after a season?"

He turns a little more, resting his elbows on the bar behind him as he looks out at the pool. "Sometimes, but usually to visit my family. I went to Barbados once with some teammates, but it wasn't like this."

I take another drink. "This is my first vacation ever. A real vacation, you know? Little weekend trips to different towns don't really count."

"Yeah. I'm definitely gonna have to do this more often. What other tropical place can we go to? Ooh, what about Saint Lucia?"

"You really want to go on another vacation with me?" I ask with a little chuckle. "What if I annoy you in the next few days?"

He scoffs. "You're not annoying."

I should tell him that my crush eleven years ago is rearing its head, and that's why I'm nervous to spend so much time with him. He thinks I got over it—over him. I want him to think that, but it's not true. I'm still very much attracted to him, and not just his looks, though of course that's the first thing people notice, but everything about him is perfect. He's happy-go-lucky, a little sarcastic, kind and caring. He makes me laugh, and when someone can make you laugh, it's hard to resist being around that kind of energy.

"Well, if we get through this vacation without a scratch, we can talk about planning a next one."

"Really?" he questions, his eyes lighting up.

"Yes, really," I reply with a laugh.

After we finish our first drink, we swim out into the infinity pool, finding a quiet space away from other guests. I float on my back, staring up at the darkening sky. My body bumps into Jarrod who gently guides me by him with his hands under my back.

"I've never been able to float," he says.

"Really? It's easy."

"It's *not* easy. My lower half just sinks and then I'm standing."

I laugh and get to my feet. "Try it."

He makes a face. "I'm telling you. It's not going to happen."

"Come on," I say, guiding him back by tugging on his shoulder.

Jarrod immediately starts flailing his arms and tilting his head forward. "I'm going to drown."

I bark out a laugh as he gets to his feet. "No, you're not, you baby. Okay, let's try it again. Here's some tips. Don't panic."

"Okay, so I failed immediately."

"Yes," I say with a chuckle. "Take a deep breath and tilt your head back. Your ears will need to be underwater."

"Okay, let's just try this."

"I'm going to hold your back this time."

He crouches low into the water and leans back. My hands find their place underneath him, one between his shoulder blades and the other at the base of his spine.

"Let your legs float up. Just relax and don't think about it. Find something to focus on."

I watch his body become parallel to the water, but I know if I let go he'll sink.

"I don't feel relaxed," he says.

I laugh and notice he's lifting his head up. I remove one of my hands and touch his chin, tilting his head back.

"It's okay. Your face won't go all the way under." His eyes connect with mine. "Point your chin to the sky."

"Okay."

"Palms up. You can move your arms to whatever position feels comfortable. Arch your back," I say, pushing up slightly where I need him to arch. "Push your chest out a little."

"What about my legs," he asks, still focused on me.

"Your legs will dangle a little. That's normal. Spread them apart."

"Devin." He sing-songs my name in a teasing tone. "So frisky in the pool."

I roll my eyes and start to remove my hands. "I'll let you sink."

"Okay, okay," he says as he immediately starts to drop.

I end up touching his ass as I push him back up before moving my hand to his lower back again. "If you feel like your legs are bringing you down, just kick them a little."

"Got it."

"I'm gonna slowly let go. Keep your chin up. Breathe."

I remove my hand from his upper back and he remains in place, then I slowly slide my other hand out from under him.

"I'm floating."

I step back as his body comes in my direction. "You're floating."

He turns in the water, and his head ends up right in front of where I'm standing. I look down at him, my stomach inches away from his hair, and I smile. He returns the grin and immediately starts to sink.

I reach out and put my hand under his head and lift him up.

"Damn," he says, getting to his feet.

"No, that was good. You'll get better."

"Well, thanks for the lesson," he says with that crooked grin of his.

"Should I start a class here?"

"No. You're mine," he says before quickly amending. "My teacher. Who's gonna teach me if you're off with a class full of people only wanting to stare at you?"

My lips twitch, fighting off a smile. "They'd only sign up for my class to stare at me? Why?"

He gives me a look like I should know why. "Come on. You're aware of your..." His eyes remain on my face, moving over every line and curve. "You're...." He shrugs, struggling with his words.

"Pretty?" I say, batting my lashes at him dramatically.

His cheeks redden. "I just think you'd probably be distracting." He clears his throat. "Let's go get another drink."

We swim up to the bar, and Jarrod avoids looking at me. I feel like something's up with him. He's straight, but for a straight guy, he keeps giving me interesting looks and complimenting my appearance. I suppose he could be a very secure man and isn't afraid to be honest about thinking a guy is attractive. Men can admit other men are good looking without having to be into guys. Perhaps I'm just seeing what I want to see.

Jarrod orders two shots and two of the same drinks we just had. "Shot?" he asks without looking at me.

"I'm good with just the drink," I reply.

As soon as the glasses are put in front of us, Jarrod downs both shots back-to-back. He finishes his Sex on the

Beach before I'm halfway into mine, and then he orders another.

He remains upbeat, and we're able to talk and laugh about random things, but I am noticing the way he tries to avoid eye contact for long periods.

As he sips on his third cocktail, he finally looks me in the eye. "Have you ever had sex on a beach?"

"Nope. It sounds romantic and passionate if you don't think too much about it, but all I can imagine is sand getting in places where it probably shouldn't."

"I'd put a blanket down," he says, his eyes already a little red. "An extra-large one under a big umbrella."

"That's a good plan. So you've never done it before either?"

"No, but I have in a pool," he says, looking out at the water.

"A public pool?" I ask, failing to hide my grimace.

He chuckles. "No. It was a private pool. You've never done anything in one?"

I give him a look. "It's probably easier to have sex with a woman in a pool than a man."

"Oh. Right."

"Plus, I'd still worry about some sort of infection."

"Have you ever had any sort of spontaneous sex?" he asks, taking another gulp from his glass, before ordering another shot.

My brows lift. "Sure."

"That's all I get?" he asks with a lopsided smile, reaching for the glass and swallowing the liquid.

"What do you want?"

His eyes lower slightly. He tries to take a step but slips.

"Maybe we should get out of the water," I say.

"I guess alcohol and pools don't really go well together."

I take his arm and make sure he gets out of the water without falling.

"Should I get you some food?"

He shakes his head, grabbing a towel from the hut nearby. "I have some stuff in my room."

We dry off and find the pathway that leads to the beach. The walk is quiet for the first couple of minutes, but he seems mostly steady, so that's good.

"Are you prone to hangovers? I have some medicine in my room."

"I don't normally drink a whole lot. This is the most I've had in a while."

"Oh."

He trips, his body jolting forward, so I quickly reach out and grab him around his torso. His left hand lands on my shoulder while his right arm wraps around me.

"You okay?" I ask, gazing up at him.

Jarrod rights himself, but we're still wrapped around each other. "Yeah. I...I tripped on something."

I look behind us and notice a deep crack. "Yeah, looks like they need to fix that."

When I turn back, I notice he's still watching me. I slowly release him from my hold, and his hands fall from my body in return.

"Thanks."

"Can't let you fall on your face," I say with a teasing tone.

He rubs his forehead. "I think that last shot is hitting me now."

"Let's get you to your room."

By the time we get to the pier, Jarrod's definitely feeling the effects of the alcohol a little more. He's a big guy, but if he doesn't normally drink, having three shots and three cocktails is gonna hit him pretty hard.

"Let me see your hand," I tell him at the door.

He gives me a lazy smile, his eyes hooded and low as he slides his hand in mine.

Amused, I grin before I slip out of his hold and press his wrist to the lock, waiting for it to beep.

"Oh, I thought you wanted to hold hands," he says with a snort.

I push open the door and guide him in. He trips over the threshold, and since I try to step in to keep him from falling, he crashes into me. His body pins my back to the wall, his hands braced on either side of my head.

"Sorry," he says quietly, eyes glassy as he stares at me.

"It's okay," I reply, pushing at his chest.

He hardly moves, but his hand comes to my face, a knuckle brushing lightly against my jaw.

My heart seizes and I forget how to breathe.

"You really are very attractive."

"And you're very drunk," I say, putting more effort into my next push.

He groans. "I'm not just saying it because I'm drunk. I said it before."

I guide him around the corner and into the bedroom. "Well, thank you."

When he sits on the mattress, he kicks his sandals off. "My shorts are wet."

"Where are your clothes?"

He flings an arm toward the closet, so I rush over and

open it up. I find some boxers and T-shirts folded up on a shelf and get one of each.

When I get back to the bed, I realize I'm going to have to strip him naked if he can't do it himself.

"Umm. I have these. Can you get out of those?" I ask, pointing to his wet swim trunks.

"It's very bright in here," he says, slurring the words together as he squints up at me.

"Sorry." I go to the switch and turn it off before clicking on a small lamp in the corner.

Jarrod stands and starts tugging the material down. He loses his balance a few times, but I keep my head turned to the side.

When I hear the covers rustling, I glance over and realize he's getting in the bed naked.

"So, no pajamas?" I ask, holding out the clothes.

He shakes his head. "Too much trouble."

I collect a trash can and water bottle and bring both nearby.

"Are you gonna be okay?"

"Probably. Room is spinning, though."

"I heard if you put a foot on the floor it'll help make you feel grounded. Or if you find something to focus on."

A thick, muscular leg kicks out from under the covers, his foot resting flat on the ground. "Can I focus on you?"

"I'm not a fixed object. If I move it might make it worse."

"So, don't move," his arm reaches up like he's trying to grab me, but it falls back down.

I grab the water bottle and uncap it. "Drink."

"Bossy."

He downs half of it in one gulp before handing it back to me. His eyelids begin drooping, and his blinking slows.

"I think..." He stops talking, his eyes closing. They open a few seconds later. "I think I..." They close again and this time don't reopen.

His breathing evens out and his face relaxes. I wait a couple minutes before I lift his leg back onto the bed so I can roll him to his side. It's not an easy task, but he unconsciously helps me after I pull on him a few times, turning to his side.

I brush the hair from his face and allow my thumb to graze across his eyebrow. He makes a noise in his throat and nuzzles into my hand.

I end up sitting on one of his chairs for an hour and a half, my attention split between watching him and the view out the back door. When I think he's in the clear and probably won't throw up, I close the curtains and slip out the front.

In my own bed later that night, I relive everything that happened earlier.

His body against mine. His finger touching my jaw. His compliments.

Tomorrow he won't remember any of it, but I always will.

Twelve

JARROD

When I wake up, I look around the room and quickly realize Devin isn't here. I'm embarrassed about how I acted last night. I never drink like that, but after realizing I was once again saying things I shouldn't, I felt like I had to drink to hopefully forget.

I told him he was distracting. I called him mine. I keep complimenting how he looks, and last night I did so while touching him. I don't understand why I'm incapable of filtering things out. Yes, he's very good looking and it's something I'm quite aware of and almost always thinking about when we're together, so it's easy to slip out. But why? Why am I so hyper aware?

I've never thought of any other guy like this. I know when people are attractive people, but with Devin, it's different. I not only think he's attractive, I think I'm attracted to him. It's freaking me out. I'm not gay. I've never wanted to be with a guy, so why am I so into him?

I slowly make my way to the bathroom so I can relieve

my very full bladder and brush away the taste of stale alcohol in my mouth. In the shower, I have flashes of Devin's face as he looked up at me when I had him pinned against the wall. My cock twitches.

It's morning. That's normal.

I reach for my shaft, needing to come anyway, because it's been a few days since I have. While I stroke, I keep seeing Devin's face. His shirtless selfie he sent me. The droplets on his flawless skin when he had come out of the water. The way his hands touched me when he was rubbing sunscreen on my back.

"Fuck," I groan, my hand moving faster.

A noise pulls me out of my thoughts and I freeze. When I hear it again, I realize it's someone at my door.

"Shit," I turn off the water and wrap a towel around my waist.

It could be Devin and I don't want him to think I'm ignoring him. Or you know, dead from alcohol poisoning.

I yank open the door and he's there with food in his hands.

"It was my turn to bring you something to eat."

I grin. "Come in."

He drinks in my appearance. "I'm guessing you just ran out of the shower considering you're dripping."

I look down at the small puddle forming under me. "Yeah. I rushed out."

When his eyes widen and then dart away, I look down and notice my erection is still pretty visible through this white towel. *Oops.*

"I got a little variety since I didn't know what you

normally eat for lunch. I have a club sandwich, cheese-burger, fries, fruit, a salad, and some baked chicken."

"All of it sounds good."

He laughs. "Well, some is for me too, but I'll let you have your pick."

When he turns to face me, his eyes travel the length of my body and once again my cock jumps, making me realize I only teased him in the shower and now he's going to want a release.

"I'm gonna get some clothes on. I'll be back."

Instead of jacking off like I really want to, I dry my body and lotion up before pulling on a pair of boxer briefs where I can tuck my erection behind the waistband. I step into a pair of shorts and forgo a shirt altogether.

"Okay, I'm ready to eat."

"You don't seem to be suffering from too bad of a hang-over," he says.

"I took some Tylenol and drank three bottles of water. Besides a tiny headache, I'm okay."

"That's good."

We sit down at the small round table in the kitchen, dividing up the food. After a few bites from my burger, I speak up.

"I'm sorry for getting drunk last night. I'm kind of embar-rassed about it."

He offers me a small grin. "You didn't embarrass yourself. I've been around people who've fallen off chairs, thrown up in people's front yards, broken dishes, and a ton of other things. You were fine."

"Well, I appreciate you dealing with me."

"Of course."

Toward the end of the meal, his phone rings.

"Sorry." He glances at the screen, his brows furrowing. "Not sure who this is. Hello?" Immediately his face falls. "Oh. Hey. No, I'm not in town. I'm on vacation. No, you don't need to know. Why?"

I can tell he's getting upset with whoever is on the other side, so I get up and start clearing the table.

"No, Mike. You know it's not. No. It's better this way. I can't talk about this now. It doesn't matter. No, I'm gonna go."

He ends the call and puts the phone on the table.

"Your ex?"

"Yeah. I guess he got a new number."

"Is he trying to get back together?" I ask.

Devin sighs. "Who knows? He's tried this before. It's not gonna work between us."

"Because you work together?"

"He's got a jealous streak and anytime I talk to anyone, he thinks I'm gonna sleep with them."

"Yikes."

"Yeah."

His phone rings again and he glances down and sighs.

"Is it him?"

"Yep."

"Answer it."

"Why?" he questions, looking at me suspiciously.

"We can give him a reason to be jealous. Maybe he'll leave you alone if he thinks you've moved on."

"I doubt it."

"Answer it."

Devin's lips curve slightly. "Hello?" He rolls his eyes at whatever's said on the other side. "No, because I'm busy."

"Hey, babe. Do you want another water?" I ask him, projecting my voice.

He smiles. "I'm okay. Thanks." Back on the phone he says, "Nobody. It shouldn't matter."

I get closer to Devin and lower my voice. "I thought we were gonna go skinny dipping. Why are you still dressed?"

Devin chokes back a laugh, covering his mouth with his hand. I hear the guy's voice on the other end get higher as he yells something.

"I gotta go, Mike. Bye!"

We both start laughing, Devin falling to the side which puts his head on my stomach. As our laughter slows, we both become aware of our close proximity. Devin sits up straight and gazes up at me with those hypnotizing eyes of his.

"Well, thanks for that. He's probably still gonna harass me, so I'll be blocking that number." He chuckles lightly and closes the lid on one of the food boxes before standing up.

I only move back a step, so when he gets to his feet, our bodies are nearly touching. My breaths are deep, sucking in oxygen like I'm going to run out of it. I inspect his face, from his crystalline eyes to his full, soft pink lips. Never have I ever been so enraptured by a man's lips before.

My fingers twitch, touching his.

"Jarrod." He says my name curiously in a soft whisper. "What's going on?"

I stare down at him, lost in the moment. Lost in my own head. I think about how it might feel to kiss his lips and then I wonder why I want to do that in the first place. My thoughts are warring in my head, but my heart is thumping hard in my chest like it wants to get to him, like it wants me to move closer.

For multiple reasons, I can't kiss him, but god do I want to.

I shake my head and step back. "Sorry. I don't know. I zoned out, I think."

He watches me inquisitively. "Okay."

"Um. I guess I should go to the gym today. Maybe I can sweat out the rest of the alcohol." I force a laugh and turn around, rushing into the closet.

"Okay. Well, I'll see you later then."

"Yeah, okay," I yell out, not trusting myself to look at him again.

It's silent for several seconds before I hear the door close. My shoulders drop with a sigh, and I find my way to the bed where I collapse on my back.

"What the hell is happening?"

Thirteen

DEVIN

Jarrod doesn't text me after I leave his place. I don't text him either, but that's because I'm really unsure about what's happening. I decide it's best to give him some space. We've spent the last several days together, and this was supposed to be a solo trip for both of us anyway.

I don't want to assume Jarrod's having some sort of sexuality crisis simply because he's been around me, but it's hard not to see the little things.

What I don't need to do, though, regardless of anything, is get involved with a high profile *straight* athlete.

Ironically enough, my production company is called Straitlay Productions, because we focus on the sub-genre of gay porn that's popular—"straight" boys. While it's fun to act in or watch, in real life, being with someone who's considered themselves straight their whole lives isn't typically as fun. You will end up in the closet with them, forced to keep everything hidden.

The following day goes by and besides going to get something to eat, I spend most of the day in my bungalow responding to business emails or watching movies.

In the past year, I've started to slow down on starring in films, wanting to focus more on the behind the scenes stuff. I've had OnlyFans for the past five years, and it's a good chunk of income on top of everything else. I think my last videos were recorded two weeks ago, but I have someone who helps manage my OF and Twitter pages and posts images and clips. Although, he did send me an email to let me know he's running low on content to post.

I log into Twitter and read through some pretty explicit comments and messages. I have quite a few people asking for new content on my OnlyFans. I suppose since they're paying for it, I should give them something.

Since I didn't bring any equipment out here, I have to be creative and find places to prop my phone. I start inside, taking photos that start out fairly innocent, but definitely suggestive. I film a clip in bed, stroking myself. I move outside and film myself showering, stroking my cock under the spray of the water.

As the sun goes down, I take some pictures of myself in my private pool, the sun offering the perfect golden hour. I remove my shorts and angle the camera to allow the viewers to see my ass just under the water.

After several more photos and short clips of teasing myself, I really need to come. Back in my bed, I prop the phone up against the lamp on my nightstand and start stroking. When I close my eyes, I see Jarrod. His broad shoulders and muscular thighs. His crooked smile and the look in his unique eyes when he stares at me. I think about his obvious erection through his towel yesterday, and I imagine all the things I want to do to him.

I moan, my body tensing up as the orgasm builds. I stare into the camera, my lips parting as it hits.

"Oh god."

My eyes close and my cum lands on my stomach in rivulets.

Once I'm done, I clean myself up and send everything to my social media manager, Carlo. Not wanting to be in this room any longer, I get dressed and decide to head to Midnight Lounge again.

"Hey there," Holden greets, running a hand through his long blond hair. "Let me guess, a Tequila Sunrise?"

"You got it. But I also want food. What do you suggest?"

"The wings are good, so are the shrimp tacos. We also have chicken skewers."

"The skewers sound good. Thanks."

He nods and puts the order in then starts on my drink. The lounge is pretty dead tonight, but I'm thankful for it. I choose to sit at the bar this time, knowing I'll at least have Holden to talk to.

"Where's the big guy?"

I shrug. "Probably in his room. We didn't come here together."

"No?"

"It was a chance reunion. We went to school together and then just happened to be here."

"Wow. Sounds like fate," he says with a wink.

"He's straight."

His face falls. "Oh." He slides me the drink. "But you like him."

"It's not that obvious, is it?"

Holden grins. "Should I lie?"

"Well, I got my answer."

"I really thought y'all were together that first night. There was something in the air between you."

I shrug. "Well, things are more complicated than you think, anyway. It wouldn't work even if he happened to be into me."

"Because he's in the NHL?"

My eyebrows shoot up. "You know?"

"Of course I know. We get movie stars, musicians, politicians' kids, athletes...adult film stars," he says, giving me a look.

"How do you know?"

"About you or the others?"

I shrug, shaking my head. "Anybody."

"We may be on a private island, but I have access to TV and internet. When it comes to you, I'm gay and watch porn. Anybody who is gay and watches gay porn knows who you are. Come on."

"Well, you know me a lot more intimately than I know you," I say, taking a sip.

"We can change that anytime, sweetheart."

I laugh, rolling my eyes. "Anyway, he doesn't know what I do."

He nods. "You gonna tell him? If he's just supposed to be your friend, why does it matter?"

"People judge you for being in the sex industry. It's nice

being here and having him. To think he may look at me differently fills me with dread. But he may look me up and find out on his own."

"It's probably better to tell him first."

"Maybe tomorrow."

Fourteen

JARROD

I'm going to have to get in touch with him at some point, because I'm sure he's wondering what's going on. I know he hasn't reached out either, but I'm the one being weird. I'm the one who shouldn't want him yet keep doing things that would be confusing—that *are* confusing.

And that's why I'm trying to keep away. I don't know what's happening. I feel...different. It's a strange feeling that I'm not even sure how to describe.

I pick up my phone to call my sister because if I talk to anyone about this, it has to be her. It can only be her.

"Hey. This is a surprise," she says with glee in her tone. "I usually have to wait three weeks and send two messages before you call me."

"Oh shush. I'm a busy man."

"Yeah, yeah. Hold on. CeCe, don't roar at your brother, please." She comes back on the phone with an exasperated sigh. "Sorry. Why didn't you FaceTime?"

"I don't know."

I do. It's because I'm not sure I can have her see me when I say what I'm thinking about saying.

"Okay, so what's up? How's vacation?"

"It's good." I sigh. "Really good. It's beautiful out here and..." I chew on my lip for a few seconds. "And I ran into someone I knew from school."

"Really?" Her voice is high-pitched. "Who?"

"I don't know if you'll know him. His name is Devin. We went to Kie Academy together, but he was in my grade, so two years younger than you."

"Hmm. I'm not sure. So y'all were friends?"

"Sort of," I say with a shrug. "We had some classes together, and he'd help me study so I could pass my tests. We didn't really hang out outside of school though."

"Oh okay, but he's there?"

"Yeah. I saw him at one of the restaurants, and we've been kinda hanging out since. It's been nice. You know it's hard for me to not have someone to talk to."

"Well, that's good. Does he know you're in the NHL now?"

"Yeah. He knew but he didn't bring it up right away. He's not into sports, so it's not like it was a big deal to him."

She laughs. "That's funny."

"What?"

"That someone doesn't care about Jarrod Bivens, the hottie of hockey."

"Did you see that article?"

"Mom sent me a link," she says with a giggle.

"Anyway."

"No, but I bet it's nice. He just knows you from school, not as a fan or anything."

"Yeah." The silence stretches between us as I try to figure out what to say next. "He uhh...he told me he had a crush on me in school."

More silence. "Oh."

"Yeah. It was a long time ago, so."

I hear her shuffling something around before she speaks again. "And are you feeling...weird about that, or?"

"No," I say quickly. "I'm not uncomfortable or anything. I don't care."

"Okay," she says slowly, waiting for me to continue.

"I'm not really sure what...I don't know. I'm feeling like...umm."

"J," she says, cutting me off.

"Yeah?"

"What's going on?"

I sigh, letting my head drop over the back of the chair, my arm slung over my forehead. "There's just been some moments. Some thoughts. I don't really know, G. I'm confused."

Her silence makes me regret saying anything. After what feels like minutes, she says, "You like him?"

"Of course. We hit it off immediately. He's fun to be around, but you know, that's normal. I hit it off with lots of people. That's typical friend stuff."

"Okay, but there's something else?"

For some reason, I start getting defensive. "I don't know, G. I don't know what's fucking wrong with me."

She remains calm. "Hey, nothing is wrong with you. I'm not saying that. I'm just trying to understand."

I sigh, sitting up, my legs bouncing. "He's good looking, but it's not hard for me to recognize when someone's attractive, so when I first saw him, I was like, *oh wow,* but didn't really think much else into it. Then we've been having breakfast together, and snorkeling, and going to the pool and all these things, and every time we're together I can't stop thinking about how attractive he is, and that's not normal. The other day I was so close to crossing a line, so now I'm avoiding him."

When I'm done talking, I release a deep exhale and wait for her response.

"So, you've never had a thought about a guy or anything?"

"Like I said, I know when someone is conventionally attractive, but I've never been like, wow, I'm really attracted to this guy. With Devin, well, first of all, he's very different from the guys I've been around."

"How so?"

"He's not like the hockey guys, you know? He's fit, but he's...I don't know how to explain it. He's...pretty." I groan at myself. "That sounds weird, I know. I'm not saying he looks like a girl, but in comparison to, say me, he is just a bit softer. Is that insulting? I don't mean it negatively. He's got abs, and his biceps are obvious, but he's got a smaller frame, I guess. I mean, he's tall, but I don't know. See? I don't even know what to say. I'm rambling and..." I sigh again. "I don't know."

When she speaks, I can tell she's smiling. "I think I know what you mean. Well, you seem to like him."

"I do, but I like all of my friends."

"I've never heard you describe your friends in this frantic, flustered, complimentary way before."

I blow out a breath. "Right, but I'm not gay, G."

"It's not just gay or straight, J."

"I know, but I've gone twenty-nine years being straight. Is it possible to just flip a switch?"

"I think sexual attraction can change for some people. Some know early in life exactly who they're attracted to, and it might take time for others. For you, if he's unlike any other guy you've met, maybe you just have a specific type for men? I'm not really sure. Maybe it's late-blooming bisexuality."

"I don't know, G. I don't understand any of this."

"Well, it's going to take time. Meanwhile, don't ignore him. He didn't do anything, and he's probably confused. Just hang out with him like you have been. See if something grows or changes."

"Yeah. I feel bad, but I'm also embarrassed. I don't want to tell him how I'm feeling, because I don't want him to think I'm just assuming he's into me because he's gay and had a crush over a decade ago. He may not even like me like that."

"Yeah, you're not even that cute."

"Thanks for keeping me humble, sis."

"You know I'm here for you. However, you got a picture of this guy? I'm curious."

"No. Oh wait, I do. One sec." I send her the bed selfie he sent me and then immediately start trying to explain. "Okay, so I know it's gonna seem weird that I have that, but it was this whole thing about how he wanted a photo for his contacts, but I refused and he searched the internet and found some, so I asked—"

"Oh damn. He's cute."

"Yeah," I say with a sigh, a dumb smile on my face.

"Like, really cute. Probably way too cute for you."

"Okay."

"Not even sure what he'd see in you, to be honest. He has to have like a million guys into him," she teases.

"All right. Thanks. I regret sending it to you."

She laughs. "I'm kidding."

"Don't tell Mom or Dad," I tell her. "Or show that photo to anyone."

"You know I won't. Go find him, though. Just ask to have lunch or something."

"Yeah, I will."

"Good. Keep me up to date and know that I love you."

"I love you, too. Thanks, G."

"Anytime. Always. Talk to you later."

"Okay. Bye."

Once I end the call, I put the phone on the table and get up to pace around the room.

Maybe Devin's the first guy I've ever found myself attracted to like this, but is he the only? Is it just him? Is Gina right about me having a specific type?

The more I think about it, I start to get an idea. Porn. I'm not a stranger to it. I watch it as often as any other guy, I guess. However, I typically stick to porn that involves a woman or two. Maybe I should look at gay porn.

I snatch my phone off the table and walk over to my bed. Instead of going to my usual site, I type in *gay porn* and wait to see what pops up.

I click the second link and find myself presented with a ton of different categories. Public, hunk, old and young, big cock, straight.

Straight? On a gay porn site?

I click it, because of course.

After watching several of the previews, I pick one that's

titled *Curious Straight Friends*. I skip ahead a little and watch a couple minutes before I decide I'm not feeling it. I skip past *Straight Studs* and *Bubble Butt Bro*, and go to another one that just has a couple of names as the title.

One of the guys has short dark hair and is fairly close in size to Devin while the other guy has longer, curlier, and much lighter hair. He's a little bit bigger than the other guy, but not by much.

They're naked by a pool and rubbing oil on each other, both already very hard. While massaging each other with the shiny liquid, they tug on each other's erections before making out a little. I skip ahead and find the dark haired guy already inside the other one, fucking him hard while the blond is on all fours.

Their bodies look good together, and after a little while, my cock comes to life. Probably normal, right? I'm watching people have sex.

Skipping forward again, I find the blond in a very flexible position, his body twisted at the waist with one leg up high as the other guy fucks into him. The dark haired guy spits into his mouth before they kiss, and I decide to go to another video.

After a few other clips, I find that I don't like everything I see, but it's the same way with straight porn. I don't like every single video just because there's a woman in it.

My hand goes into my shorts, tugging languidly as I continue to scroll. Then I find a thumbnail that makes me pause. After a few seconds, I click play and turn my phone to the side to watch on the biggest screen possible, because holy hell.

Fifteen

DEVIN

A t five-thirty, I decide to text him.

> Hey. I was gonna go to the gym tonight.
> Have you gone already today?

I wasn't really planning on going to the gym, but I figure it's something he'd respond to. I stare at the phone for a minute before I put it down and walk to my closet. Once I'm in a pair of shorts and a T-shirt, I go back to my phone but he hasn't responded.

Deciding to go whether he responds or not, I find my headphones, grab a bottle of water from the fridge, and put on my tennis shoes. With another glance at my screen, I walk out of the room and start the journey to the main building of the resort.

Inside, there's only a handful of people. One guy who's probably in his fifties or sixties, two young-looking teenagers, and a middle aged couple.

I put my earbuds in, choose a song by Wicked Hearts, and go to the free weights. After doing bicep curls, I do cable tricep pushdowns and finish with cable lateral raises for my shoulders. When I look around, I notice everyone is gone besides the teens.

After taking a gulp of my water, I check my phone but still haven't gotten a response. I make my way to the treadmill and tell myself I'll do twenty minutes of cardio before I go to his door and force him to talk to me. It's not like anything even happened. I don't know why he brushed me off so swiftly and then just stopped talking to me completely.

With my music up high, I step on the treadmill, raise the incline, and start running. It isn't until halfway into my twenty minutes that I wonder if the reason why he's disappeared is because he finally looked me up and found out what I do.

I run faster, upping the speed. Sweat drips from my forehead and my shirt clings to my skin in certain sections. I slow down for a few minutes before stopping completely. I remove my shirt and use it to wipe sweat from my face before hanging it around my neck.

As I'm cleaning off the machine, the two teens who've just been lazily using the bike machines, get up and head for the door.

Jarrod opens it up and steps in, forcing them to take two steps back. I remove my earbuds and put them in their case.

"Whoa," one of them says, eyes wide. "You're Jarrod Bivens."

He gives them a tight-lipped smile, nodding his head once. "That's me."

"Holy shit." He hits his friend in the arm. "Can you fucking believe it? Jarrod Bivens is here."

"Can we get a photo?" he asks, already swiping on his phone screen. "Nobody will believe this. We just watched that game, man. It was fucking crazy."

Jarrod meets my gaze briefly. "If I take a picture, can you give me some time to talk to my friend? Alone."

Shit. Sounds like I'm about to be reprimanded.

"Yeah, cool," one of the kids says, walking up to the side of Jarrod.

He dwarfs them, but they get on either side and take several selfies. It's hard for them to leave, both of them continuing to gaze up at him with amazement.

"Thanks, man. You got it next season."

Jarrod nods. "Okay. Thanks, guys."

They walk backwards, leaving the gym, but staying on the other side of the glass door.

"You made their day," I say before drinking the rest of my water. "Technically, guests aren't supposed to take pictures of other guests here."

He shrugs. "They're kids." His eyes dance over my torso. "Looks like you're already done."

"Yeah. Just finished."

I take in his outfit. He's wearing a pair of Adidas pants and a black T-shirt, but he has on sandals. I don't think he came to actually work out.

"Oh." He shifts on his feet, eyes wandering. "I guess you'll need to shower."

"Definitely," I say with a small laugh. "Then I'll need to eat. You hungry?"

"Always," he says with a grin.

I nod and pocket my headphones. "Want to eat at Bamboo Terrace?"

"That works." His fingers run along a piece of equipment, his eyes avoiding me. "Should I meet you there or..." He briefly looks at me before focusing on something else.

My brows furrow slightly. "You can just come to my room when you're ready. Or I'll go to yours when I'm ready. We can walk together."

"Yeah, that makes sense." A flash of eye contact before he looks at the floor. "You heading back now?"

"Yep," I say, quickly wiping down the equipment before taking my empty water bottle to the recycle bin near the door. "Coming?"

With a dip of his head, he says, "Yeah."

I notice the teens have finally left, so when I open the door we're free to leave without any distractions and make our way outside.

Jarrod bumps into me slightly on the narrow path and quickly moves over. "Sorry."

"It's fine," I say with a laugh. He's quiet, just staring at the sidewalk or at the trees to his left. "Are you okay?" I finally ask.

"Yeah." He turns his head in my direction and smiles. "I'm good."

After another couple minutes, I say, "Holden knows who you are."

His head turns in my direction. "Really?"

"Yeah. I went there last night. He mentioned it. He said he knows about almost everybody who comes here. If they're celebrities or whatnot."

"Wow. Well, at least he doesn't act like he knows."

I nod. "Yeah."

"Did he flirt with you again?" he asks after a few seconds.

"He was pretty well-behaved," I say with a smile. "Well, there might've been one comment, but you know. He was fine."

He shakes his head, a grin on his lips. "Of course."

When we get to my bungalow, I say, "Well, I'll just come out when I'm ready. Or you can come in if you're done first and I'm still getting ready."

"Okay. I don't have much to do but I may change into something a little nicer."

I nod. "I'll keep the door propped open so you can walk in."

"Cool."

Once I put one of my sandals between the door to keep it unlocked, I throw my phone and headphones on the bed and go straight for the shower. After about ten minutes, I'm out and somewhat dry as I look for my lotion.

When I hear Jarrod give a little knock on the door before pushing it open, I snatch a towel and wrap it around my waist.

"Hey."

His eyes move up and down my body. "Sorry. I came fast." Pink color fills his cheeks but he doesn't say anything else.

I laugh. "It's fine. Let me just get some clothes."

He watches me as I walk toward him, making my way to the closet.

"So, uhh. I talked to my sister earlier."

"Oh yeah?" I ask, shifting hangers.

"Yeah. Is it lame if I say she's like my best friend?"

"Is it lame if I say I don't have a best friend?"

"Really?"

I pull a dark blue V-neck T-shirt and pull it off the hanger and pair it with beige chinos.

"Yeah, I mostly have work associates. Also, I'm gonna change in here. Just FYI."

The door's partially closed but Jarrod's on the opposite side so he can't see anything anyway.

"Oh. Okay."

I drop the towel and grab my underwear from the shelf and slip them on before putting on my pants.

"Anyway, yeah, I have some friends, but none I'm really close with. At least you have a sister. Is she older?"

I pull the shirt over my head and turn around, and that's when I notice my reflection in the glass door across the room. Jarrod meets my gaze briefly before looking to the side.

"Yeah. By two years."

He probably saw me, but there's nothing I can do about it now. Let's just not bring it up.

I step out and rush over to the bathroom mirror, fixing my hair and putting on deodorant and cologne.

"Sorry to make you wait."

"It's fine, he says. "I'm at least thirty minutes away from being hangry, so you have time."

I snort as I walk to the nightstand to grab some socks. "Got it. We'll be there in time."

Once I'm done, I grab my phone and walk toward him. "Done."

"You smell good." His eyes widen briefly. "What kind of cologne is that?"

"Uhh. I think it's Chanel Bleu."

"Cool."

"Ready?"

"Yep."

We get to the restaurant in just under fifteen minutes.

"Hi, are we celebrating anything special tonight?" the hostess asks, looking between us both.

"Oh." I look at Jarrod. "Uhh no, just—"

"If we are, what's available?" he asks, cutting me off.

"Well, we have a lovely corner booth. It's private and offers a gorgeous view. We can also send over a bottle of champagne and some homemade macarons."

"Oh," Jarrod says with a smile, looking at me. "You love macarons, and it *is* your thirtieth birthday."

I open my mouth to say something, but the hostess speaks first. "Happy birthday, sir. Wow, the big 3-0. Let's get you settled."

I elbow Jarrod behind her back as she takes us to the booth, but he just chuckles.

She was right though, it's a very private area, tucked away from the main floor and hidden from prying eyes. We face the water, hidden behind the high-backed booth.

"Thirty?" I say, looking at Jarrod. "I still have six months left in my twenties."

"What? Thirty's not old. Plus you look twenty-five. You're fine. I turn thirty in four months."

"When's your birthday?"

"On Halloween."

"Really?" I ask with a squeak. "Mine is on Christmas."

"Holiday babies for the win," he says with a high five.

I smack his hand, but I swear our connection lasts longer than it should.

"It kind of sucks," I say, pulling my hand back.

"I always had costume parties," he says with a shrug. "It was fun."

"Christmas is one of the most popular holidays, so my birthday is easily overshadowed.

"Yeah, I can see how that would suck."

As we eat, our conversation flows, and it gets back to how it felt the first several days we were hanging out. Jarrod doesn't seem as tense or weird, and he's able to look at me without quickly moving his gaze.

By the end of the night, we're toasting to my fake birthday with champagne and munching on bright pink macarons.

"Would you like a photo?" the waitress asks us.

"Sure," Jarrod replies, handing her his phone.

He scoots in close, his arm stretched along the back of the booth. Our legs touch under the table and my body heats up.

Still not over this crush.

"Say, cheers!" the waitress sings.

We lift our glasses toward the camera and smile.

Once she hands his phone back to him, we both lean in to check out the picture. She took a few.

In the first, we're not really quite ready, both of us looking at our glasses. In the second, Jarrod's gaze is on my face, his smile already in place. Something about it makes butterflies take flight in my stomach. The third one is perfect, both of us gazing into the camera and smiling.

"Looks good," he says.

"Yeah. Text them to me."

"Okay."

He scoots over a little and I miss his warmth immediately.

"Jarrod."

"Hmm?" he murmurs, staring at his phone.

I think you're incredible.

I'm having the best time here with you.

I film pornographic videos and hope you don't think of me differently.

Various thoughts flitter through my head, but I don't say any of them.

"Never mind."

Sixteen

JARROD

In the last three days, everything has been perfect. We tried paddle boarding, and I did pretty good while Devin fell quite a bit, but through it all, we laughed a lot. We also went jet skiing and then I tried convincing him to go scuba diving, but he isn't a fan of the idea. Instead, we stuck a rainbow-colored umbrella in the sand and spent some time on the beach, doing some more snorkeling and swimming before lying down on a blanket and falling asleep for half an hour.

We've eaten together at least once, but usually twice a day, and we've gone to the gym together one time, Devin bailing out the other two times, claiming he only needs a twice a week workout.

Yes, I still think he's attractive, but I've been able to focus on our friendship and not worry about anything else. I really like him and we get along great, and sometimes I think I want more, but I have no clue what that even is. I don't know what I'm thinking or what I'd do or say, and I've determined

I'm way out of my element. Devin hasn't even let on that he'd be interested in me like that, and he probably isn't. I don't know shit about being with a man.

Friends. Nothing more.

"Okay, so there's two more things I want to do," Devin says, turning to look at me from his place on the couch on his deck.

"Just two? We have a good amount of time left."

"Well, we can repeat some things, but I think we should definitely go to the spa. They have a steam bath and cold plunge pool, and then this specific massage called *Euphoric* consists of a full body rubdown with some local oils. Doesn't that sound amazing?"

I smile as he talks, because he's so excited as he reads from the pamphlet.

"Yes, it does. What's the other thing?"

"Well, it's totally the opposite of relaxation and massages, but I hear there's a waterfall in the jungle. It might be nice to see that."

"Okay. Yeah, let's do them both."

"Today?" he asks, sitting up.

"It's early. I'll book the massages and we can go hike and find waterfalls then relax afterwards."

He gets off the couch with a huge grin. "Yes, let's do it."

I find that I like doing whatever makes him happy. His smile is infectious and makes my heart flutter.

Whatever that means. I'm naturally a giver, so this isn't new.

Twenty minutes later, we're both dressed for the trek through the jungle, covered in bug spray and sunscreen, under Devin's orders.

"Okay, so according to this map, the trail is here. It's uphill but not too steep."

"Let's do it," I say, hiking up the straps on my backpack.

The walk is maybe a mile, and during the journey, we pass a lot of beautiful scenery. Lush greenery, bright, beautiful flowers, and the sun peeking through the trees, creating scattered rays.

"I should be taking pictures," Devin says, pulling out his phone. "It's so beautiful."

He takes a few shots, and a short video, walking right into the path of one of the beams of the sun. Devin angles his head over his shoulder and smiles at me, the sun hitting his face and making it look like he's glowing. *He's* beautiful.

"Stay right there," I say, getting my phone. "Don't move."

He laughs. "What are you doing?"

"The sun is perfect right now. Hold on." I take a few photos, and he laughs at me, but it makes the photos better. Candid and real. "Look."

I walk over and show him. "Wow, you should be a photographer."

"It's all you. And the sun."

"Maybe I'll actually post these."

I send them to him via text before pocketing my phone. "Are you on social media a lot?"

He turns and continues walking. "Not really. Not like real life stuff. Just work."

"Well, one of these would make a great profile photo. Just give me photography credit."

He laughs. "Will do."

The sound of the waterfall gets louder as we get closer, and once we break into a clearing, we're met with frothy, white water plunging over a rocky ledge and falling into a teal-colored pool.

"Wow," we both say at the same time before looking at each other and laughing.

"We're definitely taking pictures here," I say, removing my backpack.

We drink from our water bottles and start stripping down to our shorts. I move to the water's edge first.

"Is it cold?" Devin asks as he steps closer.

"Not warm, that's for sure. Should we just go for it and dive in?"

"If I go into shock will you save me?"

"Of course," I say with a playful eye roll. "Unless I'm also in shock."

"Okay." We back up so we can run up. "On the count of three." I nod. "One, two, three."

We take off and jump as far into the center as we can. The water is cool but not freezing. I pop up first and watch as Devin's head emerges.

"Well, we're not in shock."

I laugh. "Nope."

We swim around for a while, and then I remember what my sister said and now it's all I can think about.

"Have you heard of penis fish?"

He chokes out a laugh. "What?"

"Those tiny little fish that can swim into your penis? My sister told me about it, and now I'm wondering if this water has penis fish."

Devin laughs. "I thought that was in the Amazon."

"They only live there?"

He shrugs. "I don't know."

"Let's go behind the waterfall. Looks like there's a little cave-like thing back there. Probably no penis fish."

He chuckles, but we swim around the edge and climb up the slippery rocks until we're behind the rushing water.

"Oh damn. We didn't even bring our phones," Devin says, his back to the water, his body glistening.

"I'll remember even without one."

A look crosses his face before he walks over to where I'm sitting. "We should definitely try to come back and have our phones in a Ziploc bag or something.

"Okay. We will."

Our shoulders are almost touching as we stare out at the view. It's a romantic setting, and we're hidden from any prying eyes. All I can think about is reaching over and touching his hand or his leg, or just turning my head and hoping he does the same. Our lips would be so close, we'd have no choice but to kiss.

When I glance at him, his face looks tense. His jaw is set tight, and he's gnawing on his lower lip.

I want to save it. Pull it from his teeth and soothe it with my tongue. I don't even try to make sense of my thoughts anymore. I want him in a way I can't explain, in a way I'm not sure I even understand, but god do I want him.

I shift slightly, ready to tell him. Ready to lay myself bare and hope I don't ruin this.

"Dev—"

"We should go," he says at the same time, looking at me.

"Oh."

"What time was the massage appointment?"

"Three."

"It's probably like noon now. We should go shower and eat before we show up."

"Okay, yeah."

He gives me a tight grin before he makes his way to the edge and slides into the water. Once we're back on land, we gather our things and start our hike back down.

Something's up with him. His mood shifted dramatically in a short time, and I can't help but wonder what happened.

Devin's feet move at a rapid pace, like he can't get out of the jungle fast enough. Our shoes are slightly wet and the mud under our feet is slick.

"Be careful, I almost tripped back there," I say, watching his shoes slide through the thick sludge.

"I'll be fine."

He does a quick little hop, trying to avoid the sharp rocks, and as soon as he passes them, his left foot hits the ground and he buckles.

"Oh fuck."

Devin's on the ground, gripping his ankle.

"What happened? You okay?"

"I rolled it," he says through gritted teeth. "And I hit a fucking rock or something."

I kneel down in front of him. "Let me see."

He doesn't let go, shaking his head through a grimace. "What if it's bad?"

"Then I should definitely know so I can figure out what to do."

I take his hands in mine and gently pry them from his leg. There's a cut about an inch and half long, but it's not too bad. I inspect it and find that while it's bleeding, it's not too deep.

"Can you move it at all?"

He tries, but quickly pulls his lips in, his brow furrowing as he shakes his head. "It fucking hurts."

"Okay, well it looks like I'm going to have to carry you. We can look at it in the room and see if they have a doctor we can call. The rehab side should definitely have some sort of medical professionals."

"You can't carry me the whole way."

"Why not? Think I'm not strong enough?" I tease.

He shakes his head, still in pain. "It's like another twenty minutes or so."

"But we're almost done with this jungle hike and the rest is on smooth, flat land. For the most part."

"Maybe I'll just stay here and you go get someone. They can get a golf cart or something."

"No." I bend down and scoop an arm under his knees and his back. "I got you."

Not gonna lie, I do begin to struggle after about ten minutes. Devin is lighter than me, but still a grown man.

When we get to the resort area, an employee passes us. "Oh, what happened?"

"Hurt his ankle," I say, my voice coming out strained. "We're in bungalow six. Can you have someone come check on him?"

The woman nods, reaching for a walkie talkie on her belt. "Yes, do you want to wait for a cart?"

"I'll get there faster if I go now."

"Okay. I'll send someone immediately."

Once we're in his room, I gently set him down on the bed, my arms screaming in relief. I take his leg and attempt to remove his shoe and sock without hurting him.

He grimaces and grunts, but I free him from their confines and put a couple of pillows under his calf.

"You said you had Tylenol?"

"By the bathroom sink."

I rush over and grab the bottle before getting a water from the fridge. He swallows two pills and drops back down on his pillow.

"I'm so pissed I can't go get a massage."

I give him a crooked smile. "I think your well-being is more important."

"My well-being was going to be great after a full body massage."

I laugh before going to the bathroom and running a clean cloth under some warm water. When I return, I get on my knees next to the mattress.

"I'm gonna clean this up a little."

He looks down, squeezing the covers in his fist. "Okay."

I wipe off the area, making sure it doesn't get infected while also trying to be gentle around where he may have sprained it.

"Maybe it'll feel fine in the next two hours and we can still go," Devin says with hope in his voice.

"Mm. I'm not sure about that." When his face falls, I say, "But maybe."

Soon, there's a knock on the door. I open it and an older gentleman with honey-brown skin comes in, holding a red duffle bag.

"Mr. De'León?" he asks me.

"Over here," I say, showing him to the bed. "He twisted it on our walk back through the jungle."

The doctor squats down and touches his leg softly,

inspecting the cut. He opens one of the flaps in the front of the bag and puts on some gloves before wiping the wound down again, smearing some sort of gel on it and then covering it with a Band-Aid.

He lifts Devin's foot by the heel, pressing on certain areas and moving it around, keeping an eye on Dev's expressions.

After a couple minutes, he says, "It's not broken. You can come to my facility on the other side of the island, and I can get some X-rays, but considering I was able to twist your foot with minimal reaction, it's probably a strain versus a sprain. We won't know for sure unless you start bruising. There could be some swelling no matter what, so I'd recommend keeping it elevated and icing it for fifteen minutes every few hours or so. I can come back and check on you tomorrow, but I'll leave my number if you need to get in touch. Meanwhile, I'm going to wrap it with a compression bandage. You can remove it when you go to sleep."

"Okay, thanks," Devin says. "So, I'm guessing walking is out of the question for the immediate future."

The doctor finishes wrapping his foot. "I'd keep your distances short and put little to no pressure on the foot."

"Great. Thanks," he says as the doctor starts closing up his bag.

He hands me his card. "Let me know if you need me to come back out."

"Will do. Thanks."

Once he's gone, Devin gives me a pitiful look. "Now I'm sweaty and disgusting and can't shower or get a massage."

I chew on my bottom lip for a few seconds. "I can help."

"What? No way. I wouldn't have you do that."

"You heard the doctor. You shouldn't be putting pressure

on it. Just use me as a crutch. I won't look and you can do the cleaning yourself. I'll just be there so you don't lose your balance."

He shakes his head, closing his eyes. "It's too much."

"We're doing it. Come on."

Seventeen

DEVIN

Both of us are in my shower in just our swim trunks. Jarrod tied a plastic bag around the bottom of my foot so I wouldn't need to remove the bandage, and now stands at my side, holding onto my waist with one large hand as I wash my body.

"This is weird," I say.

"It's not the weirdest thing I've done."

"What is?"

"You want a secret?" he questions, mischief burning in his eyes. "Because if I give you one, you have to give me one."

"Sure."

"I feel like this one is just as bad as the last secret I told you, and now I'm concerned you're gonna think badly of me."

I snort. "I promise I won't."

"So, back in college, I met this girl. Well, she was a professor, so she was older than me."

"You slept with your professor?" I ask, holding onto him as I attempt to turn around to let the water hit my back.

"Yes, but that's not really the crazy part."

"Go on," I say, washing my hair.

"She was pretty flirtatious and I knew she was into me, so I felt like it was gonna be an easy hookup. A few days after we started talking she let me in on a secret. She was married."

I gasp. "You had an affair with a married woman?"

"Mmm...not really."

"Oh my gosh, just get to the good part." I turn back around, and he puts both hands on my waist, looking at me as I move. He licks the water from his lips and swallows. "But before you continue, um...I'd like to clean myself, you know...in other areas."

His eyes drop down low before coming back up. "Oh, right. Do you need me to..."

"Just turn around," I tell him.

He does, and while holding onto the faucet, I shove the wet shorts down my legs, struggling to get them off my injured foot. Eventually, I do, and I'm able to wash up properly.

"So, the affair," I say.

"Oh. Yeah. So, she tells me she's married, and I'm like, what the fuck are you doing with me then? She ends up telling me that her husband wants to watch her have sex with someone else."

"Ohhh," I say. "Cuckolding. Not really *weird*, but different."

He's quiet. "Yeah, I guess. I didn't really know what that was."

I shut off the water. "I'm done, can you reach a towel?"

"Are you stable?"

"Mentally? Probably not. Physically, I'm holding onto this handle."

He laughs and walks away, returning with his back still to me while holding out the towel.

Once I dry off as much as I can, I wrap it around my waist and grab onto his shoulder. I step forward and he turns and holds onto me, slipping his arm around my waist.

"Want to get dressed?"

I shake my head. "I'll be fine for now."

Jarrod gets me to the bed and I lie down, keeping the towel closed while I rest my leg on the pillow again. He removes the bag from my foot and takes it to the trash.

"So, anyway, I didn't agree right away, but eventually, I was like, fuck it. If she wants to sleep with me, and her husband wants me to sleep with her, and I want to fuck her, then what's the problem?"

"Besides it probably being against the rules, because she was a professor," I say with a smirk.

"Right. Besides that."

"So you did it?"

He nods. "Went to their house, and she offered me a drink. We sat in the living room together before her husband showed up. He was friendly, but quiet. Then she started making moves."

"Wow."

"Yeah, it was quite the experience."

"Sounds like it. Did he touch himself at all?"

Jarrod nods. "Yeah. Not in the beginning, but eventually he started jacking off from a chair in the corner."

"Well, you had fun in college," I say with a grin.

"I suppose so." He pushes his damp hair from his fore-head. "Mind if I shower?"

"No, go ahead."

"I'll be quick. Be thinking about your secret, because I'm not forgetting."

"Oh. Well, take your time."

He disappears back into the shower, and I try to think of something I can tell him that's not the one secret I can't stop thinking about.

Before I know it, he's done and strutting toward me wrapped in his own towel. He plops down on the bed next to me.

"Okay, secret time."

"I thought of something."

He rolls onto his side, and the towel opens slightly. "Hope it's juicy."

"Not as juicy as cuckolding. Should it be sexual?"

"Sexual keeps it fun," he says in a husky tone.

"Okay, well..." I think over all of my sexual situations and try to find one that's not related to porn and work. "Oh, when I was twenty, I was a stripper."

"What?" he exclaims, his lips parted. "For real?"

I laugh. "Not like in a club. Some friends of friends were having a bachelor party and wanted a couple guys to come strip for them, so me and my friend said we'd do it. We got paid well for it, so it was fine."

His brow furrows. "It's not like you needed the money though."

I swallow and look up at the ceiling. "I moved out when I was eighteen. My parents wanted me to follow their footsteps, but I didn't want to. I had plans for other things that they didn't approve of. So, I was on my own when I left their house. I didn't take any of their money for anything."

"Wow."

I look over at him. "And now we're even."

He gives me a look. "Mine was a little juicer, but I guess we can call it even."

I shift. "Think we could go to the spa tomorrow?"

Jarrod's quiet for a while. "I can give you a massage here."

My head snaps in his direction. He's still on his side looking at me. "Why?"

I don't mean to question him and certainly not in the way it came out, but I don't know why he's being so nice and attentive.

He shrugs. "Why not? You're an injured patient."

Jarrod tries to joke and keep things light, but I have a feeling he uses humor as a distraction sometimes.

"You don't have to massage me, Jarrod," I tell him, looking back up at the ceiling. "I can wait."

When he doesn't reply right away, I face him again and find a soft and vulnerable look in his eyes.

"Let me. Please."

My brows dip briefly, confused, but he seems very serious now.

"Okay. Sure. Am I gonna owe you another secret after this?"

I try to go back to the joking nature and he happily responds.

"Probably like five, actually."

"Only if it's a good massage."

"It's gonna be *very* good."

I slowly roll to my side, careful to keep my towel in place, then I flop onto my stomach with a grunt, readjusting my leg on the pillow.

"Do you have references?"

His voice comes from the bathroom area. "You'd be my first, but I've had massages, so I know a few things."

I laugh. "Okay."

The bed dips to my left from his weight and then he says, "It's gonna be cold for a second."

The cool lotion hits my back before he starts rubbing it in. His hands are large with a few calluses, but the strength in them feels good as he squeezes my shoulders.

His fingers push into my shoulder blades, moving lower down my back. He takes his time and uses more lotion as needed, tracing small circles on both sides of my spine. With his whole hand, he applies more pressure from the base of my spine all the way up to my neck.

"Oh god," I moan. "This feels good."

After a pause, he says, "I told you."

He does it for another ten minutes before I feel him move down toward my legs. I didn't expect him to do anything besides my back, and while I *should* stop him, I don't.

His lotion-slicked fingers begin rubbing the back of my left thigh, taking it in both hands and squeezing, his thumbs making half circles.

I bury my face in the pillow in the hopes of muffling any moans, but Jesus Christ his fingers are dangerously close to touching parts of me I've been dying for him to touch.

"Does this feel good?" he asks in a shy tone, like he needs encouragement. All of his bravado from before is gone.

I turn my head to the side. "Yes. Very good."

He moves to the other thigh, his legs touching mine as he reaches over. This time, his finger skates right under the crease of my ass and a groan slips out.

Jarrod moves lower, working on the calf of my uninjured leg before getting off the bed and taking my foot in his hand. He squeezes the arch, running his thumb up and down. Holy fuck, why am I getting turned on?

I shift my body, needing to reach under the towel to adjust my erection.

"You okay?" he asks, his fingers working their way up my leg again.

"Yep."

His fingers skate over the back of my thigh, reaching the inner part, and when he slides upwards just an inch, his fingertip barely touches my scrotum.

My eyes roll into my head and I bury my face into the pillow as I groan his name. "Jarrod."

It's a plea. I need him to stop. He has to stop touching me, because I want nothing more than to feel him all over. The longer his hands are on me, the more I'm going to grow accustomed to it. To know what it feels like to be touched by him and know I'll never feel it again is torture. Bittersweet fucking torture.

Call me a masochist, because I don't tell him to stop. In fact, my hips wiggle slightly, wanting more. Hoping he slips again. Please, God, let him touch me once more so I know what it's like to be ruined, because that's what'll happen. I will become ruined under his touch, unable to think about anyone else, unwilling to want anyone else.

Without warning, I spin around, needing this to be over.

I can't keep doing this to myself. At the waterfall, we were sitting next to each other, enjoying an idyllic day with a picturesque view. Everything about it was perfect. I never wanted it to end. I wanted to wrap myself around him and never let him go. I want more than he's capable of giving. It's why we had to leave.

When I flop to my back, my towel comes apart, and though I'm quick to try to bring it together again, my erection is obvious. There's no hiding it. It's begging to be seen and touched.

His eyes move to it. I go to open my mouth to apologize, though I don't know why. It's not like I did it on purpose. But then my eyes notice something. His own towel is tented.

My eyes slowly peruse upward, tracing every muscle in his torso until I meet his gaze.

Jarrod's voice is soft when he says, "Dev."

Eighteen

JARROD

His embarrassment quickly transformed to confusion before shifting into what looks like desire. Meanwhile, I feel self-conscious as I grab my towel and twist it to the side, needing the split to be farther away from my dick.

"Jarrod."

I scurry off the bed, standing on the opposite side from where he's lying. "I'm sorry."

"No, don't—"

"Dev, I don't know what to say. I'm...I really don't know."

I look around for my things, spotting my backpack on the floor.

"Don't leave," he says, sitting up.

"I should. I need to."

"Jarrod," he says in a firm tone. "It's fine."

"I'm not gay, Devin!" I shout.

He blanches. "I didn't say you were."

"Good, because I'm not."

"Are you saying there's something wrong with being gay?" he questions, his face hardening.

I snatch up my backpack and march toward the door. "I didn't say that."

"You're not saying much."

"There's nothing to say," I say with a bite. "Nothing at all. We're spending way too much time together, I think."

His face reflects the hurt I caused. "Then leave."

I want to apologize and explain why I'm reacting this way, but I don't know how. "Fine."

Rushing through the door, I stomp all the way to my room and throw my bag against the wall when I get in. I hurriedly pull on some boxers and climb into bed. This day needs to be over.

I hate myself for reacting the way I did. It was my opportunity to be open and honest, and instead, when faced with it, I turned into a coward. I lashed out and became defensive. He doesn't deserve that, and I want to take it back and apologize, but I need to figure out exactly what I want to say and how first. I need to tell myself the truth before I tell anyone else.

THE NEXT DAY I text and call Devin, but he ignores them all. I go to his door and bang on it for ten minutes, but he never opens up.

I feel bad for leaving him alone when he's hurt and could use somebody. I go right down to Midnight Lounge and approach Holden.

"Hey, big guy," he says with a smile. "Been a while since I've seen you."

"Hey, can you do me a favor?"

He looks around and leans in close. "Did you hear about the weed?"

"What?" I ask, my brows furrowing.

"Oh. That's not what you want?"

"No. I need your help with Devin."

"What's going on?"

I scratch the back of my neck, looking off to the side. "Well..."

"You messed up. That's the classic *I fucked up* move right there."

"He's ignoring my calls and won't open the door."

"Relationship problems?" he questions with an arched brow and smirk on his lips.

"I'm not...we're not together."

"Right," he says with a nod.

"Anyway, he hurt his ankle yesterday, and now he's in there alone, so I just want to make sure he's okay."

His face softens. "Definitely doesn't seem like you care about him at all."

"Could you just..." I bite back the rest of my response. "Please."

"Fine. Give me his number."

"I don't know how I feel about giving his number to you."

He crosses his arms, giving me a smug look. "Afraid I'll take him from you?"

I bite my lip. "Can you go to his room?"

"Ooh. I might really get the chance to take him then."

"I swear to god," I say, slapping my hands on the bar.

"Make sure he's okay and don't fucking touch him. Don't flirt. Don't do anything but ensure he's fine."

Both of his eyebrows shoot to his hairline, but he still looks amused. "Okay. Which bungalow is it?"

"Six."

"I'll be there in fifteen. Don't be around though. He won't open up if he sees your hulking figure through the peephole. I'll let you know how it goes."

"Thank you," I say, trying to hide my annoyance. "I'm in eight when you're done."

I march back to the bungalow, hating that I had to enlist Holden's help, but needing to make sure Devin's fine by any means necessary.

Thirty minutes go by before I have a knock on my door. I snatch it open hoping it's Devin, but it's just Holden.

"Is he okay?"

"He's fine. Hobbling around a little, but fine."

"Did he say anything? Has the doctor come to see him?"

"Doctor came earlier this morning. It's a light strain. Nothing to worry about."

I rub the hair on my chin. "Did he..."

"Talk about you? Oh yeah, he's pretty mad. Wouldn't say much about why."

"I've been trying to apologize."

He tilts his head. "What happened?"

"It's none of your business."

"Maybe not, but based off what I've seen, and how you're reacting, I'm going to assume you're feeling a certain type of way." He dips his chin and raises his brows. "I know he really likes you. I know you're pretty high-profile, too. But I also know you two have this energy—this chemistry. It's rare and beautiful, and I don't even see it in all the newlyweds we get here. Whatever you're feeling is valid and normal, but don't let it turn into hate. We get enough of that from other people, you know?"

I ingest his words and nod. "Thanks for your help."

"Anytime."

Devin avoids my calls and messages for the rest of the day.

I WAKE up and check my phone and still don't have a response. When I leave my bungalow to get breakfast, I do it knowing I'm just going to bring it back to my room. I hope to get a glimpse of Devin on the way there or back, but I don't.

I struggle getting the stupid door to unlock with my bracelet because I'm carrying so much food, and to make matters worse, my sandal gets caught on the threshold as soon as I'm walking in. I plunge forward, losing my shoe and almost smacking my face against the wall. I kick off my other sandal in frustration as I take the food to the table.

Instead of eating, I go to my bed and pull out my phone. I click on my photos app and spend a ridiculous amount of time staring at the pictures I have of Devin. First, the selfie, then the ones of us at the restaurant. In one of them, I'm staring at him like he's the most amazing thing I've ever seen. And it's true.

The ones from the hike are beautiful too, but there's really something special about that selfie. It feels intimate. Taken just for me.

I reach into my shorts and feel like a preteen trying to jerk off to a still photograph, but I don't care.

And then I remember...Devin does porn.

I stumbled across the videos that day I decided to look into gay porn and it blew my mind. He's incredible. His body, his prowess, his confidence.

I was shocked at first. I didn't know what to think. I almost didn't watch them, because it felt like an invasion of privacy. He obviously kept this from me for a reason, and here I am watching him. But doing so filled me with warring emotions. I wanted to kill every man he was with for being lucky enough to touch him. They got to know him in a way I haven't. They felt his mouth, his cock, and his ass.

As I continued to watch that day, I imagined me being one of those guys. I inserted myself in his videos as his partner and it was incredible. I came so hard.

And multiple times.

Then, I decided to stop watching. I couldn't do it anymore. He was texting me about the gym, and I knew I needed to make a decision.

Do I tell him I know? Would that make him uncomfortable? All I knew was that I was a thousand percent attracted to him. Some of the other guys were attractive too, but I guess my type is everything Devin encapsulates. Right now, I'm not willing to say I'm into guys—plural. I'm into one. One very perfect guy, and I probably ruined it with my fear.

I tried to just go back to friends and act like I never saw the porn. It felt wrong that I got to see him that way without his knowledge, but now I'm desperate to see him in any capacity.

I type in his stage name in the search bar of a gay porn

site and watch as the videos pop up. This time I click on the solo ones, not wanting to watch him with anyone else.

I pull my shorts down and settle in. In this video, he's sitting on a chair, staring right at me, stroking his dick. I mimic his moves and pretend we're doing this in the same room together.

He starts talking dirty and drives me crazy. He speaks like he's talking just to me.

Do you want to stroke my dick for me?

I nod in response.

I wish your cock was filling my ass.

I nod again. "Yeah."

You're so fucking big. I bet you'd make me come so hard.

"Fuck, yes." I stroke faster.

I turn up the volume and close my eyes, listening to his sultry voice utter filthy words as I get myself closer to release.

"Devin, fuck," I groan just as cum shoots from my cock, landing on my shirt.

I drop the phone next to me and open my eyes just as I hear a soft click near my front door.

"Hello?"

When nobody replies, I assume it was just the wind and then get up to go to the bathroom.

Nineteen

DEVIN

Twenty minutes after I'm back in my room, my phone goes off.

> Hey. I know you're mad, but I really want to talk to you. Can we meet today?

Fury burns in my veins, heating me up to a scorching degree. I went over there after a barrage of messages begging me to talk to him. His door propped open with a shoe led me to believe he was hoping I'd come over and have a conversation.

Ready to hear him out and lay everything on the table, I instead came face-to-face with Jarrod jerking off to porn. *My* porn.

I stood there frozen in shock for a few seconds, hearing my own voice come from his phone as his hand slid up and down his shaft.

He knows and who knows how long he has, but he never

told me. Instead, he chose to watch the videos and use them to get off all while telling me he's not gay.

It feels weird and I debate within myself on whether I have a right to be angry. I recorded them. They're available to watch online for anyone. I can't control who sees them, but the thought of Jarrod watching them makes me feel uncomfortable.

> How long have you known?

Known what?

My frustration grows, but I swallow it down and try to figure out how to continue this conversation.

Dev, please. Can we talk? I overreacted. I was nervous and scared. I'm feeling all these things, but I really want to talk in person.

Part of me wonders if he only wants to make up because he's seen the videos. He wants to try things with me because he knows what I do—the sexual things I'm capable of. Jarrod wants to use me like everyone else. I can give him what he's curious about.

> I can't believe you found out what I do and didn't say anything. Instead, you sit over there jerking off to me. You yell at me about how you're not gay, like I was forcing you into something, and then you watch me. You watch me do things I don't even want you to see. I can't believe it. I can't believe you.

He doesn't respond, but I watch when the message is read and I never see the bubble pop up to show he's writing.

Two minutes later, he's banging at my door.

"Devin, please. Open up. We need to talk. Please, Dev. I can explain. Let me explain."

I walk closer to the door, my heart in my throat. "No, Jarrod. You had time to talk to me, and you didn't take it. You keep running from me, leaving me to sit in your absence to question what the hell is going on."

"I've been texting you!" he yells. "I've called and come over. *You're* ignoring *me!*"

"So you watch my porn to make yourself feel better? If you can't see me, you just go watch me?"

"No!" His fist hits the door with a heavy sigh. "It's not like that."

"It's exactly like that. I've noticed the little things, Jarrod. The lingering looks and small touches. Something's been happening and I never pushed or questioned because I knew it may have been very hard for you to wrap your head around. Instead of opening up and being vulnerable with me, you watched me in some of my most vulnerable moments. You chose to live out your fantasies without having to actually include me. You didn't allow me to experience what's been growing with you. You did it on your own, behind my back, and I don't even..." I walk away, running my hand through my hair before I step closer to the door. "I don't want this. Whatever it was or could have been. I don't want it. You've taken a very intimate thing from me. I know I put myself out there, but that's for strangers and people I'll never know or care about. If you wanted to see me naked, you should've let me be the one to show you, instead of watching me on the internet."

"Dev. I'm sorry. Please."

He sounds desperate and sad, but I remove myself from the situation and go into the bathroom where I turn on the shower and drown him out. I attempt to wash away this unpleasant feeling that clings to me. I put any hope I had down the drain with the water, and I plan my trip out of here. I can't chance a run-in. I almost feel embarrassed to face him.

When I get out of the shower, I'm met with the sounds of a storm. The rain is whipping against the bungalow, the wind picking up speed. I watch the turquoise water ripple with waves under a gray sky.

I pull out my laptop and start searching for flights. As I'm looking them up, I get alerts informing me of a tropical depression potentially forming into a tropical storm nearby. Nobody believes it will escalate further than that, but the rain and wind will be here for at least a couple days.

With another glance outside, I know my plans for a hasty escape are going to be put on hold. Great.

I slam the laptop closed and turn on the TV. I watch the weather channel for a while and then decide to clean up. It's not like there's much to clean considering the maid service was in here two days ago, but I tidy up to keep myself busy. There's hardly anything to do on a tropical island when there's a storm beating down. I watch the water slosh back and forth, hoping like hell these bungalows aren't on their last leg.

By five o'clock, the weather has only gotten worse and

the sky is even darker. My phone dings next to me as I lie in bed.

> Devin. Let's talk. Please.

> As soon as this storm passes, I'm leaving. There's no point.

> You're not supposed to leave for another week and a half.

> Things change.

He doesn't reply, so I settle in under my covers, the TV on and the rest of the lights off. My eyes flitter from the screen to the water, unsure which is more interesting while I zone out and try not to think about Jarrod.

Twenty minutes later, I hear a clanging against the deck and wonder if I should've checked to see if anything could fly off. I'm assuming their furniture is sturdy enough to withstand some wind, but I might have left a few things out there.

Too late, because there's no way I'm going outside now.

Another noise has me sitting up because it was louder. I squint my eyes and watch a dark shadow move from the lower deck to the upper deck. It unfolds slowly, getting bigger as it moves closer.

"What the fuck?" I mutter under my breath, moving from the bed to approach the glass door.

When my eyes adjust, I gasp. It's Jarrod. He's soaking wet, his clothes clinging to his skin as the wind whips him in the face.

I slide it open. "What the hell are you doing?"

He hurries in, standing just inside the door as I close it. I face him, his body shivering slightly as he soaks the floor. He's not even wearing shoes.

"You said you were gonna leave."

"Jarrod, this is insane."

I rush to get a towel and bring it to him.

"You make me insane," he replies, taking it from me. "I had to see you before you left. I knew you wouldn't open the front door and knew you kept the back unlocked."

"So you were prepared to break in?"

"Yes."

I rip my gaze from his face and go to my closet. "Get out of those clothes."

When I return, he's standing in his shorts, using the towel to dry himself off as much as possible.

"My clothes are a little smaller, but it's better than nothing, I guess."

I hand him a pair of boxer-briefs because they'll stretch a little, as well as a pair of lounge pants that are elastic in the waist, and a plain T-shirt.

He takes them, his eyes focused on me, but I go to the kitchen to allow him some privacy while I make a cup of coffee.

Before I'm done, Jarrod's in the kitchen, wearing only the pants. They're a little short on him, but it's better than having wet clothes.

"Dev."

I hand him the mug, but as soon as he takes it, he puts it back on the counter. I walk past him and gather his wet clothing, taking them to the shower where I can hang them up.

He follows me, ripping them from my hands and tossing them on the floor. "Stop it. Look at me."

"I can't!" I yell, meeting his gaze for only two seconds before I turn my head. "I don't want to see the way you look at me now that you've seen me through a different lens."

His thumb and forefinger grab my chin and turn my face to look up at him. "Devin, I see you. *You.* Not a persona, not a pseudonym or actor. Just you."

I shake my head and step away from him. "You don't. You can't."

He moves forward, not allowing me to run away. With a sigh, he says, "I've known for days, Dev. I knew before we shared macarons together. I knew during the hike, paddle boarding, jet skiing, countless other meals and trips to Midnight Lounge. I found out a week ago. Did I ever treat you any differently?"

I blink rapidly, trying to absorb his words. "What?" The word leaves my lips in a breath.

"Can we sit?" he asks, taking my wrist in his hand.

I nod, following him to the edge of the bed. I put some space between us. "How?"

He rubs his palm over his jaw. "Well, uhh...I had been talking to my sister about how I'd been feeling. I told her about you." I look at him then and notice the way his cheeks turn pink. He turns his attention to the floor. "I wasn't sure if I was just attracted to you or what. It's new to me. I never felt attracted to any guy before. Anyway, I thought maybe I'd look at porn...you know, to see."

I nod, looking at the floor as well. I can't blame him for that. "Okay. And then you found me."

"I did. I was surprised. I didn't know what to think. I

thought to ask you about it but didn't want you to feel uncomfortable. I figured you didn't tell me for a reason, and I was waiting to see if you would."

"I wanted to. I thought about it a few times," I say, running a hand through my hair before I lean back on my palms. "But I didn't want you to judge me. I was afraid it would change everything, but I also feared you'd find out on your own. I knew I should've mentioned it."

He shifts, turning to the side and bending his knee so it rests on the mattress. Our eyes meet and we're quiet for several seconds.

"I wish you would have, but I understand why you didn't." He reaches out and tugs on the hem of my shirt. "But Dev, you have to know I'm not judging you. It's definitely a different than usual kind of job, but I understand that it's a job."

A lump forms in my throat at his easy acceptance and non-judgmental way of looking at it. It's hard to come across people who don't cringe or make snide comments.

"What I said still stands," I say. "And it may be ridiculous, but I hate that you watched them."

He bites down on his lip. "After that first day, I didn't. I stopped looking completely, but then today..." He sighs. "Today I was desperate. I missed you. I needed you. I wanted to talk. I wanted to tell you how I felt but you weren't open to it, and so..." His shoulders drop. "Well, you know."

I sit up straight and look at him. "Jarrod, what does all this mean? What's even happening?"

His lips downturn. "I don't know much yet, but I can tell you everything I do."

"A secret for a secret?" I ask with a small grin.

He nods, his lips curving. "I like you, Devin. From the moment I saw you at the restaurant, there was something about you that drew me in. I didn't want to be away from you. Your energy was inviting, your eyes are hypnotizing, and your smile intoxicating. I sort of hated when you went on that date with that guy, and then when you told me he turned out to be a dick, I wanted to hurt him for hurting you. I've wanted to kiss you countless times. I've stared at that selfie you sent me for an embarrassing amount of minutes. I don't know that I can say I'm attracted to guys, because it's only you. You're the only one. I have no idea what happens from here. We have two different lives, but god, I want something to happen. I'm clueless about a lot of things, especially when it comes to this, but I know without a doubt that what I feel for you feels like something worth exploring."

I swallow, my eyes focused on his as his declarations wash over me. "It's a good thing I'm a little less clueless then."

His smirk begins to form. "That's another fear. You're way more experienced." He clears his throat. "In lots of things, and I'm afraid you'd just be disappointed, because I don't—"

I put my hand on his, cutting him off. "Kissing, hugging, touching...it's all done the same. It may feel different, but there's no extra steps. You've touched yourself, so you know what feels good."

Jarrod nods, his blush creeping in as he stares at me. "I haven't done a couple other things."

I bite down on my smile. "It's okay."

His thumb brushes over my knuckles. "What's your secret?"

We lean in toward each other. "My crush never ended. It just reignited the moment I saw you."

"So, you *do* want me?"

I move in even more, my lips inching closer to his. "More than I've wanted anybody."

"Can I kiss you now?" he asks.

"Please."

Twenty

JARROD

I tilt my head to the right as his goes to the left, and my eyes, half-lidded, search his gaze, waiting for him to change his mind. Closer, I feel the soft tickle of his breath above my lip and inhale what he exhales, wanting to share his air. Just as my lips touch his, my hand moves to graze across his cheek and he leans into it.

We kiss, our lips coming together in gentle pecks. Devin scoots in, his hand on my thigh before his tongue swipes across my bottom lip.

I suck in a shuddering gasp, my breath catching when his tongue meets mine for the first time.

He's slow and gentle, like he's handling me with kid gloves, afraid I'll break under his touch. But I want him fervently.

I reach out and grab him by the waist and bring him to my lap, forcing him to straddle me. Devin gasps before wrapping his arms around my neck and going in for another kiss. With my hands on his back, I devour him in the way I've been dreaming about for weeks. I explore his mouth with my tongue as his fingers thread into my wet hair. My arms pull him in tighter, wanting to erase any space between us, because we've had enough of that already. When Devin moans, I swallow the sound, hoping the memory of it stays within me forever. I never want to forget the noises he makes when he's with me.

His hips move and I groan as he grinds over my erection. We pant heavily into each other's mouths as we continue to make out, his teeth teasing my bottom lip with a nibble.

My cock jumps and I know he feels it when he moans again, rocking into it. He doesn't stop moving, and I have to grab his hips and squeeze, my eyes closing as I pull away from the kiss.

"You okay?" he asks with a heavy breath.

I shake my head. "I'm gonna come if you don't stop."

He drops his forehead to mine with a chuckle. "You scared me."

"My heart is trying to escape."

He puts his hand on my chest and I open my eyes to look at him. "Lie back."

Slowly, I lower myself to the mattress, and he follows, lying on top of me.

"I can't really believe this is happening."

He smiles against my lips. "Nothing is happening. Yet."

I swallow and he rocks into me.

"Oh god."

"Don't worry. We'll move slow. Snail's pace."

"Snail?" I question, my hands underneath his shirt, rubbing up and down his sides. "What about a turtle's pace?"

"Turtles can move pretty fast," he says, peppering kisses along my cheek and jawline.

"That's fine."

"Mm," he moans against my throat, his tongue licking across my Adam's apple. "What are you ready for?"

He punctuates the question with another rock of his hips, sliding over my erection. I release a shuddering breathy moan. "Um. I don't know."

"Do you want to come?" he whispers, his lips coming up to brush against mine with the question.

I kiss him. "Yes."

"Okay," he replies with another kiss before sliding down my body until he's off the bed. "Take off your pants."

I shove them down my legs as he digs into the drawer of his nightstand. When he turns back to the bed his eyes land on my cock, his tongue darting out to lick his lips before he crawls toward me.

"Wow."

"Stop," I say with a nervous chuckle.

He looks at my face before allowing his gaze to move down again. "No, really. I'm..." He pauses, nodding his head.. "Okay. Well, congratulations on that."

My cheeks heat up, but then he climbs between my legs and the warmth spreads through every vein in my body, setting me on fire.

"I want to see you," I say, reaching for a pillow to prop under my head. "Take off your shirt."

He reaches down and grabs the hem, pulling it up over his head and tossing it on the floor. "Better?"

"Kind of," I say with a smirk.

"Mm. Turtle's pace, remember?"

"Fine."

He grabs the lube he took out of the drawer and pours some into his palm. When his fingers wrap around my shaft, I suck in a deep breath. His teeth sink into his bottom lip as he stares at my cock in his hand.

"Fuck," I hiss as I watch his hand move.

Devin brings his other hand to my shaft, one above the other, both of them rotating in opposite directions while moving up and down.

"Holy shit," I say on a breath, closing my eyes.

He continues to stroke, hand curling around my head and driving me absolutely insane. I can feel myself throbbing in his hand and wonder if his cock is leaking like mine.

"You're so fucking thick," he says huskily. "It's perfect."

"Jesus," I breathe, opening my eyes again. "You got me so hard."

Instead of removing his hands to get more lube, Devin spits directly onto the top of my cock, his saliva dripping down the sides and making it slick again.

"I love it."

"Fuck, I love it, too," I moan, thrusting into his fists. One of his hands moves lower, cupping my balls, gently squeezing. I suck in a staccato breath. "Holy fucking god." A fingertip runs along my perineum, making me gasp again. "Devin. My god."

His other hand continues to stroke up and down my shaft. "I can't wait to see your cum," he breathes.

"I...I can't...oh my god. I'm so close."

Devin sits up higher on his knees, one hand running up my stomach as the other works my cock. His own erection is stabbing at the material of his pants, trying to get free.

The visual of him and his sex appeal paired with the skillful way he's touching me has my balls tightening as my orgasm builds.

"I'm gonna come." I manage to get the words out before it happens.

The first spurt shoots up and lands on his fingers before more erupts like lava and lands on both of us.

"Fuck yes," he moans, straddling one of my legs as he watches me break apart.

My body trembles as I pull in quivering breaths, and then I notice Devin adjusting his erection in his shorts.

"You have to come too," I say on a breath.

He shakes his head. "I'm happy with you coming."

"Please," I beg. "I can just watch."

I can tell he's desperate for a release by the tension in his face. He doesn't argue any further. Using the hand he used to stroke me—the one with some of my cum on it—he wipes up more from my stomach and tugs his shorts down with his other hand.

His long shaft pops free, curving slightly to the left, the pink tip engorged. I swallow when I see precum drip from the slit.

"It's not gonna take much," he says, smearing my cum on his shaft before stroking.

"Holy fuck," I exclaim, unable to take my eyes off of him.

With his free hand, he grips my thigh, closing his eyes as he works himself to release.

"God, Jarrod," he moans, green eyes opening and landing on my face. "I'm gonna come on you."

I nod, biting down on my lip, ready for it.

His back bows and he leans forward, aiming his release

for my lower stomach. It lands in thick, white streams before dropping in small, circular pools.

"Oh my god." It comes out in a revered whisper.

My eyes flicker to his face where he looks completely blissed out, his sexy, soft lips parted into an O, his eyelids heavy and half closed as he meets my gaze.

"So good," he whispers, body jerking with aftershocks.

He's so beautiful I can't take it. I sit up and grab him, pulling him back on top of me, mess be damned.

His cock slides over mine and we both groan into each other's mouths as I plunge my tongue between his lips.

"I have another secret," I whisper against his cheek.

"Hmm," he murmurs.

"I don't think I'll ever be the same."

Twenty-One

DEVIN

I wake up feeling warmer than usual, the room bathed in darkness while the rain continues to fall outside.

Turning my head, I find Jarrod lying on his side next to me, our bodies touching only slightly. I smile when I see him, his face relaxed and peaceful.

Last night was not how I expected the day to end up, but I'm definitely not disappointed. The man swam through windswept waters in a storm to get to me, afraid I'd leave before he'd get the chance to talk to me.

Listening to his side definitely gave me the added perspective I needed. I can't change that he's seen my videos, but I always expected it to happen. What I didn't anticipate were the feelings that grew in such a short amount of time. That's what made it harder. I wanted an intimate moment with Jarrod, and though I was never sure it would happen, I'd rather have him see and experience me in person before knowing everything beforehand.

I get his curiosities though. He was struggling with his

own feelings, and watching porn isn't an abnormal thing to do. I just happen to be one of the biggest faces in the gay porn industry. But he was right, I never felt him judging me. He never looked at me differently. Even when telling me about it, he didn't ask why I'd choose this. He reacted better than most people.

With a glance at the clock, I see that it's only one in the morning. We passed out shortly after cleaning ourselves up and lying back down.

Jarrod shifts slightly, his legs moving under the covers before his arm reaches in my direction. His hand skates over my lower torso, which means he rubs over my erection.

My cock doesn't seem to realize or care that it hasn't even been six hours since my orgasm. I woke up and so did it.

I suck in a breath as he pulls his hand back slowly, rubbing it again.

"Mmm," he moans, waking up. He freezes when he realizes where his hand is and pulls away. "Sorry," he says in a husky, sleep-filled voice.

"Don't be."

"How long have you been awake?"

"Just a few minutes."

"What time is it?"

"A little after one."

He turns to his back and stretches, his biceps flexing in the process, then rolls to his side and scoots closer to me. After a minute, his fingers walk up my ribs before splaying across my abs. I grin up at the ceiling.

"You owe me a secret."

I angle my head to look at him. "Do I?"

He nods, a small smirk on his lips. "My last one was that I'd never be the same."

"That's not really a secret."

"Humor me."

"Fine," I say with a low laugh. "Remember when you asked what moment I had that made me realize I was gay?"

"Yeah."

"It was tenth grade, and I had already been questioning things. I never looked at girls the way other guys did. I never found them all that sexually appealing. Pretty? Sure. Did I want to touch them? Nah. Anyway, I remember being late to gym one day and rushing into the locker room to change. Most everyone was already on the basketball court, but there were a couple guys still changing. One guy was sitting on a bench, his shirt off while he tied his shoelaces. I quickly stripped out of my jeans and into my shorts, but then this guy stood up, showing off muscles I had no idea kids our age could have. He gave me a friendly smile as he pulled his shirt over his head and ran his hand through his hair to get it back in place. I felt myself frozen in that moment, knowing I needed to look away but also finding it very hard to. It was no longer just his body, but the way I felt when he looked at me. His smile made my stomach do flips, and he had the most unique eyes I'd ever seen—one split into two different colors."

Jarrod's lips part as he watches me. "Oh."

"I knew before then. Deep down, I always knew, but when my stomach started doing cartwheels over a smile, I was like, *yep, I'm gay*." I laugh. "It's easy to find people attractive, regardless of sexual identity. Appearances are surface level. When you look at someone and *feel* something, then you know it's far more than realizing they're cute. They've now altered something in you."

He holds me a bit tighter, his arm wrapping around my waist. "And you're why I'll never be the same again."

I smile at him and brush a wavy lock from his forehead. "As long as you remain who I've always liked."

"Of course." His hand moves across my stomach, fingers sliding under the waistband of my briefs. "The only difference is that I want to do more things with you. To you."

His voice drops as his hand moves lower into my underwear.

"What kind of things?" I ask quietly.

"I want to touch you."

"Mm."

"Kiss you."

His fingers graze over the underside of my shaft as it sits heavy against my stomach.

"You are a good kisser," I reply breathily.

Jarrod begins tugging my briefs down, so I lift my hips to help in the process.

He swallows. "I want to know what it's like to have you in my mouth."

I moan as his fingers wrap around me for the first time. "Mmhmm."

"I want your mouth on me."

His fist moves slowly up my shaft.

"Yeah," I say on a breath, closing my eyes and thrusting into his hand.

"And I want you to be happy."

I reach out and pull him by the shoulder, bringing his

mouth to mine. I kiss him and he continues to stroke me under the covers.

I'm frantic with need, my body writhing under his touch as his tongue tangles with mine.

"Jarrod," I pant into his mouth.

"Does it feel good?" he asks, and I know it's a genuine question coming from him.

"Yes, baby. It's good."

He groans and devours my mouth once more, his fist moving faster as his naked body rocks into mine. His erection slides over my hip and I want it in my hand, mouth, ass...any and everywhere.

"I'm already so hard," he murmurs between kisses.

"I feel it." I moan. "Get on top of me. Straddle my legs."

He doesn't question it. As he gets up, I kick my underwear all the way off and find the lube on my nightstand. I pour some on my dick and start stroking.

Jarrod eyes me with a lust-filled gaze, his thick cock pointing at me. "You look so good," he breathes.

"Come find out how I feel."

His muscular thighs rest on either side of my own, and I reach out and rub some of the remaining lube on his erection.

"Oh god."

"Slide it against mine," I tell him.

He leans forward, his fists holding him up as he rocks his hips.

"Holy shit."

"It's so good," I breathe, grabbing onto his waist.

"Holy shit," he repeats.

I smile. "I love how thick and heavy your cock is on top of mine."

"I love the way you talk," he groans.

"Sit back. Let me see how we look together."

He listens, and I reach out and take our dicks in my hands, stroking them together.

"Oh my god," he says quietly, fucking into my hand.

"You do it," I tell him. "Stroke us both."

Jarrod bites his lip but he takes us in one hand, rubbing us together. "So good," he whispers, almost to himself. "Holy fuck."

I put my hands behind my head as I gaze up at him. He's stunning. So big and muscular, and yet so soft and gentle.

He moves his hand faster, sitting up higher. His free hand lands on my stomach, traveling to my chest.

"You're so fucking incredible."

"You are," I reply. "You're doing so good."

His eyes close and his head drops back. "Oh god. Don't praise me."

"Not your thing?" I ask, bringing one hand down to grab his.

"No, I think I just found out it is."

"Mmm."

I bite down on my lip and bring his hand to my mouth. I kiss his palm first before taking a finger and sucking it.

His gasp is loud followed by a sexy moan. His hand slows on our shafts as he watches me suck a second finger into my mouth.

He moves them, gliding the tips over my tongue.

"Mmhhmm," I murmur, encouraging him to fuck my mouth with his fingers.

Jarrod's face is flushed, his mouth in a permanent O as I hold his wrist and help him. I feel his fingers at the back of my tongue and suck on them like I want to suck his cock.

"Devin," he breathes. "Yeah."

I remove his fingers from my mouth and guide them back to our shafts.

"Make me come," I say in a gravelly whisper.

"Oh god."

"I want to come so bad."

"Me too," he moans, stroking faster.

"You're so fucking sexy." His eyes close at the compliment. "The way you're stroking us..." I push my head deeper in the pillow. "It's driving me crazy."

"You like it?" he questions with hooded eyes.

"Jarrod, you're fucking perfect. My cock is throbbing and leaking. I love it."

"I'm so close but I don't want it to end," he admits.

"If you come now, we can find a new way to come later," I say through pants. "Maybe you can come in my mouth."

He squeezes his eyes shut. "Yeah."

"You like that idea?"

"Yes," he hisses, his hand moving faster.

"I can't wait to have you in my mouth. Oh, that's it. Just like that, Jarrod," I beg, my breaths coming in short bursts. "You're about to make me come."

"Fuck," he grunts.

"Oh god. You're so good. So fucking good."

"Yes," he cries out, his entire body tensing up as cum shoots from his tip, landing on my stomach. His breaths are shuddery, his voice basically a whimper when he says, "Oh my god. Yeah. Oh shit."

"I'm coming. I'm fucking coming. Oh god."

Jarrod's fist never stops moving, and my release joins his on my stomach. I cry out, gripping the covers in my fists as his slippery cock slides over mine.

"Fuck," he curses one last time.

"Jarrod." I hide my eyes behind my arms as I try to catch my breath. "Holy hell."

The bed makes a noise when his body flops down next to me. He sighs, his leg falling over mine.

"That was incredible."

"Yes," I say on a heavy breath.

I drop an arm from my face and find his hand, squeezing his fingers. He looks at me and squeezes back, that crooked smile making my stomach flip again.

Twenty-Two

JARROD

The storm rages through the night and into the next day, but it's fine, because we don't want to leave anyway. I left once to run back to my bungalow and grab everything I needed, just to come straight back to Devin.

We showered together, naked this time, but Devin was sure to keep us at a turtle's pace, afraid he'll overwhelm me if we do too much too fast. Meanwhile, my cock is like the Energizer Bunny—he just wants to keep going and going.

But it was nice to just be together, both of us stripped bare, touching and rubbing while kissing under the spray of the shower.

Someone drives a golf cart out here to bring us food, and after eating, we crawl into bed and turn on the TV.

"*What can we expect from the San José Bobcats next season, Bob?*" the broadcaster asks, still talking about the fucking playoff game.

I groan and drop back onto the pillow. "I don't know why

they act like I'm suddenly the worst player in the league now. We'll be fine."

He touches my wrist. "I'm sorry. I saw a little bit about it when I first got here."

"It was a good game...until it wasn't. We couldn't make a shot at all in the third period, and then I allowed two to get in. I know it's not the first or last time it's gonna happen in the NHL, but when you're that close to the finals, you can almost taste the win. I could feel the weight of the trophy." I sigh. "It sucks, and obviously I take that loss, but I know we'll be fine."

He rubs his thumb over my hand in a comforting gesture. "You will be." Devin goes quiet for a little. "Would you have come on vacation if you had won?"

"Not when I did, because I'd have been in the finals."

Devin doesn't say anything for a while, and then, "I was reaching a breaking point. I've been in the industry since I was nineteen. I got really lucky five years in and grew to a level I never thought possible. I've slowed down on starring in films, but I do little solo things for OnlyFans. I also have my own production company now."

"No shit?" I ask, turning to face him.

He grins. "It's called Straitlay Productions."

After a few seconds, I ask, "Straitlay?"

"Our particular company focuses on a specific trope in gay porn which is *straight* guys."

I snort. "Ironic."

His lips twist to the side. "A lot of people like watching the 'straight' guy try things with the gay guy. It's new, it's exciting, and people get a kick out of watching him realize how much he likes it. Obviously, it's meant purely for entertainment. There's a slippery slope. Sometimes, in real life, these 'straight' guys are dealing with internalized homophobia, and while they may be curious, they can immediately regret messing around with a gay guy and turn violent. It's happened to one too many people that I know personally. Porn is entertainment, and within it there are a lot of storylines that are okay because it's fake."

I take his hand in mine. "Have you ever dealt with that?"

"Once. It didn't get too bad. He started blaming me for tricking him or forcing him into it, and then started yelling and throwing things. I was able to get away before it got much worse."

"I'm sorry."

He shakes his head. "It's just important to remember that real life isn't as perfect as we make it look in movies and books. I'm aware my videos are fantasies, and I have to hope nobody finds themself in a situation that we make look perfect only for it to be a nightmare for them." He sighs. "Anyway, I made an announcement that our company would pay actors more than what most do, so we've been swamped with a lot of new guys wanting to work with us. I have some other business deals with sex toy companies, and I just felt like I was being torn in different directions, needing to make everyone happy. But *I* wasn't happy. I was just working and busy and stressed. Everyone needs me for something. Guys I try to date expect me to be a certain way because of what I do, and when I'm not in full porn star mode, then they feel a certain way. They don't understand that I'm acting in these films. My real life isn't supposed to mimic my porn life."

He sighs, running a hand through his hair. "Then of course there are my parents. They're always in the back of my head. I did this almost to spite them. Don't get me wrong, I enjoy my job, and I'm glad I've expanded and grown it beyond filming a scene here and there, but I started it to piss them off. I became an actor, but not the kind they wanted, and what's funny," he says with a humorless laugh, "is that I kind of want to act in movies now. Non-pornographic ones. But I don't want to get in with their connections. I'd love to do some indie films, and I wonder if it's even possible now."

I squeeze his hand. "Devin, I think you can do anything you want. You broke away from a wealthy family where you could've had anything. You started over and still made your way to the top of your industry. You're successful and you should be proud. But you should also be happy, so if that means trying something new, then do it. I know you have it in you to be the best at whatever you put your mind to."

I turn to my side and smile at him. "Thank you. I guess, even though we came here because of less than perfect circumstances, it ended up being the perfect time."

With a swallow, I lean forward and plant my lips on his. "It's hard to be mad about losing that game if I think about not having this opportunity if I had won."

"I don't believe everything happens for a reason, but I think sometimes we get lucky and the universe puts us where we need to be when we need it most."

I curl into him, laying my head on his chest as I throw one of my legs over his. "So, you mentioned sex toys."

He laughs. "So, you heard that part?"

"I definitely did."

"What do you want to know?"

"Everything."

He gently rubs his palm up and down my arm. "I recently had a dildo come out."

I get up and spin to face him. "Like, it's yours? Your actual dick?"

Devin grins. "Yes, they made a mold of it, so it looks as close to the real thing as possible."

"The veins and everything?"

"Yep."

"Where would one buy one of these?"

He smacks my arm. "You have the real thing."

I chuckle and lie back down on him. "For now."

The knowledge that this will eventually come to an end sits heavy between us, filling the room with silence. We haven't talked about leaving or what happens once we do. We have some time, so we're trying to enjoy it.

"They want one of my mouth next."

"Oh damn. Well, you know, keep me up to date on that."

"Or," he says, pausing for a while. "You can learn a little about it now."

My heart skitters to a stop before thumping hard in my chest. "Yeah?"

"Yeah." He slips his arm from under my neck and moves to straddle me. "But only if you want."

I hold his hips in my hands. "I've been dying to be between those lips."

Devin bites down on his bottom one, looking sexy as fuck. "I don't know if you found this out while watching the videos," he says, lowering himself down my body. "But I don't have a gag reflex."

"Fuck."

He pulls my basketball shorts down my legs, taking my

boxers down with them. His fingers wrap around me first, stroking teasingly.

"I love how you feel in my hands."

"I love how your hands feel on me."

"Let's see which you prefer," he says with a wicked smirk before opening his mouth and taking my tip between those pink, full lips.

His warm, wet mouth envelopes me, teasing my head with sensual licks as his hand squeezes and strokes. I watch, enraptured by the visual and intoxicated by the feeling. His tongue slides down my shaft, licking my balls before sucking each one into his mouth one by one.

"Oh god," I all but whimper.

Devin runs his nose along my groin, planting small but wet kisses in the crease. My hips buck, dying for more.

With one hand at the base of my shaft, Devin takes me in his mouth, slowly sliding my cock across his tongue and to his throat. When his eyes lift upward, meeting my gaze, I let out a cry of pleasure.

His mouth feels incredible, but the way he's maintaining eye contact with me as he devours my cock is hard to take. I may come in thirty seconds if I continue to watch him like this.

I close my eyes, draping an arm over my forehead as I chant, "Oh my god, oh my god, oh my god."

Devin moans around my length, slurping his way back up to the tip before swallowing me down again.

"Holy shit," I grunt, my hand reaching down to thread my fingers through his hair.

He grabs it and puts it at the back of his head, moaning as he looks up at me again. I watch as he takes me to the back of his throat, his lips touching the skin around the base of my dick, his chin grazing my balls.

"Oh shit," I gasp.

He pulls off of it, saliva dripping down the sides, his lips pressing against my balls again as his hand strokes my erection.

"I love the way you fill my mouth," he moans.

"Fuck, Devin. I love the way you take it."

His eyes find mine again before he wraps those perfect fucking lips around me, sucking my cock in a way I've never been sucked before.

I'm not trying to say I have the biggest dick in the world, but it's not small, and I know it's quite thick. Most girls haven't been able to take it all the way, and they definitely don't take their time worshiping it the way Devin's doing.

He continues to take me deep, slurping and moaning like this is as good for him as it is for me. Devin plants kisses along my shaft, his hand cupping and squeezing my balls. He swirls his tongue around my head, teasingly sucking only on the tip while his hand moves up and down.

When I'm all the way in his mouth again, both of my hands find a home on the sides of his head, and my hips thrust up. Devin moans appreciatively as I fuck his mouth, his beautiful eyes flickering up to watch me.

"Your mouth is too good," I say between grunts. "It's so fucking good, Devin."

He murmurs around my cock, his cheeks hollowing as he sucks. My orgasm builds, my balls drawing up tight as my muscles tense. I never want this to end and yet can't wait to come in his mouth.

Devin eases off my cock, his hand stroking fast as he

peers up at me from between my legs. "You gonna come for me?"

I nod, moving my hands to the sheets below me. "Yes. So close."

"I can't wait to have that cum down my throat."

"Holy shit," I say through a sharp inhale.

His mouth is on me again, staying high at the tip so his hand can move up and down my shaft. It's probably only thirty seconds before I'm hurtling through the heavens, making my way to cloud nine as my orgasm hits.

Devin takes me deep, moaning around me as I let out a roar everyone on the island can probably hear.

"Ahhh! Oh god. Fuck. Shit."

"Mmm," Devin moans as my cum explodes into his mouth and down his throat.

"Fuck, fuck, fuck," I curse, squeezing the hell out of the sheets.

He eases up my shaft, and I open my eyes just in time to watch him swallow everything down. He bites his swollen lip. "So good."

"Shit," I say with an exhale.

His mouth closes around my tip again as his hand squeezes and tugs, getting every last drop out of me.

I have a full body shiver once he pulls away completely.

"No toy will ever be as good as that." I exhale loudly. "Holy fuck."

He chuckles and I look down to watch him swiping a finger under his lip. "So, you don't want one when they come out?"

"I didn't say that," I say with a smirk. "Come here."

Devin crawls up my body, straddling me as he leans

down. I take his face in my hands and bring his mouth to mine, licking my taste from his tongue.

"You're so hard," I whisper, feeling his erection against my stomach.

"Mm. I really enjoyed sucking your dick."

"I think you need to come," I say, my hands running up his back.

He moans, kissing my lips. "That would be nice."

"Do you think..." I pause, letting what I'm about to say settle in my brain. "Do you think I can return the favor?"

He sits up, his ass on my lower stomach. "I think I'd enjoy whatever you wanted to do."

I reach out and run my palm over the hard length pressing against his pants.

"I want to try," I say, licking my lips. "It may not be as good as—"

Devin cuts me off by taking my hand in his and squeezing. "Hey." He shakes his head. "It's going to be great, because it is you. Everything you do will be better than I'm used to, because it's real and because..." He trails off, watching me carefully. "I want you in a way that I've never wanted anybody. Not once in my life did I think this would ever happen between us. You are my dream come true."

I stare at him for several seconds, emotion squeezing my heart. I grab onto him and spin us around, pinning him on the mattress below me. I've never felt so feral in my life. His words, though romantic and sweet, have turned me into an animal.

Twenty-Three

DEVIN

His large, naked body rests on top of me as he kisses me with furious passion. His hands pin mine above my head, and he grinds against my erection.

"I don't know what you've done to me," he whispers huskily into my neck. "You take my breath away while simultaneously granting me exactly what I need to feel alive."

He kisses down my neck before hastily sitting up to pull my shirt over my head. His mouth travels across my chest and down my sternum, licking a path to my belly button. Jarrod scoots down, taking my lounge pants with him.

My cock strains against the confines of my briefs, and he groans with pleasure when he looks at it. His large hand runs up the shaft, closing his fingers when he gets to the top and stroking downward.

He kisses it through the material, making me writhe and moan beneath him.

"Jarrod," I pant.

A noise rumbles in his throat before he slips his fingers

in the waistband and pulls them down. My cock slaps against my stomach, engorged and ready.

Once he has me completely naked, he settles himself between my legs, reaching for my shaft. His fingers close around me, moving up and down the length as he studies the size of me. I watch as his tongue slides out to lick his lips and then his eyes flicker up and meet mine.

"Please," I whisper, my hips unable to keep from undulating.

Jarrod rises up enough to take me in his mouth. He's slow and gentle at first, getting an idea of how it tastes and feels. When he closes his lips around my shaft and takes me deeper, I moan, thrusting up before remembering this is his first time.

I've had a lot of sexual encounters, most done for the sake of work. I've struggled with finding the separation, and understanding I don't have to put on a show in my personal relationships. I've dealt with how my partners felt when they thought I wasn't enjoying sex simply because I wasn't over-acting like I do in porn.

I don't have to put on a show with Jarrod. I'm a thousand percent into everything he does, and it doesn't matter if it's his first time. I don't care if he's still cautious and learning. He's Jarrod. He's exactly who I want.

However, I'm aware of the newness of it all for him, and I'm holding back because of it. I don't want to overwhelm him or push him into an uncomfortable setting, so I try not to thrust into his mouth.

His hand travels up and down my shaft as he sucks on the head, his tongue sliding over the protruding glans.

"Jesus," I whisper, watching his mouth work.

Those unique eyes find me again, watching to see how I'm reacting to what he's doing.

"It feels so good," I tell him, my stomach rising and falling with deep breaths. "You're doing so good."

Jarrod moans and takes more of me into his mouth. He goes as far as he can before he gags. The sound makes my cock twitch and has my eyes rolling back into my head.

"Yes, baby," I moan, reaching down to gently run my fingers through his hair.

He does it again, taking me across his tongue until he can't anymore. He pulls away with a small gasp, saliva dripping from his mouth.

"Holy fuck, you're so sexy," I tell him.

Jarrod groans and strokes with fervor. His tongue slides across my slit before he envelopes the tip in his mouth. I accidentally tug on his hair a little hard, but when I go to pull away, he reaches up and brings my hand back.

"You like it?" I ask, gripping the strands a little tighter.

He murmurs something, his head nodding as he continues to suck me into his mouth. I'm an advocate for a little pain during sex, but I didn't want to overstep before finding out exactly what he's into. But I guess there's only one way to learn, and that's to communicate.

"Would you like it if I fucked your mouth a little?"

"Mm," he moans, gaze lifting to mine. He eases off my dick, his hand still gripping the base. "I think I'm willing to do whatever you want," he pants, his lips more pink than usual.

My brow raises. "Hmm. I like that. Get up."

Jarrod moves to the side of me and I stand, walking to the

front of the bed. When he joins me, I see his cock is already hard again.

"Get on your knees for me," I tell him, pointing to the glass floor where the fish swim below us. "You tell me if you ever need to slow down or stop."

He nods, getting to his knees. "I don't think I'll want to," he says, his mouth opening to tease my cock. "I want everything, Devin."

I take my dick in one hand and stroke his cheek gently with the fingers of my other. I slip my thumb into his mouth and he sucks it.

My teeth dig into my bottom lip before I remove my thumb from his mouth and replace it with my cock.

Jarrod's hands hold onto my upper thighs before they curve around and feel my ass.

"Mm," I moan, pushing into his mouth.

I stare down at him, loving the view of this huge, muscular man on his knees for me, my dick sliding between his lips. His cock is fully engorged again, the tip leaking.

He moans as his hands squeeze the flesh of my ass before traveling to the backs of my thighs. I hold the back of his head with my hand and move my hips, still careful to not go too deep.

Taking a half step back, I stroke my dick while keeping the tip right at his lips. "You like having my dick in your mouth?"

He nods several times. "Yes."

"Your cock is dripping for me."

Jarrod moans, sticking his tongue out to taste me again. "I'm so turned on."

I tease him, sliding my dick into his mouth, but only giving him a couple inches before I slide out again.

"Touch yourself." He listens, grabbing a hold of his shaft. "Fuck, you look so good on your knees." I repeat my teasing, giving him a few inches before pulling out. "Where do you want me to come?" I ask, pushing into his mouth again before he can answer.

"Anywhere," he pants once I pull out, jerking himself faster.

"In your mouth?" I ask, sliding into it again. "Your face?" Another push inside, this time deeper. "Your chest?"

"Fuck," he breathes, tugging on his cock. "Yes. All of it. I don't care."

"Mmm. So needy. So desperate."

"Yes, yes," he chants, his muscles flexing with his movements.

"God, Jarrod. If I could take a picture of you just like this, I would. So fucking perfect."

I stroke my length, continuing to slide the tip into his mouth. He desperately tries to close his lips around my shaft, wanting all of me. His greediness drives me wild, and when I push into his mouth again, he surprises me by taking me deep, one hand pressing into my ass so I can't move away.

He chokes, backs up slightly, then does it again.

"Holy fuck," I gasp.

His body shakes as he jerks his cock, hard and fast. As soon as he pulls away, gasping for air, his mouth open with saliva making his chin glisten, his face contorts. "Oh god."

I shift slightly so I can watch as he comes, the liquid falling to the glass window on the floor.

The visual is intoxicating. Here's this massive naked man

on his knees, so turned on and frenzied with lust that just sucking my dick has made him come for the second time in thirty minutes.

He looks up at me, his body spent, cum on his hand and still dripping from his tip. His skin is flushed and glistening with sweat, and it's so fucking beautiful.

I keep up with my strokes, stepping forward to shove it into his mouth one last time. His exhaustion doesn't show as he grabs my hip and bobs his head up and down.

After just a couple minutes, I feel my release building. At the last second, I step back.

"I'm coming," I breathe. "I'm coming. Fuck!"

My cum shoots out, landing on his chin and falling to his chest. He moans and brings me forward, forcing me to finish releasing into his mouth.

"Jesus fucking Christ," I cry, gripping his head with one hand. "Oh my god."

After several seconds, I ease back, my legs Jell-O. Jarrod's licking his lips as he peers up at me, and then his lips form that crooked smile I love so much.

"That was fun."

I smile, biting my bottom lip as I bend down and kiss his lips. "I have a secret," I whisper against his mouth.

"Hmm?"

"I don't think I've ever been this happy."

Twenty-Four

JARROD

The weather clears up, and Devin's no longer trying to flee the island, so the two of us fall back into the routine we had before, except now there's more kissing and touching.

Today, we're out on my deck. Devin is relaxing on the couch with his shirt off while I sit in the small, private pool next to him.

"So, you have your own coach?" he asks, looking at his phone.

I laugh. "Are you researching hockey?"

His head turns and he gives me a smile. "Maybe."

Warmth spreads through my chest as my heart flutters. "Yes, goalies have their own coaches."

Devin scrolls through his phone a little longer. "And you wear more gear than everyone else?"

I fold my arms over the edge of the pool as I watch him, my smile frozen on my face. "Yeah, well, I use my whole body to block a puck flying at the net, so you definitely want to be protected."

He nods, scrolls some more. "Seems like it's really hard. Lots of up, down, right, left. And that stance looks uncomfortable."

"Yeah, it's pretty physically demanding, but you get used to it. It's more mentally taxing some days. You know?"

"And you have your own win/loss record? How does that work?"

"If the goalie lets in a game winning shot, that loss goes on his record. Even if another goalie was in earlier and let in three pucks, the one on the ice at the time of the other team scoring the game winner gets the loss. And the goalie in the net at the time their team scores the winning goal is credited with a win."

Devin shakes his head. "I feel like I get it, but also, I'm not sure. Better not push it. I think I'm done learning today."

I laugh and push myself out of the pool. "Thanks for trying."

He puts his phone down and grins at me. "Please don't try to learn anything about my industry."

I grab a towel and dry off a little before I make my way to Devin. "No? I think I should study it at least...you know, to learn a little more."

He reaches up for me, and I lie across his body, trying not to crush him completely. "I can teach you," he says.

"Mm. Well, you know I have a thing for teachers."

I plant a kiss on his lips as one of his legs wraps around me. "I don't have a husband willing to watch us."

"Thank god for that," I say with a laugh. I slide my arm

under his body and flip us around, so now I'm the one lying on the couch and he's on top of me. "But tell me something else about your industry. Not the filming or anything, but what you've created."

He settles in, half on me, half between my body and the cushions of the couch. "My production company produces films, and we have those available on a website that people access with monthly memberships. I've directed quite a lot now, and that's just another thing I'd be willing to expand on. Outside of adult films."

"That would be cool."

"Yeah. And I guess I should've mentioned it before, but the sex industry isn't as dirty as people make it seem. We do frequent blood tests and make sure everyone is clean. So, you should know, I'm negative. It's been a couple months since I've been with anyone anyway."

"Me too, and I haven't been with anyone in almost six months, I think."

He drags his fingertip down the middle of my chest, both of us falling into silence for a while.

"What happens when we leave?" he asks, finally bringing up what I've been trying not to think about.

"I don't know," I reply honestly. "I haven't wanted to think about it."

"Is this just a fun vacation fling?"

I rub his arm. "It's more than that, Dev. You know that, but I don't know what the future holds for us."

"Yeah," he replies quietly. "I understand. I mean, I still have to work."

My body stiffens slightly. "Right."

"It's not real, Jarrod. What I do with other people isn't real."

"It's hard to think about, I won't lie, but I'm also aware you've had your job for a lot longer than you've had me in your life. Plus, I'll be busy with pre-season training and then the season itself."

"So, we have now."

I squeeze him into me. "We have now."

We stay on the couch for a while before we eventually get up and go snorkeling again. Once we shower and get dressed, we find our way back to Gardenias where we eat dinner and enjoy a drink. At the end of the night, we find ourselves in my bed, a tangle of limbs as we make out like we're teenagers.

The next few days mimic the same routine—lots of showering together, eating, and venturing somewhere on the island to do some sightseeing. We laugh a lot, and it's easy to forget this isn't our reality. This will come to an end, and the real world will rear its ugly head and force us apart.

Our distance isn't too far. We're in the same state, just six hours apart. A doable trip when we have time, but what does that mean? Would that mean we're dating and monoga-mous? Would that mean I have to come out?

I don't feel like I need to say, "Hey, world. So it turns out I'm bisexual and I need you to know." Why is it anybody's business? I like Devin. He's a man...so what? But I know the reality of the situation. If the media gets wind of this, it'll be on every headline for the foreseeable future. The *Hottie of Hockey* known for dating high profile Hollywood girls is now with a man. They won't care about what my team is doing. They won't notice if we're doing well and have the potential of going to the finals. It'll only be, *Bobcats' Jarrod Bivens is dating a man. Will Bivens' new relationship interfere with the team's season?* I can see them already. It's not fair to me, nor my teammates. But I can't imagine not seeing Devin again. In fact, I'd be downright miserable if I knew I'd never see him again.

DEVIN

We have a day and a half left.

Jarrod already extended past his original departure date which was five days ago, and he's been staying with me in my bungalow.

The first two weeks were spectacular as reunited friends having a good time, but the last week and a half has been even more incredible. Our friendship has already grown by leaps and bounds, and now we've crossed into an intimate relationship where, at least on my end, feelings are becoming involved.

We haven't had sex yet, because it's been nice enough to touch and kiss and keep things restricted to hands and mouths. Honestly, I've never been more satisfied. Intimacy is many things, and though we haven't had sex, we've gotten to know each other on an intimate level that rivals some of my more serious relationships.

But with our looming separation on the horizon, I want to take that step, hoping like hell it's not the one and only time, but also thinking that if we leave here and never see each other again, at least we'll have had one time. One beautiful moment that will stay with me forever.

"Want to go to the waterfall today?" he asks.

"Yes."

So we do. We bring a plastic bag, take the mile hike, put our phones safely in said plastic bag, and swim to the waterfall. Safely tucked behind the rushing stream, we take out our phones and document our time together.

Jarrod takes photos of me, and I take some of him. We both take selfies together, happy to have these memories to look back on once we leave.

"Have you thought about what I said before?" Jarrod asks, crawling over my body until I'm on my back.

"You've said many things I think about constantly."

He smirks, lowering his lips to my ear. "Like how much I love the curve of your cock, or how the way you say my name with that quivery voice when you're about to come makes me feel like a god."

I arch my back, pushing my hips up into him. "Yes," I say with a moan.

He grinds into me, his lips kissing my neck. "Well, those are good ones, but I meant when I said we should come back. Do another vacation together."

My nails lightly trail over the middle of his back. "So, you're not annoyed by me."

He chuckles. "Not at all."

I swallow. "Will that be the next time we see each other?"

"No. It can't be. I won't survive a year without you."

I cling to him, wrapping my arms and legs around his

body, wanting nothing more than to merge us together. Where he goes, I'd have to go, and vice versa.

"I think we should go to our room now," I breathe.

"Yeah?"

"Yes."

"Okay."

He stands up, reaching down and pulling me to my feet. We make quick work of swimming through the water, and while hurried, we're careful to avoid injury on the hike down. We stop and take more photos, suddenly desperate to document every moment.

I let Jarrod shower first, knowing I'll take extra time to prepare for what's about to happen. After I'm done, I keep just the towel around my waist and make my way to the bed where Jarrod waits in just a pair of basketball shorts.

He's lounging on the pillows, one arm tucked under his head, his left knee bent as he flips through channels. When he sees me walk in, he immediately turns off the TV and puts the remote on the nightstand.

I get the lube and toss it on the bed before I climb onto the mattress, lying on my back. Jarrod's on me in a second, kissing me softly while his left hand slides down my side until he reaches the towel. He moves slightly to undo it and open it up, his hand finding my cock.

"I want you inside me," I tell him, freezing his movements. "Is that okay?"

He nods, licking his lips. "Yes. Of course. I just...I don't know..."

I reach up and cup his cheek. "Let me teach you."

Jarrod gives me another small nod, and I get up and push

him to his back. I remove his shorts and start sucking on his cock.

"Fuck, Dev," he breathes. "I'll never get over this mouth."

I take him deep, his tip knocking at the back of my throat while I cup his balls. I cover his cock with my saliva, then ease away, lowering myself between his legs.

With my hands on the underside of his thighs, I push upward, spreading him open for me. My mouth finds his perineum, my tongue sliding up and swirling around his balls before I do it again.

"Oh fuck," he moans.

This time I let my tongue travel lower, finding his tight hole.

"Jesus fuck!"

I glance up and find him pulling a pillow over his face.

"Want me to stop?"

"God no," he says into the pillow.

My lips curl up before I descend back in between his cheeks, my tongue licking around his hole.

Jarrod writhes and wiggles, muffled noises finding their way to my ears. I continue to eat his ass, getting it nice and wet before I pull away slightly and slide a finger through the crease, lightly pressing against the entrance.

"Devin. Fuck. My god."

I get onto my knees and take his shaft in my left hand. When I pull it up straight, I watch as a string of sticky pre-cum stretches from his stomach to the tip of his dick.

"Oh, baby. You're so wet for me."

He groans, thrusting into my hand before removing the pillow from his face and looking at me. "I'm so fucking turned on."

While staring into his eyes, I slide two fingers between his cheeks. "When you do this to me, you'll push in." He nods. "One finger at a time, and with lube."

"Okay."

"Once I'm stretched, you'll put more lube on your cock and slowly push inside."

"Fuck," he grunts, hips lifting. "Okay."

I crawl over his body, my cock coming to rest on his stomach. "You don't have to be gentle with me. I'm a big boy."

He smirks, grabbing my hips. "I may be new to this, but I want you to remember I'm even bigger. Don't feel you have to be delicate with me either."

I bite my lip. "Okay. Are you ready?"

He quickly rolls over, pinning me beneath him. "Are you?"

Twenty-Six

JARROD

My heart feels like it's going to explode in my chest based on how hard and fast it's beating, but not even the threat of a heart attack would make me stop.

I kiss down his chest, making my way to his abdomen where I lick every dip and curve of his muscles. When I get to his cock, I hum with excitement, ready to devour every inch of him. Over the past few days, I've gotten more comfortable with performing blowjobs, finding that turning him on turns me on. His grunts and moans of pleasure make me feel incredible. And let's not even talk about his words of praise.

Mimicking his actions, I get his shaft nice and wet, playing with his balls before I go lower. Devin lifts his legs for me, spreading them apart and showing me his perfect, hairless ass.

He's so smooth and soft, his hole pink and inviting.

"Fuck."

I dive in, my tongue dancing around the puckered area. I

grab his hips, lifting him from the mattress and bringing his ass to my face. I lick, suck, and kiss everywhere.

"Yes, yes," he moans.

With the tip of my tongue, I push inside his hole, gently penetrating him.

"Holy shit," he cries, grabbing my forearms.

My cock throbs, aching to be inside him. I've never fucked anybody in the ass, let alone a man, but holy shit do I want it desperately. I want to feel him clench around me.

With that thought, I lower him to the bed and remove my shorts. He quickly passes me the lube, and I pour it in my palm, coating my fingers. I start with one, like he said, carefully pushing inside.

Devin moans, his lips parting as his eyes close. "Yes. Keep going."

I slide my finger deeper, stopping at the first knuckle. He's so fucking tight I don't know how I'll even fit. When Dev grabs his cock to start stroking, I push in all the way before beginning to move it in and out in cautious movements.

"Does it feel good?" I ask.

"So good," he whimpers. "Fuck. Give me another."

I pull out and bring my middle finger to my index, taking the same careful measures as I move them both inside.

"You're so tight, baby."

"Mm," he moans. "Finger me." He sucks in a deep breath. "Faster."

I obey, curling my fingers up inside his hole. Devin sucks in a breath, a gasp leaving his lips as he fists the covers at his side.

"You okay?"

"Baby," he pants. "You're hitting my prostate."

"Oh." I stop moving.

"No. It's good," he breathes. "But I'll come quick if you keep it up."

I chuckle and keep my movements shallow, rotating my wrist as I try to loosen him up. "I can't wait to be inside you. My cock is leaking all over the bed."

Devin's back arches and he bears down on my fingers, taking them deeper. "Give it to me, Jarrod. I'm ready."

Gently, I remove my fingers and reach for the lube, slathering it on my cock before rubbing my slick fingers over his hole once I'm done.

"Start slow," he says in a breathy tone. "When I'm comfortable, I'll let you know, and then you can let loose."

With a growl, I bite down on my lip and grab the base of my dick. I tease him with the tip before I carefully push inside, watching him stretch around me.

"Holy shit," I say with a quivering breath. "Dev. Oh god."

My eyes flutter closed before I slide in a little deeper, feeling his ass pull me inside. So tight and warm. The moment I slip past the resistance, we both groan.

A turning point in my life—my first time fucking a man, and it's not nearly as frightening as I thought it would be. I'm overcome with lust and need, but mostly, my heart sings in my chest.

I continue to take my time, memorizing the way everything feels while trying to understand my internal feelings. It's unlike anything I've ever experienced, and not just the physicality, but the emotion.

"God, you're so big," he moans.

"I'd apologize, but—"

"Don't you dare apologize," he pants. "Squeeze more lube on your shaft."

I take the bottle and pour the clear liquid onto my shaft, using my fingertips to smear it in. This time, when I push forward, I slip in farther. When I'm buried deep, I lean over him and plant a kiss on his mouth.

"I'm never gonna want to stop."

"Good," he whispers against my lips. "Now, everything from here is basically what you're used to."

I kiss along his cheekbone. "Nothing has or ever will be like this, Devin. I know what fucking is, but this...this isn't that."

He wraps his arm around my neck and pulls me closer, sealing our lips together. I move my hips, pulling out a little before I move back in. I inhale the moan he releases and breathe my own back into him when I thrust a little deeper.

"Jarrod," he cries, his legs wrapping around me.

"Baby," I croon, dusting his cheeks with kisses.

I ease away, needing to see more. More of him. More of us. When my back is straight, I peer down at our meeting point, watching as my shaft disappears into his ass. A rumble of appreciation sounds in my throat, and when I let my gaze move up to find his face, I nearly buckle.

He's exquisite. His flawless skin is flushed red, his beautiful face contorted into an expression of bliss—brows drawn in, soft pink lips parted as he sucks in breaths.

"Jesus." It doesn't feel like just a word this time, I utter it like a prayer to the heavens, giving thanks for what I'm blessed to witness and take part in.

"More," he begs. "Please. I need all of you."

I drop down, bracing myself on my forearms as I begin to

pummel into him. It doesn't make it less romantic, or any less like love making. I may fuck him hard and deep, but with each stroke, I pour a little more of myself into him. I'm his. A hundred and fifty percent. And I want him to feel every part of me.

"You have me," I tell him.

My hips don't stop moving, rocking back and forth while our mouths desperately seek each other out. My orgasm threatens to explode out of me any minute, my entire body trembling with pleasure.

I pull back, bringing one of his legs to my shoulder while I reach for his cock with my free hand.

"Jarrod." It's that quivering sound I love so much. "Jarrod, please."

"What do you want, baby?" I ask, stroking his length, feeling the pre-cum on my fingers when I get to the top.

"You. More. Everything. To come."

I stroke a little faster as I keep the rhythm in my hips. "I'm yours. I'll give you whatever you want, and your cum is what *I* want. So I'm gonna make sure you get there. Don't worry."

He whimpers, closing his eyes as I bring him exactly where he wants to be. His cock swells in my hand and my balls draw up.

"I'm so close," he says on an inhale. "Jarrod, I'm going to come."

"Come, baby. Let me see how much you enjoy having me inside you."

Devin's back arches, his mouth agape as he cries out. "Oh god."

"That's it," I growl.

"C-coming. I'm coming."

Watching his cum shoot straight into the air, falling onto my hand and cascading down to his stomach sets me on fire. I release his cock, and he replaces my hand as I grab onto his waist.

"I'm going to come. Devin. Your ass feels too good. Your cock looks...oh my god."

My fingers dig deep into his flesh, and I worry I may bruise him as I dive deeper and deeper, but I have to.

"Yes, please. Yes. Come," he cries.

My body tenses and my release pours out of me, my body slowly collapsing on top of him as I give him every drop of my desire.

"Devin."

"Jarrod."

Twenty-Seven

DEVIN

After we wash up, I crawl under the sheets instead of eating snacks with Jarrod. My body aches as I curl up, watching him at the table as he shoves mini muffins into his mouth.

Our sex was the most exceptional experience of my life. I know some people believe sex is sex. You can do it with anyone. And I suppose that's true, but to have a truly wonderful experience is to have sex with someone you care about. I know it sounds cheesy, but sometimes cheesy is true. My heart was in it. There was no acting, no exaggerating, and it was because it was with Jarrod that it felt otherworldly.

He was right. We weren't simply fucking. What we did has the power to break my heart, because I don't know what's happening after we leave this island. All I know is that when he leaves, he's taking part of me with him, and I've finally learned what it's like to be whole.

"You falling asleep over there?" he asks with a lazy smile.

"Maybe," I reply, my blinking becoming slow. "Someone wore me out."

He chuckles. "I'll be over there soon."

"Mmkay," I reply, my eyes closing. "We'll have dinner..." I force my eyes open. "Later. Once I've had a..."

"Nap?"

My brows lift but my eyes remain closed. "Hmm?"

His laughter reaches my ears before the sound of the chair scraping across the floor does. I'm vaguely aware he's moving around, but exhaustion swallows me.

At some point I startle, feeling the bed dip. His arm wraps around my waist and pulls me into him. I'm pretty sure I grin, or at least I want to.

Jarrod's nose touches the skin behind my ear before he speaks. "I have another secret."

Once again, I raise my brows in question, though he can't see. I attempt to murmur a response, but sleep is calling my name and pulling me into darkness.

"I think..."

"Time to wake up, sleepyhead," Jarrod says, pushing my shoulder. "It's dinner time and the muffins have long worn off."

I stretch my limbs, rolling onto my back, feeling the tenderness in my ass when I do. "How long have I been asleep?"

"Two hours."

"Mmm," I grumble, rolling to my other side.

"Uh-uh," he says, yanking the covers off me. "You have to feed me or I'll get grumpy."

I reach into my underwear and adjust the semi I have. "Feed you what?"

His eyes track my movements, his nostrils flaring slightly. "Don't tease."

"Who's teasing?" I say, sliding my hand inside to stroke myself.

He growls, walking away just to come back and throw clothes at me. "Get dressed. Let's eat, and then I'll devour you."

"Fine," I say with a grumble.

"Did you take a nap with me?"

"For a little."

"Were you talking to me when I fell asleep?" I ask.

He turns to face me. "Probably, but it's okay. I knew you were pretty out of it."

"Sorry."

"It's fine," he replies, changing into a pair of gray chinos.

I get out of bed to use the bathroom and fix my hair, and Jarrod saunters over in a black tee that fits him like a glove.

"You look nice."

His eyes sparkle. "It's our last date."

"Our *last*?"

He wraps his arms around me from the back, looking at me in the mirror. "On the island."

"When was our first?" I question with a grin.

"Oh, I'd say when we had champagne and macarons."

"We were just friends."

"I had feelings for you then. Does that count?"

I spin around in his arms and lock my hands behind his neck. "This can be our first and last...on the island."

He nods. "Okay."

"So, what should I wear?"

His cheeks pinken as he bites down on his lip, fighting a smile. "Can I make a suggestion?"

I raise a brow at him. "What's that?"

"The black shirt you wore that first night to Midnight Lounge? The sheer one?"

I scrape my teeth across my bottom lip. "You like that one?"

Jarrod nods. "That was the first time you took my breath away. I was so shocked and felt like I was staring the whole night. It looks good on you."

My lips press against his. "Then I'm wearing it."

As soon as I'm dressed, Jarrod stares at me with hunger in his eyes. A different kind of hunger.

"Maybe I made a mistake."

I laugh, walking toward him. "Nope. Don't get any ideas now, big guy. We're eating dinner first."

"But I just want to..." He lets the sentence trail off.

"Say it."

His eyes find mine. "I want to fuck you."

My stomach does a flip as warmth spreads through me. "Mm."

Jarrod steps up to me, his finger making a path from the hollow of my throat down the middle of my chest, coming to a stop where the shirt finally meets above my belly button.

"I want you so bad," he whispers, his fingers splaying

across my stomach, slipping into my shirt. "Will it hurt...if we do it again?"

"I'll be fine," I say with a small smile. "But we're gonna eat first. Come on."

Jarrod groans behind me. "Fine."

On the walk to the restaurant, Jarrod slips his hand in mine. I look up at him, surprise covering my features. He shrugs with a small smile curving his lips.

"Gentlemen," the hostess greets. "Right this way."

She escorts us to a half circular booth, not as private as before, but still along the edge of the restaurant with a view of the water. After our order has been taken, Jarrod sighs.

"I can't believe it's already been a month. It went by so fast."

"I agree. I don't know if I'm ready to go back to the real world."

"I guess I have a little more vacation left. If you count sitting in a room with two toddlers who constantly fight each other a vacation."

I snort. "I'd like to see you with them. They probably love you."

"I don't wanna brag, but I am their favorite uncle."

"You don't have any brothers."

"Shhh."

I roll my eyes and laugh. "How long will you be with your sister?"

"Not too long. I have to head back to Cali and get started on conditioning and training. But not before being checked out by our doctor and making sure everything looks good. I had some injuries last season, but nothing major."

"Damn, so off-season isn't really *off*, is it?"

"I'm lucky I got as much time off as I did this time. And that's really because I didn't talk to anyone about it," he says with a grin. "Coach may have something to say, but I've been working out here a little, so it's not like I've fallen off track completely."

"What's your schedule usually like during the season?"

His brows lift and he exhales. "Well, I think our first full month we'll have eight away games and six home games."

It's my turn for my brows to reach for my hairline. "Fourteen games a month? Holy hell, that's a lot."

He nods. "I love it, though."

"That's good. It's always best to love what you do."

"What's your schedule looking like when you get back?" he asks.

With a sigh, I say, "Check in with my agent, because I'm sure he's having a panic attack. Finalize the deal with the sex toy line for the new masturbator sleeve."

"And send me one," he pipes in.

"Right. And send you one," I say with a wink. "I have a meeting with my production manager. She's responsible for the budgets, shooting schedules, hiring, and what have you. I just need to make sure everything's running smoothly."

He begins fiddling with his napkin. "Do you have any uhh...movies scheduled?"

"My agent has one he's begging me to do. I've definitely taken a step back from them, but I'm the face of the company. It all started because of me and what I do, and people want to continue watching me, so it's hard to break away."

Jarrod nods, his lips twisting to the side. I can tell he's

probably feeling uncomfortable, and I understand it. He's reacted really well to everything, but nobody is immune to experiencing jealousy. My job is the main reason why none of my relationships have worked—and why this may not either.

A waitress stops by with our food, allowing us a small reprieve from our uncomfortable conversations. Once she's gone, the silence is back.

"Have you ever filmed with a woman?" he asks, taking me by surprise. I'd thought he'd want to change the subject completely.

I move my fork around my rice. "Yeah."

"Really? What'd you think?"

I laugh. "I don't prefer it, but the scenes were also with another man, so it was okay."

"Give me a storyline for one of them."

"Uh. A couple invites their new neighbor over and the wife seduces him. The husband catches them screwing on the couch, but then gets turned on and joins in."

"Ah. His 'first time'?"

I chuckle. "Yep."

We eat in silence for several minutes before Jarrod speaks again.

"I don't know what we're doing from here. We don't live too far away from each other, but I know my schedule is pretty busy. When I'm off, I'd like to see you if you're free, but it might only be for one night before I have to leave again. It's gonna be like that for a while. One or two days here or there. You can come to me, too, but..." He looks nervous and I know what he's thinking.

"You're not out. I know," I say with a nod. "We'd have to be careful."

"I don't want you to think I'm ashamed of you. I'm not. I —" He stops himself. "I think you're amazing and I don't feel like I owe anyone an explanation for who I like or why, but I'm aware of how the media latches onto things. They're vultures. They hover over you and as soon as they find you vulnerable, they attack and tear you apart. I'm not just thinking of myself here."

"I know." I give him a nod and my heart begins to fracture.

This isn't going to go anywhere. He's hockey's biggest star. Any news of us would ruin him and overshadow his talents. It shouldn't be that way, but it will be. He won't come out, and I don't blame him. Saying you're bi is one thing, saying you're with a very out and proud gay porn star is a whole 'nother. I can't be mad, but it doesn't make it hurt any less.

I put my silverware down and look at him. "I think I need to make a decision for both of us."

He sits back, his brows drawing in with concern. "What do you mean?"

My heart lurches up my throat, wanting to choke me before I manage to say the words I know need to be said.

"I think we both know things will end with us once we leave here."

He leans forward, ready to argue. "No—"

"Jarrod," I say, cutting him off. "It's not going to work. Believe me, I wish there were a way, but leaving the island thinking we're in some sort of relationship is only going to make things more complicated. We'll leave, keep in touch, plan little rendezvous where you're flying in and out on the same day or where I'm sneaking into your place for your one day off. It'll give us hope and we'll think it'll work, but over time, it's going to get harder. We're going to *fall* harder. The distance will eat us up. You'll hate knowing or not knowing what I'm doing during my workday. Even if we're seen in public in the most platonic way possible, the headlines will question why Jarrod Bivens is friends with a gay porn star. Your teammates will ask questions. You will be forced to lie or come out. You will have to defend yourself and our friendship. It will be difficult for you, and I will be left brokenhearted."

"Dev," he says softly.

"You know it's true. I'm not asking you to make major life decisions for me. I don't want you to be worried about anything. I don't want your season to be tainted with rumors and questions if we're ever photographed together. I want you, Jarrod. More than I've ever wanted anyone or anything, but if we try this, it's only going to drag out the pain and heartache."

"I don't want this to be the end," he says passionately. "It can't be."

I pin my lips together. "I don't want it to be either. I hope you believe me. I've never felt like this before," I say, hand at my chest.

Jarrod rubs at the hair on his jaw, frustration radiating from him. "I don't like the way this is making me feel."

"I know."

His arm juts across the table, grabbing my hand. "I'm sorry." His eyes look so sad, drooping at the edges.

"Don't," I say, squeezing his hand. "You don't have to apologize."

"Can we go back to the room now?"

I nod.

The whole way back, we hold hands, knowing it's the last time.

Twenty-Eight

JARROD

The night is now tinged with sadness. More than that. It's doused with despair. My heart aches in my chest knowing this is it—the last time I'll be with Devin. I understand where he's coming from. What he said makes sense, and I feel bad because I know it's my fault. He's out. His industry and co-workers aren't going to care who he's with. It's because of me that we can't be who we are or do what we want.

We slowly get undressed, taking quick glances at each other, the mood unequivocally changed. I don't want this to be the end. It's been one of the best months of my life, but I also know he deserves a hundred percent.

I'm glad he didn't hear me earlier. It would make things much worse had he had heard my whispered secret while he was going to sleep. We would've been forced to talk about it, to dive deeper into it. I told him I think I love him. And I do think that. How do you end something that's felt so right from the beginning?

A lump forms in my throat and I turn away, putting my clothes on a chair because I almost can't stand to look at him. He's sad because of me, and I've only ever wanted him to be happy.

Soft hands touch my back and wrap around my middle. "Come on."

I spin around and hold him, inhaling his scent as I squeeze him tight. "I don't want this night to end. For the first time in my life, I don't want to see the sunrise."

He pulls away, his hands cupping my face as he stares me in the eyes. "You will see many sunrises. We'll watch the same one, and we'll remember the time we had here."

I grab him and plant a ferocious kiss on his lips. I walk him back to the bed, both of us tumbling on top of the covers, unable to stop touching and kissing. We say with our bodies what we can't say with words. It doesn't make sense to utter love declarations or promises we don't know we can keep. We just show each other how desperate we are for the other.

Naked, we lie facing each other, our legs intertwined, hands roaming, tongues tasting. My cock rubs against his as I grind into him.

"Jarrod," he breathes against my lips.

I look at him and tell myself I don't see his eyes glistening. I don't see the sadness. I only see the lust.

Reaching down, I take hold of his dick and stroke. He does the same. Our mouths never stray far from each other, moaning and whimpering with each tug.

"I'm gonna come," I say on a pant.

"I'm so close," he responds.

"Oh, fuck!"

I bury my face into his neck, trying to keep my pace on his shaft as my body's overcome with jerky movements.

"I'm coming," he cries, and I instantly feel the warm release on my hand.

"Yes," I breathe. "Yes, yes."

"Oh god."

When our bodies are spent, we flop onto our backs, sucking in deep breaths. We may not have had sex again, but it's for the best. This was still a perfect, intimate moment. And our first time—our only time—was incredible. It was done without dread or sadness. I want it to remain an untainted memory.

Devin reaches over and finds my hand. I squeeze his three times for three words. He repeats it back to me.

THE MORNING IS SOMBER, the gray sky encapsulating the mood for the day. Both of us get ready, the silence stretching between us as we pack.

At the door, Devin turns around and takes in the room. It's where some of my favorite moments took place. I understand wanting to mentally say goodbye.

He gives me a small grin when he spins back around, and then I pull open the door and we walk onto the pier.

Matteo and another employee wait for us to take our luggage back to the main building. We load everything into one cart and sit together in the other.

After checking out, we're taken to a boat that takes us from Black Diamond. We watch as the bungalows disappear from sight and the trees shrink into the distance. We witness this dreamy vacation spot fade and eventually vanish as we're taken closer to the bigger island that holds the airport.

Everything moves too quickly. Before I know it, we're checking in our luggage and standing in the terminal, having to go to separate gates.

"Well," Devin says, leaving it at that.

"Yeah."

"I really had the time of my life, and you're the reason why. I went to Black Diamond to get away and be alone, but I think if you hadn't been there, I would've left within a week. You made it fun and relaxing. Without you I would've been bored and tired of myself."

My lips draw up into a crooked grin. "It was...life changing. I'm so thankful for you. For our friendship. For...everything."

His chin dips with a nod. "Me too."

I grab him and hug him tight, inhaling his scent one last time. "Bye, Devin. Thank you for the memories I'll never forget."

I hear him swallow as he tightens his hold. "Bye, Jarrod. Thank you for reminding me what's important."

Though I'm not too sure what he's referring to, I give him one last squeeze before I pull away. Both of our eyes shine with emotion.

"Bye," I say again.

"Bye."

We turn away from each other and walk in opposite

directions. I never turn around to see if he does the same. If I catch a glimpse of his face one more time, I may never leave.

My heart splinters, a small piece left behind with him. It doesn't register right away that without it, I'll never be whole again.

August 29th

"It's almost September and you haven't done anything but solo scenes. What's going on with you?" my agent, Steve, asks.

"Nothing is going on with me. I'm working, aren't I?"

"Angelo is still wanting to do that movie with you. He's a rising star, Devin. You two together would be explosive. Everyone wants to see it."

I rub my fingers over my forehead. "Let me get back to you. I have to go meet Melissa about the mouth sleeve."

"Is it done?"

"I have to approve it."

"Oh, did you get my email about the article with *Flash*? They want to do a Q & A. Some *Ask a porn star* type thing. You'll also need to have your five favorite toys you'd recommend."

"Yeah, I got it. Tell them I'll do it."

"When you see Melissa, ask her about the anal sleeve. I'm not even sure why they didn't start with that. Do you know how many people are gonna want that one?"

"We've started the discussion."

"Great. Let me know when it's time to sign contracts."

"Will do."

"Think about the movie, Devin. I'm serious."

"Okay," I say with a sigh. "Talk to you soon."

I end the call and drop the phone to my desk. I know I should do the movie. I'm aware Jarrod and I aren't together and haven't even spoken since we left the island. I just keep thinking about how he'd feel if he knew I'd been with someone else. Then I wonder if he's already been with someone else, and the spiral begins.

I've debated texting him. More times than I'd like to admit, to be honest. But I'm the one that said this shouldn't extend past Black Diamond. I can't talk to him because I'll never want to stop. And then what? We're exactly where I said we shouldn't be.

Jarrod's aware of my job, and it doesn't make sense for me to turn down opportunities, It's not like we're together. I should tell Steve to go ahead and get the ball rolling. I'll film with Angelo and just like all the other times, it won't mean anything.

Before I can send him a text, I get an email alert and open it up. It's from a director friend of mine who I talked to about doing another movie. My smile grows as I read, and I end up sending Steve a completely different message.

Thirty

JARROD

October 30th

"All right, guys. Game night. After we beat Vegas tonight, we've got two days off, and we're gonna go out and celebrate Bivens' birthday tomorrow."

Cheers erupt in the locker room after our captain's announcement. "We may be in Sin City and all, but let's not get in too much trouble." He shoots a glare at Stafford, who last time we were in Vegas, got extremely drunk and took a piss right in front of the hotel.

"I learned my lesson," Stafford says, holding his hands up.

"Bivens is turning the big 3-0, so let's celebrate right, and the first way we do that is by winning this fucking game."

We roar our excitement before heading to the ice.

We're in our first month of the season, and out of the fifteen games so far, we've won eleven. Hopefully twelve after tonight.

I can't help but wonder if Devin ever watches any of these games. I know he said he's not really into sports, but he did start looking into it at the island. It might be too hard for him, which I get, but I definitely play thinking he's watching.

"How's the knee?" Cory asks as we make our way through the tunnel.

"It's fine. No worse than usual."

He nods. "What do you wanna do tomorrow night? A bar? Strip club? Ooh, we could go to that brothel. It's been on TV."

"We are not going to a brothel," Eriksson grumbles, moving past us.

"Just because you're married doesn't mean all of us are," Cory replies. He elbows me. "Whatcha think?"

"Let's start at a bar and see where we end up."

"Cool."

The game starts and our center, McKinney, scores within the first five minutes. Ten minutes into the second period, one of the Knights breaks away and comes at the net. I move past the crease area to hit the puck, but the guy body checks me, sending me flying back.

As I get back to my feet, I see Cory flying my way, followed closely by the rest of my teammates.

Cory shoves the guy into the boards. "Don't touch my fucking goalie!"

"Fuck off!" the guy yells back, pushing Cory into the back of the net.

We all move into the trapezoid, fighting or yanking people off our own players. The guy who hit me checks me with his shoulder as he tries to skate off, and I push him back into the boards. Cory moves in to defend me when the guy charges.

The refs start blowing their whistles and break everything up. When it's all said and done, we have penalties for interference, charging, boarding, and fighting. Multiple people end up in the penalty box for anywhere between two and five minutes, Cory included, and though I get a penalty, someone takes my place since I have to remain in the net.

Five minutes into the third period and they score on a tap-in.

"Fuck!" I yell.

We're down to four minutes left, tied 1-1, and the Knights are flying at the net. I squat low, trying to stay in center, watching the puck and hoping like hell the defensemen can push that shit to the other side.

The smacking of sticks against sticks gets louder and closer, and then they shoot. I drop down, ready to stop the puck with my hand and then there's snow in my face. It's the same fucking guy that hit me earlier.

I shove the puck away and get up, pushing him into the net, nearly bending him over the top as I swing for his head. "What the fuck, man?"

We're soon crowded, my guys coming in to have my back, and his teammates having his. All of us are surrounding the goal, fighting it out.

"Fucking snowing the goalie now? What the hell, man?" one of my teammates says.

"Didn't even work, you fucking dumbass!" I yell.

The refs come in to break it all up, and once again people are sent to the sin bin for fighting and unsportsmanlike conduct before we can continue.

The game clock reads 1:58 when we score again, and we're able to keep them from scoring for the remaining seconds, coming away with the win.

In my hotel room later that night, I want more than anything to text Devin and tell him about the game. I keep having the urge to reach out. It's been months and it hasn't gotten any easier. All I do is think about him.

I look through my photos from our time at Black Diamond and realize I never sent him half the ones I took. Would it be weird to send them now? Am I just looking for an excuse to reach out? Maybe. But what if he wants them?

I go to our text thread, which I've saved, and start typing.

Thirty-One

DEVIN

October 30th

"I t's Sexsposá day," Cam deadpans as we walk through the hotel doors. "Yay."

"Don't sound so excited," I say with a laugh.

"You know I hate this shit."

"Why do you come?"

"Well, let me rephrase. I don't hate meeting the fans, but the insider mixers and meeting people I don't care about or seeing people I really never wanted to see again." He makes a face. "I could do without all that."

"I get it. My ex is gonna be here."

"Yeah. I have two that'll be around, too. Remind me, why do we date these people?"

I snort. "We are these people."

"Exactly. We should know better."

I met Cam a few years ago after we did a scene together, and while we're hardly best friends, we're closer than I am to most people. He's one of the most popular gay porn stars right now and in the top one percent of OnlyFans.

He's very good looking; his dark brown skin is flawless and ripped to perfection. If we weren't in the same industry, and if I was interested, he'd probably fall in with my typical type. At least physically. However, I'm not his. I've found out he's more into femboys, and while I may not be hyper masculine, I'm not what he's looking for.

This weekend we're in Vegas for Sexposá, an adult convention that hosts hundreds of porn stars and lots of vendors. There are award shows, not only for the performers, but for sex toy products. There's an interactive experience that allows people to learn more about BDSM, burlesque performances, and panels to learn more about the business.

"How'd the panel go yesterday?" Cam asks as we make our way to the elevators.

"It was good. I like talking about the business from the other side of the lens, you know? Plus, I met a guy who I may collaborate with. He's in the lube business, so we can help promote each other and potentially reach new audiences."

"That's good, man." He looks at his watch. "I'm gonna go meet someone at the bar real quick. But I'll see you tomorrow."

"All right. Goodnight."

He turns and heads back while I keep going toward the elevator. We just had a late dinner after a full day today. I'm ready to pass out so I can be energized for tomorrow. At least the schedule is easier. We only go until eight o'clock, and it's mostly meeting fans, signing autographs, and taking pictures.

When I get to my room, I toe off my shoes and start stripping down to my underwear. After a quick shower, I brush my teeth and make my way to the bed. I grab my phone to set the alarm, and plug it in, and come to a screeching halt when I see I have a text from Jarrod.

> Hey, I forgot to send these to you. Thought maybe you'd like to see them. If not, feel free to delete and ignore, but...I don't know. Hope you're well.

The text is accompanied by at least ten photos, most taken from our time at the waterfall and some he snapped on the deck of his bungalow.

My heart gets lodged in my throat. It's been four months. I wasn't sure he'd ever text, and while I've waited for the day he would, I've also dreaded it.

He was thinking about me, possibly even staring at these photos, remembering those days. But what now? Do I simply say *thank you?* Do I ask how he is and start what will end up being a really long text conversation that could lead to a phone call, that will eventually lead to my heart breaking all over again?

I type and delete a variety of messages. Nothing I say feels right. I don't know how to talk to him like he's not the most amazing thing I've had in my life. How do we go back to just Jarrod and Devin—old high school acquaintances?

It takes me an hour before I respond, and apparently he sent the message an hour before I saw it, so he's likely asleep.

> Thank you. I'm glad you sent them. Hope you're well, too.

The message feels wrong, and it makes my stomach roll with displeasure. It's so curt. It's a response you send to a co-worker you hardly like. It's a pleasantry meant for someone you barely know. It's not the response you should send to the man who flipped your world upside down and brought you a happiness you never thought possible.

I turn off my ringer and put the phone face down on my nightstand. I don't want to know if he responds or not. I force myself to go to sleep, my heart aching, my stomach in knots, and despair rolling in.

Thirty-Two

JARROD

October 31st

I stare at his text message for the twentieth time today. It was polite enough but offered no insight into how he was feeling. He could've deleted the whole text thread right after responding. He acknowledged me but didn't care to continue talking. However, he did say he was glad I sent them, so that means he wants to keep them, right?

I run a hand through my hair, tugging on the strands in frustration. I hate this. I hate not being able to talk to him the way I want to. I want to ask him a million questions. I want to FaceTime him so I can see his face. I need to tell him how much I miss him and how often I think about our time together.

"You okay?" Cory asks as he leaves the bathroom and enters my bedroom.

"Yeah, I'm good."

"You ready? I think some of the guys are at the bar down in the lobby. Stafford wants to go to the hotel next door."

"Yep. I'm ready."

I get up from the bed and put on my shoes. I wasn't sure what kind of place we'd end up in, so we all went for business casual vibes. I went with black pants and a ribbed knit, polo sweater. It's lightweight so I won't get too hot inside, but warm enough for when we're outside. Cory has on a green, long sleeve, Polo button up and sand-colored chino pants.

"All right, birthday boy, let's get it."

We leave the hotel room and find six of the guys from the team in the lobby. They all lift up a shot glass when we approach, boisterous cheers and out of sync *happy birthdays* yelled in my direction.

"To Bivens!" Tipton shouts, handing me a glass of dark liquid. "May your thirtieth year be the dirtiest yet."

"Yeah!"

"To thirty!"

"You're old as fuck."

I shoot Popov a look. "Fuck off, Pop. You're twenty-nine."

"Yeah, but I just turned twenty-nine, so I'm basically twenty-eight."

"Yeah, yeah, but you're the one with a bad hip," Andersson says, nudging Popov as he raises his glass.

We clink them together and swallow down our first shot of the night.

On the street, we pass card flickers and walk over the advertisements of escorts with stars on their tits and a promise of a good time if we call the number on the card.

"Hey, Pop. You're still a virgin, right?" Cory teases. "Get

you a girl in twenty minutes," he says, pointing to one of the flickers on the street wearing a shirt that says just that.

"Ha ha. I'll have you know I just had a girl on my dick before we flew out here. When was the last time you got laid?"

"When was your dad out of town again? Last week?"

"You were with his dad?" Stafford asks with a laugh.

Cory pushes him. "It was to insinuate I was with his mom."

Everyone laughs and the teasing continues until we get to the next hotel.

"Holy shit it's packed in here," Pop says.

"There's a convention or something happening," Stafford replies, pointing at a sign that reads Sexposá.

"Ah shit, a porn convention?" Cory asks, rushing to the sign. "Damn. It just ended."

My stomach clenches and my eyes scan the advertisement. It doesn't specify who's here, just that it's a major convention for the adult film industry.

"We should've stayed at this hotel. I could've ran into my favorite porn star. I wonder if Dazzling Diamond is here."

"That's her name?" Stafford asks.

"Don't act like you don't know her. She's got double D's," he says, holding his hands out in front of his chest. "Black hair and a tattoo that wraps around her neck and down the middle of her tits. God, I hope I see her."

"Right, because you'd have a chance," Pop says.

"There's a bar over here," Tipton says, ignoring the porn talk.

All of us linger between two high top tables near the bar,

drinking and watching the highlights of our game that's on the TV behind the bar.

"Look at that fucking guy!" Cory says, watching as the center from the Golden Knights body checked me into the net. "He really had it out for you."

"I was mostly pissed about the snow," I say.

"Oh shit, look at me. That's the quickest score I've had in a long time," Stafford says, watching his goal go in five minutes into the game.

We get another drink and start walking to the casino floor, all of us spreading out between slot machines and blackjack tables.

I haven't been drunk since that night at Black Diamond when Devin had to take care of me, but I feel myself getting pretty tipsy already. It's my birthday, so I feel like it's a good excuse to drink and have a good time with my teammates.

After Cory loses three hundred dollars on blackjack, less than ten minutes after sitting at the table, we find Eriksson, Tipton, and Lars at a roulette table. Stafford and James are nearby trying their hand at craps, and a cocktail server is walking toward me.

"Good evening, sir," she says with a friendly smile. "What are you drinking tonight?"

"Jack and Coke."

She gestures to my mostly empty cup. "I can take that for you and bring you another."

"Thank you," I reply with a grin.

"You're most welcome."

Once she walks away, Cory's at my side. "Oh shit, she's hot."

"Yeah," I say with a little shrug.

"I watched the whole encounter. She thinks you're hot, too."

I roll my eyes. "They're friendly to everyone. It's their job."

"She's probably pretty good at another *job*, if you know what I mean."

I make a face at him. "Anyway, I'm gonna go take a piss real quick. If you see her, just grab my drink for me."

"Or I'll send her to the bathroom."

Not bothering to respond, I wander through the maze of slot machines until I find a sign for the bathrooms. Once I'm done, I wash my hands and head back into the sea of smoke and people.

Before I can get far, I stop dead in my tracks.

Devin.

He's here.

He's wearing a black button up with the first button coming together right at the top of his abs, leaving his chest visible. A dark, emerald green blazer highlights his eyes and I can't seem to close my mouth.

When I finally snap out of it, I realize he's with someone. A handsome Black man with muscular forearms visible because the sleeves of his ivory sweater are pushed up.

They're laughing at something, leaning into each other like only people who are close would do.

This is why he responded the way he did. He's with someone.

Thirty-Three

DEVIN

"Oh man, I can't even guess as to how many boxes of dildos I signed," Cam says with a laugh.

"Me either. For once, I was overwhelmed with the amount of dicks coming at me."

Cam barks out another laugh. "I can't look at them too long, because then I start really inspecting it and judging my own shit. Like, I know my dick looks good, but I see it from up here. Does it really look like that from underneath?"

I snort, almost choking on my drink. "It was really surreal to see it for the first time."

With a glance around, I try to spot the cocktail waitress who's supposed to be getting me another drink. Instead, I find a very frozen Jarrod Bivens.

"What the..." I let it trail off, my eyes stuck to his as he stares right back.

"Who's that?" Cam asks.

I lick my lips and swallow. "Um. A friend."

"Hmm. Y'all ain't looking at each other like friends."

"I haven't seen him in a bit. I wasn't expecting this."

I take a step forward and Jarrod does the same, swallowing up the space between us with long strides.

"Hey," I reply, nerves strangling my vocal cords, making the one syllable word come out shaky.

"Hey," he replies without his normal cheer.

"What're you doing here?"

It's the wrong thing to ask. The wrong four words to come out of my mouth. I should've said, oh my god, I'm so happy to see you. I've missed you. I can't believe you're here. Instead, I question why he's existing in the same place I am.

"I had a game," he says, eyes flickering back to Cam. "Yesterday."

"Oh," I reply, inclining my head. "That's right."

Something flashes in his eyes. "You knew?"

"It was on at the restaurant I was at."

I knew he was playing last night, but I didn't expect him to still be in town tonight.

"It's your birthday," I say, remembering suddenly what day it is.

He nods. "It is."

"Happy birthday. Are you here with anyone?"

"Some of my teammates are around." His eyes once again find Cam who's lingering two feet behind us, acting like he's not paying attention. "And you're with?"

I instantly realize why he's acting the way he is. He thinks me and Cam are together.

"Cam," I say, turning and gesturing for him to come forward. "This is my friend, Cam. Cam, this is Jarrod."

"I wasn't going to say anything," Cam said, taking his hand. "But you play for the Bobcats, right?"

Jarrod gives him a practiced smile. "I do."

"It's really nice to meet you. I didn't know Devin knew a famous hockey player. What the hell other secrets are you keeping from me?" he asks, smacking my arm with the back of his hand.

I chuckle nervously. "He's a friend from school."

"Congrats on the win last night. Devin didn't even mention knowing you as we watched at the sports bar."

I feel my cheeks heat up, and since I don't know what to say, I change the subject. "So, when are you heading back home?"

"Tomorrow afternoon."

"Wow," I reply, allowing my eyes to roam up and down his body.

"I'm gonna go get our drinks," Cam says. "I think the waitress got lost."

"Okay."

Once Cam's gone, I feel my shoulders relax as I sigh. "God, Jarrod. It's so good to see you again," I say, taking a step forward before thinking better of it. "Are your teammates nearby?"

"Just hug me, Dev," he says, holding out his arms.

As soon as we're connected, everything feels normal again. My heart flutters and I take a deep inhale, breathing in his scent. It's like the weight of the world is off my shoulders and I'm carefree again.

"I'm sorry I didn't respond the way I wanted to," I say. "With Cam here...and people. I don't know."

He pulls away and gives me a grin. "It's okay. So, he's your...friend?"

I smile. "Yes. Friend."

"Why does this feel awkward?" he asks, putting his hands in his pockets.

"I'm not sure," I say with a laugh. "We're in the real world. There's tons of people around."

He nods. "We're not being ourselves."

I chew on my lip. "Thanks for the pictures. I wasn't sure how to respond and I regretted the one I gave you instantly."

"I debated sending them at all. I figured you didn't want to hear from me."

"Jarrod, it's not that I don't want to hear from you. It's—"

He holds up his hand. "I know. I'm sorry."

"There you are!" a loud voice calls from behind me.

I turn and find a very tall guy with wavy brown hair coming toward us, his eyes a little glassy and a smile on his lips.

My eyes fling back to Jarrod, and I find him standing a little more stiff. Nervous.

"You found me," he says.

"Did that waitress find you, though? I talked to her for you, and she's one hundred percent interested. I told her you were in the bathroom, but maybe she went to another one."

Jarrod's eyes slide over to me, his expression hard to read. "I told you she's just friendly to everyone. I'm not interested." His eyes land on my face, like he's making sure I get the message.

"She's not that friendly to everyone. She was giving Pop a hard time a couple minutes ago. And oh—" He stops talking, finally realizing I'm not just another patron at a slot machine, but someone who was talking to Jarrod. "Sorry."

I give him a friendly smile, dipping my chin slightly.

"Cory, this is Devin." He pauses. "A friend from school."

"Oh, cool," he replies, his voice loud. "I'm Cory." He shakes my hand and turns back to Jarrod. "Stafford wants to leave soon, and I think Eriksson and Tipton are probably going back to their rooms. Married guys," he says, rolling his eyes.

"Okay. Uhh, yeah." He looks at me again before talking to his friend. "I'll find you in a minute. We were just catching up."

"Sure. Yeah." Cory nods at me. "Nice meeting you."

"You too."

Once he's gone, Jarrod exhales. "I was not trying to hook up with the waitress."

"It's fine."

His face darkens. "Is it?"

"Jarrod, I don't have a say in what you do."

"So, you don't care if I sleep around with whoever?"

"I didn't say that."

"Are you...have you..." He cuts himself off. "Okay, I'm sorry. I don't mean to get mad. It's just...this is hard."

"This is why I said we couldn't keep in touch."

"I know," he replies with a bit of a bite, before softening his tone. "I know."

"I hope you have a good birthday," I say, coming in for a goodbye hug. "I think about you constantly and hope for only the best."

I squeeze him, bringing him flush against my body. "I miss you."

"I miss you, too."

I have to pull away and flee before I break down, so when I take a step back, I barely look at him before I walk off.

"Dev."

My steps halt but I only angle my head slightly, unable to look in his eyes again. "Yeah?"

The silence stretches and I figure he must be rethinking whatever he was going to say. Part of me hopes he begs to spend the night with me, the other part hopes he doesn't, because I won't know how to respond.

He clears his throat. "Goodnight."

"Goodnight."

Thirty-Four

JARROD

December 24th

With two days off for the holiday, I decided to visit my parents in my hometown. My sister flew in with her husband and kids yesterday, so it'll be a fairly nice family reunion that hasn't happened in at least three years. I either see my parents while Gina's still in Chicago, or she visits them when I'm at an away game. Our schedules hardly line up, but this year we get to be together for Christmas.

I pull up into the circular driveway and park in front of one of the three garage doors. My parents have always had money. A ridiculous amount of it, so it's fair to say I come from a very privileged background. I never went without anything and was probably given more than I needed. They were pretty good parents though.

The house they live in now isn't the one I grew up in. This is a grand Mediterranean house with way more bedrooms and bathrooms than they need, but Mom likes that it's a guard-gated community with exclusive access to tennis and racquet courts, and dad fell in love with the fully outfitted cabana.

I pass the palm trees that line the walkway and find myself in front of the black double doors. As soon as I'm inside, I hear the screeching of children followed closely by, "Connor, no!"

I drop my bag and rush down the hall, jumping through a doorway to stop my nephew in his tracks. He squeals with excitement, his chubby cheeks jiggling with each step. I pick him up and bring him to my hip, finding a half smooshed jelly covered piece of bread in his hand.

My sister flies around the corner, stopping with an exhale when she finds me with him. "God, that kid's fast."

"Maybe he'll be the fastest skater on ice," I say, tickling him.

"No sports. Not for my precious babies."

I roll my eyes. "Mommy doesn't know that I already have lessons planned for you as soon as you turn five. Just three more years to go, buddy."

"Please," she says, coming to take the bread and wiping his hand with a wet wipe. "I saw what happened to you yesterday. I'm not letting my son get treated like that."

"He'll be a grown man, G. Not a toddler."

"Still my baby." She takes him in her arms and gives me a hug. "How are you, though? You okay?"

I bend my leg slightly. "Knee's kinda hurting me, but I'm fine."

"Dad isn't home right now, and Mom wants to know if you can go to the store for her."

"What? I just got here."

"I'll come with you. You know the area better than me. Plus, I'm able to get away from these precious little devils," she says, rubbing her nose against Connor's.

"Where's Matt?"

"Out back with CeCe. But don't let her see you yet or you'll never be able to leave. Let me drop off Con and then we can run out."

Ten minutes later, we're pulling out of the community and heading toward the nearest stores that are still open.

"She still needs wrapping paper?"

Gina shakes her head. "I think she forgot we were all coming. Yesterday she was out buying toys for the kids. *Yesterday.*"

"Old people," I say with a laugh.

DAMN NEAR THIRTY MINUTES LATER, we end up in Sherman Oaks and Gina sees a sign for a mall.

"Malls are always open, right?"

"I don't know about always, but let's see."

We're in luck, sort of. The mall is open, but it's fucking packed. It takes forever to find a parking spot.

Inside, Gina gets distracted from the task at hand and ends up shopping for much more than wrapping paper. She finds small gifts for her kids, something for Mom and Dad, and asks me what I want.

"That's not how it works, G. You're supposed to know and love me so much you already know what I want."

She rolls her eyes. "Anyway. Go away, then. Let me find something for you. Go get some wrapping paper."

"You were just talking shit about Mom forgetting to get gifts and you're just now getting mine?"

She gives me a smile. "Uhh. I've been traveling! Do you know how stressful it is to travel across the country?"

I cross my arms and give her a look. "Yes."

"With kids!" she amends. "Close to a holiday."

"Yeah, yeah."

"Just go," she says, shooing me away.

I wander around, peeking into stores to see if it looks like they'd have wrapping paper. I feel like this wasn't the best place to go. Most stores are just selling things you need to wrap.

Spotting a line to a smoothie vendor, I make my way over and wait. The older lady in front of me has a bag full of wrapping paper.

"Excuse me, ma'am."

She spins around, looking me up and down. "Yes?"

"Can you tell me where you got that wrapping paper?"

She smiles slightly. "Sure." Pointing to our left, she says, "If you turn right there by the sunglasses store, they have a little pop up shop. They'll be there offering to wrap presents for you, but you can also buy wrapping and boxes for yourself."

"Thank you," I say with a polite grin and dip of my chin.

"Sure," she replies, turning back around.

After I get my strawberry banana smoothie, I turn around and head back down the line, but I stop in place when I spot a familiar head of hair and an exquisitely dressed body.

"Devin?"

His head lifts from looking at his phone and his brows raise when he sees me. A smile slowly stretches across his lips just as mine curl up on one side.

"What's happening?" he says with a chuckle. "Are we gonna keep running into each other now?"

I step forward and hug him, our arms wrapping around each other briefly, separating faster than I'd like.

I accidentally kick the bags at his feet. "Sorry."

He waves a hand. "It's fine. Nothing important in there."

"No presents?"

He chuckles. "I don't really celebrate."

"What?" I exclaim, stepping forward with him when the line moves. "Oh. Is it a religious thing?"

Devin shakes his head. "No. I just don't have anyone to celebrate with." He laughs. "I don't mean that to sound as pitiful as it does."

My lips draw down in the corners. "You aren't going to your parents'?"

"We haven't spoken in a while."

"But your birthday."

His eyes meet mine. "I'm just going to relax at home and watch movies. I'll be fine. I promise."

I bite down on my bottom lip as I debate on saying what is threatening to leave my mouth at any second.

"Why don't you come to my parents' place?"

His head snaps up. "What? No." He shakes his head, moving up in line. "It's really fine. I won't intrude like that."

"They're only half an hour from here. Where do you live?"

"Woodland Hills. About twenty minutes away."

"You're so close. Come on, Dev. We're having dinner tonight. At least come for dinner."

He steps up to order, his eyes sliding in my direction. "Can I get a large, peach and mango smoothie?"

"Dev."

He faces me. "You know it's a bad idea, right?"

"Is it?"

He's probably right, but everything in me is telling me I need him with me tonight.

Devin pays for his drink and we walk away, finding a spot where we're out of the way of the crowd.

"Jarrod."

"Please."

His eyes drink me in. "You have to understand it's not because I don't want to be with you. I want you more than I can explain, and that's why I'm hesitant. Taking steps toward you is easy, but it's the walk away from you that kills me. Every time I do it, another piece of my heart breaks off and I'm not sure how many more times I can do it before it stops beating entirely."

My hand twitches, wanting to reach out and take his. "Maybe the universe keeps putting us together for a reason."

He inhales deeply, looking away. "Don't do that, Jarrod."

"What?" I ask, moving closer, my body drawn to him like a magnet.

"Don't give me hope."

He's right. I get caught up in my feelings when I'm around him, and I'm saying things like it's not me keeping us from being together.

"I'm sorry, Dev. I just want—"

"There you are!" Gina's voice calls out, two bags in each hand as she maneuvers through people.

"Hey," I reply, easing away from Devin. "I had to get a smoothie."

She gives me a look. "And the wrapping paper that we came here for?"

"Oh, you're one to talk with all those bags. But don't worry, I know where to get it. I just ran into Devin."

My eyes dance to him. I watch as realization hits Gina's face. She looks at him, her brows rising when she meets my gaze again.

"Oh. Oh. Devin. Right." She plasters a smile on her face and places two of the bags down, extending her hand toward him. "It's so nice to meet you, Devin."

Ocean green eyes slide to me as he shakes her hand, an amused grin on his face. "You're his sister."

"I am!" she squeals. "He talked about me?"

Devin pulls back, a genuine smile on his face now. "Yes, and I'm aware that he also mentioned me."

Gina looks way too happy. "Maybe."

I roll my eyes. "Anyway. Gina, Devin was just saying he doesn't have plans for Christmas, so I—"

"None?" she questions, eyes wide. "Well, you gotta come hang out with us. I promise it's gonna be pretty laid back."

Devin does his best to not look at me like he wants to kill me for putting him on the spot. "It's a family holiday."

"Absolutely not," Gina says. "It's a holiday for loved ones, blood related or not."

I give him a wide grin, hoping he caves.

"Okay. Sure, yes. I'll be there."

"Yay!" Gina squeals. "Well, I'll see you later then. J, tell me where to get the wrapping paper and I'll go get it."

"Pass the sunglasses shop and it should be over there. They'll be wrapping presents."

"Okay."

Once she's gone, I face Devin and immediately apologize. "Okay, I'm sorry, but I was desperate. I can't only see you for ten minutes again. Not now when we're so close."

"It's okay. It'll be nice," he says with a soft smile. "Um, text me later?"

"Of course."

He grabs his bags and hesitates briefly before coming in for another quick hug. "See you soon."

"Can't wait."

Thirty-Five

DEVIN

Christmas Eve Night

S tanding in my walk-in closet, I debate my outfit for the evening, not knowing if they have a more dressed up standard or if they just wear everyday clothes. You never know with the exceptionally wealthy. I've never met his parents, and my heart hammers in my chest knowing the first meeting happens tonight, right before the biggest holiday of the year.

They don't know what happened between us, but meeting the parents of the guy you have feelings for is quite the occasion regardless.

> Hey. The address is 3311 Clerendon Oak. Dinner is at 6:30 but you can show up sooner.

> Okay. What is the dress code?

> Lol. You don't need a tux or anything. I think my sister has a red and white striped shirt on because she wants to be a candy cane I guess. I'm wearing a cream-colored Polo and jeans. Just wear whatever you want.

I look back in my closet and find a green Polo shirt. If he's wearing a Polo, that's what I'll do. Green for the holiday spirit, I suppose. I snatch a pair of black chinos to go with it, hoping to fall perfectly between casual and dressed up, unsure what his parents will be wearing.

After getting dressed and spraying a couple spritzes of cologne, I go into my kitchen and grab an unopened bottle of wine from my wine fridge. My phone vibrates in my pocket.

> Are you coming now?

I smile as I read his message.

> It's only 5:16

> It takes approximately 36 minutes to get from Woodland Hills to Beverly Hills. Depending on traffic. It could be longer.

> I'm assuming you looked at Google Maps.

> Maybe.

> I'll leave now.

> Yay!

I shake my head, a smile on my lips as I gather everything I need and head to my garage. I put the bottle of wine in the backseat of my white Jaguar XJ and slip into the driver's seat.

When I get to the guard, I tell him my name and the address of Jarrod's parents' house, grateful Jarrod had already called ahead to let him know to expect me.

I pull up to the grand home, parking behind a silver Range Rover. I send Jarrod a text to let him know I'm here, but when I look out my window, I see him hopping off the last step of the porch.

Reaching to the back, I grab the wine and then step outside, letting out a deep exhale.

"The guard told us you were on the way," he says.

"I brought wine," I say, holding up the bottle.

He smiles. "You didn't have to."

"Are your parents cool with me being here?"

"Of course. They're not awful people. I promise."

My body is still tense as I follow him inside. The house opens up to a spiral staircase on the right, the ceilings stretching to the second floor.

We quickly pass a living room on our left, walking down the long hallway, bypassing a formal dining room that has three arched openings to enter through. Straight ahead is the kitchen and that's where he leads me.

A woman with shoulder-length hair stands in front of the sink washing her hands. She's wearing wide leg white slacks and a green blouse, her hair a mix of blonde and white.

When she looks up, her eyes light up and a friendly smile curves her lips. "Hello," she sings, turning off the water and reaching for a towel.

"Hey, Mom," Jarrod says. "This is Devin. This is my mom, Shirley."

I walk forward and extend my hand. "Thanks for having me on such short notice."

She gives me a quick once over as she shakes my hand. "Oh, it's no problem. We'll have plenty of food. Full disclosure, I did not cook any of it."

I laugh and present her with the wine. "I brought this."

"Oh. Thank you," she says, taking the bottle and placing it on the counter. "Jarrod tells me you two went to school together."

"Yes, ma'am. Kie Academy."

She nods. "Well, it's a small world, is it not?"

"I was gonna show Dev the back before dinner," Jarrod says.

"That's fine, dear."

I offer her another smile before I follow Jarrod out of the kitchen. We enter another sitting area that has French doors that lead outside.

"Wow."

"It's pretty nice. Kinda reminds me of Black Diamond," he says, glancing my way.

I take in the pool and hot tub in the middle of the stamped concrete. There's three sets of tables and chairs on one side, taking on the appearance of a small bistro, while on the other side are chaise lounge chairs, outfitted with black and white striped cushions. There's no grass in sight, but there's plenty of huge potted plants perfectly placed, and the entire yard is surrounded by massive palm and pine trees, and lush green shrubbery.

"Yeah," I reply after a pause.

"Come here. Let me show you this part."

He jogs around the pool, moving to the far end just to disappear down some stairs.

"It's a two story yard? What the hell?"

He laughs. "Down here is the lower terrace, and it has a full cabana, so there's a kitchen and bath."

"Wow," I say, spinning around and noticing that to my right is another few steps that lead to a long grassy area that looks like a soccer field. "This is really nice. I'd just live out here."

"My dad practically does."

"Where is he?" I ask, following him under the cover of the kitchen area.

"His office. Gina and her husband are in their room fighting the kids to get dressed."

He turns around, leaning against the grill. "You look really good."

I bite my lip. "You do, too."

I rest against the wall opposite him, leaving five feet between us. We study each other in silence, the tension growing thick.

The urge to touch and kiss him has me forcing my feet to the ground, hoping they seep into the cement to keep me in place. His eyes roam over my face and I know he's thinking the same thing. We want each other too much to be left alone and be expected to behave.

After another long thirty seconds, we both make the same decision at the same time, pushing away from the edges of the room and meeting in the middle.

His arms wrap around my back as my fingers slide

through his hair at the back of his head, our mouths coming together for the first time in six months.

Our tongues twirl around each other, our breathing turning heavy fast as we begin to rub our bodies together, desperate to feel each other in all the ways imaginable.

"I've missed this," he breathes, scratching his beard across my cheek as he kisses my neck.

"That's not a good enough word," I say, bringing his lips back to mine. I suck his tongue into my mouth, drawing a moan from his throat.

"Then tell me what is," he says, his hands disappearing under my shirt.

"My heart aches in your absence. It physically hurts sometimes. I think it only beats in hopes of finding the piece you took from it, longing to be whole again."

"Fuck," he groans, smashing his mouth against mine. "Devin, I—"

"Hey, J?"

His sister's voice has us breaking apart, both of us wiping at our mouths and adjusting our erections.

"Jarrod?"

"Yeah, we're down here," he yells.

"Oh," she says. "I'll wait up here."

I chuckle. "Do I have whisker burn on my face?"

His palm gently rubs over my cheek. "Not too bad"

"I messed up your hair a little," I say, fixing the strands in the back.

"That wasn't enough," he says, coming in close, his thigh brushing against mine.

"Don't start now. Your sister is waiting."

He growls, planting a soft kiss on the corner of my

mouth. "I'm going to take that as an invitation for something later."

Before I can argue, he walks out. "Is dinner ready?"

"Yeah," she replies.

I follow him up the stairs and Gina has amusement twinkling in her eyes. "I'm glad you came," she says when she spots me.

"I'm thankful for the invitation."

Gina walks ahead and Jarrod spins around, walking backward as he whispers, "I'll be really glad if you come."

I shoot him a look but he just laughs. I missed that sound.

Thirty-Six

JARROD

"Dad, this is Devin. Devin, this is my dad, Charles, and my brother-in-law, Matt."

Devin shakes my dad's hand first. "Nice to meet you. Thanks for having me for dinner tonight."

"Of course," my dad says with a smile. "Try as I might, I can't eat all the food," he continues, putting a hand to his slight pot-belly.

Devin chuckles along with him good-naturedly, moving to Matt. "Nice to meet you."

"You too."

"And those little rugrats are the best niece and nephew anyone can ask for," I say, pointing at Connor and CeCe who are scribbling in a Christmas themed coloring book on the floor of the kitchen.

"They're cute," Devin says, offering a smile to Gina and Matt. "How old are they?"

"Four and two," Gina replies.

"All right, everyone, dinner is on the table," my mom says, strolling through the kitchen.

As G and Matt grab the kids, I direct Devin to the dining room. Mom ordered in all the food we'll be eating tonight, but that doesn't make it any less delicious. There's a turkey in the center of the table, already carved, plus honey ham, and several different sides.

They've removed the chairs we won't need, leaving two on each long side and one at each end. The kids will be sitting at a small table next to Gina that Mom set up.

"So, Devin. Tell us a little about you," my mom says.

He shifts nervously in his seat as he scoops mashed potatoes onto his plate. His eyes land on me when he hands me the dish.

"Well, I own and run a production company, and I've done some directing. The acting bug is calling, though, so I guess I don't fall far from my parents' tree."

Mom nods, her eyes finding mine briefly. "Oh, well, that sounds nice."

I told her before he got here not to mention his parents, because it's obvious their relationship is strained and I didn't want him to be uncomfortable.

"What kind of production company?" my dad asks.

"Well, nothing big like Paramount or Warner Bros," Devin says with a nervous chuckle. "Probably a little more niche specific."

He bangs his knee into mine under the table.

"Oh, Mom. Did I tell you I'm going to Dallas in a few days? Maybe I can see Aunt Lana."

"Are you?" she questions. "Will you even have time to visit her? I don't know if she'll go to a game."

Devin's hand touches my thigh, giving me a thankful squeeze.

I reach down and cover his hand with mine before I bring it back up to grab my water.

"I guess we won't be there too long," I say.

"That's too bad. You know, she has a neighbor who's about your age. She's a nice girl. A *normal* girl."

"Mom, the girls I dated were *normal* girls."

"They're in showbiz, honey." She seems to realize what she's said and looks at Devin with wide eyes. "I'm sorry. I didn't mean—"

He holds up his hand with a gracious smile. "It's okay. I understand."

"It's not that I don't like actors, but when it comes to the girls he was *dating*, you could just tell they were a little...I don't know, self-involved."

"Mom."

She holds her hands up in defeat. "Okay."

We get through the rest of dinner without any more talk of Devin's career or my exes, so everything goes smoothly. By eight o'clock we're all in the living room getting ready to watch *Santa Claus is Comin' to Town* because the kids are with us.

"This movie is from nineteen-seventy," I mutter.

"Shush," Mom says. "It's a classic."

"It's fucking scary," I whisper, leaning into Devin as I prop my feet on the table. "Look at the face of Kris Kringle. I'm gonna see that in my nightmares."

Devin laughs, trying to cover it with a cough.

"Jarrod," Mom scolds. "It's for the kids."

"Exactly. Shouldn't they be watching *Frozen* or something less weird and old?"

We're thirty minutes into the movie when Gina comes in from the kitchen to tell the kids the cookies are ready. After they place the cookies and milk for Santa, we all watch a little bit more of the movie before the kids start falling asleep.

Once Gina and Matt take the kids to bed, Dad gets up from the couch and Mom follows.

"Goodnight, kids. Devin it was so nice having you. You're welcome anytime, you hear?"

"Yes, ma'am. Thank you." He stands and shakes their hands again. "Merry Christmas."

"Merry Christmas," they both say before disappearing through the doorway.

"Well, what now?" I ask.

"Tell me about your season. How's it going?"

"You're not watching?" I ask. "Have you learned more than the puck goes into the net?"

Devin laughs. "I learned there's a lot of fighting, and that you get in on it."

"Only sometimes," I say with a crooked smile.

"Players get put in timeout."

I snort. "The penalty box. Yeah."

"Your team seems to be doing pretty good."

"We are." I pause. "Every time I play, I wonder if you're watching."

"I try to catch them all."

I nod. "How's your work been?"

"It's good. I'm actually trying something new." He looks embarrassed when he says it.

"Like what?"

"I got a role in a movie. Not a Hollywood blockbuster or anything, but a decent role in a mid-budget film."

"Really?" I exclaim, turning to face him. "That's amazing."

"I start shooting next month," he says, a smile on his face. "It's a queer film about a guy who's been hiding his sexuality because he lives in a small, Bible Belt town in Mississippi. He falls in love with his married neighbor, who, get this, is the new town pastor."

"Ooh. Scandalous."

He laughs. "I'm excited. It's only forty days or so of filming."

"That's really awesome, Dev. I'm happy for you."

After a few seconds, he says, "I've still filmed videos, you know, for my usual job." My body tenses. "But I want you to know, I've only done solo scenes."

"Why?"

Devin lifts a shoulder. "I was already slowing down and focusing more on the business side, and the company is doing well. Plus with the toys I have selling, and now with hopefully breaking more into serious acting roles, I don't—"

I put my hand on his. "Why?" I ask again.

He sighs. "I can't bring myself to do it. I don't want to go back to feeling nothing when I know what it's like to be fulfilled." Devin takes a breath. "You know my tattoo?" I nod. "You opened that window for me. I finally experienced that serene feeling. I was so happy there with you. I knew..." He swallows, picking at an invisible thread on his pants. "I just knew I needed a change in my life to have a chance at something incredible."

There are a million things I want to say and ask, but right now, I want to give him the peace he's given me.

"I haven't been with anyone else either."

We stare at each other, locked in the moment.

"We still have busy schedules ahead of us," he says, leaning in.

I nod, matching the movement and feeling too embarrassed to say I'm still nervous about what going public would mean.

"I want you, Devin. I don't have the answers you might be looking for past that. All I know is that the longing I feel for you is stronger than anything I've ever felt before. I believe that everything I need and want is encapsulated in you."

Something akin to pain flashes in his eyes. The green orbs, usually so full of light, are sorrowful, but yet, he leans in and kisses me.

Thirty-Seven

DEVIN

The pain of hearing how much he wants me is like a knife to the chest, because I believe him wholeheartedly when he expresses his feelings, and yet, he's not saying he's ready to be with me publicly.

I get it, but it still hurts. If I had known doing porn would keep me from being with the love of my life, then maybe I would've thought twice about it. Yes, it was done in spite, but I'm not ashamed of my work. I do, however, want to be better for him. I want there to be something he can point people to that's not my naked body with someone else. The movie is supposed to be that. And hopefully there will be more movies to come.

I'm sure Jarrod doesn't want to be with a gay porn star, but I'll always be that, even if I quit. I can try to transform into something more, but I don't know if it'll ever be enough.

I want him more than anything, but I don't know if he'll ever have me. Even so, I twist the knife in my chest a little more, breaking off another piece, because I have to be with him one more time, even if it means shattering my own heart.

"Come to my room," he whispers through kisses.

"What about your family?"

"This house is massive. My room is clear on the other side."

I nod and he pulls me from the couch. We try to keep our steps quiet as we rush through the expansive home and find our way to his bedroom.

Once inside, he closes and locks the door, wrapping me in his arms and pulling me into him. Any pretense of acting like we don't want this or overthinking what this means goes out the window. We're behind closed doors, together again in the way we've both wanted for months.

He reaches for the button of my pants just as I grab the hem of his shirt. Once my fly is open, he pulls the shirt over his head, dropping it to the floor. My eyes take in his torso, carved to perfection by what has to be daily workouts. He seems even more muscular than before.

I swallow before removing my own shirt. Jarrod looks at me like I'm a glass of water and he's been in the desert for weeks.

We strip out of our remaining clothes, and before I can think to make a move, Jarrod is dropping to his knees.

"Such an eager boy," I tease, running my hand through his hair.

"You don't know how much I've missed this," he says, his hand taking my cock and stroking with reverence.

"I might have an idea," I breathe.

"I need you in my mouth," he declares quietly, looking up at me with lust in his eyes.

"Take me."

His lips part and then he slides me across his wet tongue, his hand still at my base. Jarrod devours me. Worships even. My stomach quivers with shaky breaths as I watch him lick my entire shaft. He strokes me while sucking and teasing my head, and then he's taking me deep, nearly choking on it.

"Fuck, baby," I groan, tightening my grip in his hair. "You're so good."

He moans, turned on by my praise. Pulling away, he looks up at me. "I want you to fuck my mouth."

"Oh god," I say, pleasure rolling down my spine, giving me chills. "Those words coming from you are gonna be my undoing."

He gives me a quick grin before scooting back against the end of the bed. "Come on."

I don't question what he wants, I only walk over to him and thread my fingers through his dirty blond locks and force his head back. With my shaft in my other hand, I push into his mouth.

"God, you look so good with my dick between your lips."

He blinks, giving me a short nod, murmuring something around my shaft. I thrust my hips, fucking his mouth just like I've fantasized about for months. His fingers squeeze my thighs, but I keep going until he gags.

When I pull away, he brings me closer. "More," he begs. "Keep going."

I do. I hold his head in both hands, burying myself until he chokes again. Saliva coats my shaft and falls to his chest, but he continues to moan and his hand travels to his own erection to get some pleasure.

He looks so desperate and undone.

"My turn," I say, stepping back. "Get on the bed."

Jarrod wipes his mouth as he stands up, getting on the mattress and lying back.

I crawl between his legs and run my palm up his thick cock, the veins protruding and his tip pink and slick with precum.

"My god, your dick is so perfect."

"Please," he begs, gently stroking my hair as my fist moves up and down his length.

"You want my mouth?" I tease, flicking my tongue underneath his head.

"Yes. God," he grunts, thrusting his hips.

"You gotta be patient," I say, placing soft kisses along his shaft.

"It's been six months, Dev. Please."

"I like when you beg."

"Oh my god," he groans, his hips unable to keep from moving.

I barely close my lips around his engorged tip, teasing him with the softest graze of my teeth.

He gasps, sucking in a loud, shuddering breath. "Oh shit. I'm gonna come so fast."

I slide him all the way to the back of my throat before releasing him. "Do you want to come in my mouth?" I do it again, swallowing his length. "Or my ass?"

"Fuck. Stop talking about it." He grips the covers tight in his fist, his eyes squeezed closed.

With a grin, I take him deep again, stroking and sucking in tandem. I reach for his balls with my free hand and massage them, pulling another sinful moan from his throat.

"Yeah," he breathes. "So good. So fucking good." After a

few more minutes, he squeezes my shoulders. "Okay, okay.
I'm getting too close."

I back away with a chuckle. "That's the point."

"Not if I want to come in your ass," he says, begging to
move.

I rest on my knees and watch him get up to walk to his
bag, returning with lube.

My teeth sink into my bottom lip. "How do you
want me?"

"Every way possible."

I drop down on my hands, my ass exposed to him. "Like
this?"

"Holy fuck."

Jarrod rushes over, tossing the lube to the mattress
before getting behind me. His hands squeeze my cheeks,
spreading me open.

"I don't understand how you're this sexy," he says.

Before I can reply, his tongue is dancing over my hole.

"Oh shit," I cry, biting down on my lip to keep myself
quiet.

Jarrod spends the next five minutes eating my ass, his
tongue dipping in and out, his moans and grunts animalistic
as he greedily consumes me.

I end up dropping to my elbows and biting the covers to
keep from making too much noise. My cock drips between
my legs, and now I'm sure I'll be the one to come too fast.

Cool air hits my ass as he pulls away, and then I hear the
lid to the lube popping open. His fingers spread the cold
liquid over my hole before he begins pushing one finger in.

"Jarrod," I breathe.

"Yes, baby?"

My heart nearly explodes. "I want you so much."

There's a pregnant pause. We both know I don't just mean now, physically and sexually. I want him. All of him. All the time.

He doesn't respond with words, choosing to move his body to the side, leaning down to kiss me while his finger moves inside. I lift up to meet his mouth, kissing him passionately while emotion clogs my throat.

Jarrod pulls away after a while, sliding another finger inside. "I love your ass," he says, dipping his fingers in and out. His other hand reaches under and grabs my cock. "I love this, too."

I moan, dropping my head. "Mmm."

"I love the noises you make." He puts a third finger inside me. "I love the way you take me."

"Jarrod," I whimper.

"And I love the way you say my name when you're turned on."

His fingers slip out and the lube is opened up again. After he coats himself, he lines his tip at my entrance and begins to slowly push in.

"Fuck, baby. Oh god, you're so big."

"Mm. And I love the way you compliment me."

One hand goes to my hip, holding me in place while he pushes inside.

"Yes, fill me up," I moan as he pushes past the ring of muscle.

With both hands on my waist, he finishes entering me. I feel a tinge of pain, the slight burn of him opening me up, but I crave more.

"God. I love how tight you are. How your ass grips my cock."

So many uses of the *L* word. It's driving me crazy.

"It's yours," I whisper. "I'm yours."

His movements still, and then his hands run up my back, squeezing my shoulders as he rotates his hips.

"I'm yours too."

I can't deal with this emotion. I can't hear him say he loves anything else about me. My heart can't take any more.

"Fuck me, Jarrod," I say, shoving my ass back. "Hard. Let me feel you for days after you leave me."

"Dev," he says quietly, his hands going back to my waist.

I move, feeling his cock slide out an inch or two before I throw myself back, engulfing his shaft. "Fuck me."

He groans, squeezing my hips, and then he's thrusting. Hard and deep strokes have fireworks exploding behind my eyelids.

"Yes," I cry. "Yes, harder."

Jarrod grips me tight, moving my body more than he's moving his. He slams me onto his cock.

"Fuck," he grunts.

"Yes. Harder. Deeper!" I yell.

"I don't want to hurt you."

You already are.

"I want you to," I say instead.

I can't tell him the truth. I can't say I'd prefer temporary physical pain over the agony of his absence. Because for as long as I'm not with him, the ache in my heart will never go away.

"Dev."

"Jarrod, please." My voice cracks.

He thrusts, giving me what I want. What I asked for. He buries himself to the hilt, pulling out just to slam into me again.

We grunt and moan, curse and whimper. Our bodies collide in the way I wish our hearts would.

"I'm about to come," he says through a shaky breath. "Oh god, Dev."

I can only offer up moans in response as he pummels into me, ripping me apart in more ways than one.

His cock twitches, his release pouring inside me as his grip tightens on my body. He fights to keep his noises down, leaning over my back and crying into my spine.

After a few seconds, he carefully pulls out, and I wince in the process. Turning to my back, I watch him as he grabs his erection and positions himself to slide into me again.

He teases my hole with his tip, his eyes full of wonder as his lips part.

"Watching my cum drip out of you is the hottest fucking thing," he says, using his head to push it back in.

"Fuck," I groan, feeling him slide all the way inside.

I take my cock in my hand and stroke, knowing it's not gonna take long to reach release. Jarrod thrusts in and out, his muscles rippling with every movement. Being able to see him will make it easier to come. I get to witness the euphoria on his handsome face and watch his powerful body move.

Our eyes connect and my heart clenches.

Have you ever looked into the face of the person that means more to you than anyone ever has knowing they'll never be yours? It's excruciating.

"Come for me, baby," he says quietly.

I close my eyes and give my cock a few more strokes before I shatter.

"Jarrod," I cry, my eyes flickering open briefly to witness the look on his face.

"Oh yeah," he moans. "Oh god, I love it. I love watching you come. I love..." Multi-colored eyes find mine. "Everything. I love everything."

My body jerks as I finish coming, tears burning the backs of my eyes when I close them.

Thirty-Eight

JARROD

By the time we're cleaned up and dressed again, it's almost eleven. I want him to stay here until twelve, so I can at least spend a minute of his birthday with him, but he seems anxious to go.

"Are you okay?" I ask as he slides his phone into his pocket.

"Yeah," he replies, giving me a passing glance.

"Dev," I say, stepping in front of him and forcing him to look at me. "I—"

"Please don't," he says. "Whatever it is, please don't say it."

"I want to explain myself."

"How can you? Or why?" he questions. "I already know, Jarrod. It's why I didn't want this to happen. I didn't want to see you. I didn't want to be with you."

I flinch. "What?"

He sighs. "You're not ready for me."

"I am!" I say, immediately realizing I'm not sure if that's

an honest answer. "I...I like you, Devin. A lot. A sickening amount, probably. My thoughts are filled with you. You're in my dreams, my fantasies, and..."

"Am I in your future?" he questions, staring me straight in the eye. "Because that's really all that matters. You can fantasize about me all you want, but—"

"Don't say it like that." I grab his hands. "I didn't mean for it to sound so cheap. You're everything."

"Why is everything not enough then?"

I shake my head and look away. He pulls his hands from my grip.

"I don't know. I'm scared. I still don't really understand, and—"

"Like I said, you're not ready for me."

"Look, I know I'm the asshole in this situation!" I shout. "It's my fault. I'm keeping this from being what we want. I hate myself for it. I hate seeing the hurt in your eyes, Dev. It fucking kills me, but god, I want you. I want you so bad, but—"

"But you can't be with a porn star, right? You can't lower yourself to the seedy, disgusting level at which I operate. You're the golden hockey boy that everyone worships and being with me would taint your aura."

I jolt back, my brows furrowing. "No! What the fuck? I've never thought that, Dev. Ever! Don't put me on a pedestal. I don't think I'm better than you and I've never once looked down on you or what you do. It's me!" I say, slamming my hand on my chest. "*I'm* not good enough for you."

His brows dip, his lips downturning. "What are you talking about?"

I run a hand through my hair. "I don't know anything,

Dev. I'm clueless and I feel so out of my depth. I can't even admit I like guys, because I don't. I only like you. You're the only one. What does that mean for me and my sexuality? I've been with women my whole life until you. In the last six months I've not looked at another man the way I look at you. I haven't looked at *anyone* the way I look at you.

"I don't know what to tell people. I don't know how to answer the questions I'll get. And yes, I'm selfishly thinking about myself and my teammates. I don't want what's already a promising season to be overshadowed by me if I decide to say I'm in...I'm with a man. I'm terrified of what that'll mean for my career, and I know that's selfish. That's why I'm aware I'm the bad guy here. You don't deserve what I'm putting you through, but I can't cut you off. I can't do it, Dev. If there's ever an opportunity for us to see each other, I'm going to take it. It has to be you that stays strong, because it won't be me. I'm weak when it comes to you."

Tears sting my eyes, so I turn around and give him my back, unable to meet his gaze anymore.

I hate being aware that I'm the problem and knowing what the solution is but unable to bring myself to pull the trigger. It tears me up, leaving my insides a shredded mess.

Devin's arms wrap around me from behind, his cheek pressed against my shoulder blade. I reach up and touch his hand and a tear falls down my cheek.

"I'm sorry," I whisper.

"It's okay."

A sob breaks free, and I spin around and clutch him to me. Because it's not okay. It's far from it, and yet he's still trying to give me peace.

My tears fall steadily as I bury my face in his neck,

holding him tight. When I hear him sniffle, my heart shatters, because I've only ever wanted him to be happy. It's what gave me joy back on the island. His happiness brought me mine, and now I'm the cause of our heartache.

I pull away, holding him by the arms, looking into his watery eyes.

He reaches up and wipes tears from my cheeks with his thumb. "I should go."

"I didn't intend for this night to end this way," I say.

"I know."

"I guess I shouldn't have pressed you to come. You probably knew this is how it would go."

He wipes another tear from my other cheek, pressing a quick kiss to my lips. "I'm weak, too." Stepping back, he takes a breath. "Jarrod, I want you. I want to be with you more than I want anything else. I understand that it may come off that I'm being selfish in thinking we should be able to be together. I get that I've had many more years of being out and being comfortable with myself. My job isn't like yours. I know you exist in a different environment. I don't want you to do anything that makes you uncomfortable, but, god, I'm constantly uncomfortable."

My brows furrow. "How so?"

"By not being with you the way I want. By not being able to talk to you or call you. Every day that we're apart my heart feels like it doesn't know how to beat. I tell myself to move on and find someone else, but the thought of actually doing it makes me sick. I can't imagine being with anyone else anymore. It's like I'm just going to be alone and unhappy forever. Waiting. And I don't deserve that. You don't deserve it either.

"You have the right to happiness just like everyone else. Your teammates get to date and marry whoever they want. They've never had to run that by anyone else, I'm sure. They get drunk and get into car accidents. They get into fights at bars. They cause a lot of negative press, don't think I don't know. And you're worried what being with someone you care about will do. You have to be concerned that something that's supposed to be positive and good will hurt your team. Isn't it bullshit?

"All I'm saying is I know you're concerned about the consequences or hardships in the aftermath of saying you're with a guy. I know it's a big deal. I'm just worried you're not considering the consequences that we'll endure—that we *are* enduring. And until you're ready, there can never be anything more."

I absorb his words, each one hitting me like an arrow, sending pricks of pain throughout my body. As much as it hurts, I know he's right, and there's nothing else I can say. As the saying goes, *actions speak louder than words.*

I bring my shirt up to wipe my face, sniffing. "Let me walk you out."

Our journey to the front door feels like it lasts a lifetime, the silence and pain between us weighing us down. Somehow, though, when we're outside, it feels like it went by too fast.

"I brought you something," Devin says. "But now I'm not so sure I should give them to you."

"I want it. Whatever it is."

He reaches into his backseat and gives me two wrapped boxes. With a small grin, he says, "Don't open them in front of your parents."

"I got you something, too."

"My gifts aren't sentimental," he says. "So, I hope yours isn't either."

I walk to my car and open the door, finding the gift bag I brought from my place.

"It's probably something you'll never use," I say, handing it over.

He takes the bag and holds it, looking at me. "I'll open it tomorrow."

"Me too," I say, holding up his boxes.

Devin opens the door and puts one foot inside before turning to face me. "Bye, Jarrod."

"Bye, Dev."

February 14th

"**A**nd that's a wrap," the director says.

Everyone around claps and cheers, excited to have finished filming such an emotional and touching movie.

It's been forty-five days since we started, and during that time we've split filming between the towns of Canton and Bay St. Louis, Mississippi.

"I'm glad we filmed this now instead of the middle of summer, aren't you?" Elias asks, a smile on his lips.

"Yes," I reply. "I don't know how we'd have gotten through those scenes in that church considering it doesn't have air conditioning."

Elias nudges me with his elbow. "We'd have just been a little more sweaty than we already were."

I smile, looking away.

He's an attractive man and openly gay himself. Playing

my love interest, we spent plenty of time together, and he's not only good looking, but really nice as well. He's been in a few other movies, and while mostly independent films, he's on his way to an Oscar. I know it. His acting is outstanding.

"When are you flying back home?" he asks.

"Tomorrow. You?"

"Day after tomorrow. You gonna come celebrate with us tonight?"

When he asks, Elena, the woman who played his wife in the movie, comes and wraps her arm around his waist.

"I'm not sure," I reply.

"Come on," Elena says. "We should all celebrate. This is a big fucking deal!"

My eyes move to Elias and he's watching me with a hopeful expression. "Okay," I say.

"Yay!" they reply in unison.

"In the meantime, I'm gonna go shower and nap," I say with a chuckle.

When I get to my Airbnb, I strip off my clothes and jump under the warm spray of the shower. My first non-pornographic movie is done and I can't stop smiling. Whether it makes a hundred dollars or a million, I'm beyond grateful for the opportunity. I'm hoping this is a stepping-stone that'll lead me to other projects, all of which I want to get on my own without mention of my parents or use of their connections.

When I get out of the shower, I flop onto my bed and turn on the TV before responding to my messages.

It doesn't take long for me to fall asleep, and when I wake up to my phone's alarm at seven-thirty, I promptly turn it off and roll over. The voice from the TV gets my attention, and I realize Jarrod's playing. I reach for the remote and turn up the volume, propping myself up on the pillows to watch.

They're only ten minutes into the second period, but already up 2-0.

My phone buzzes next to me with a text from Elias.

Hey. We're meeting at Louie's at 8:30. Do you want to ride with me?

Okay, that works. See you soon.

I spend the next twenty minutes in bed, riveted as the Predators tie the game with only five minutes left in the third period.

I start getting dressed through commercials, popping back in front of the TV as soon as it's back on. Who knew I'd be into hockey...or any sport for that matter.

Even though I've not spoken to Jarrod since Christmas, if the game is on and I'm free, I always make sure to watch. I guess I like torturing myself.

The commentators voice rises as I'm going through my closet.

"And Bivens is behind the net, trying to get to the—Oh! And he's hit by Schanter. Headgear is off and he is down. Here we go."

I pivot around, the cheers and yells from the audience are loud and my eyes scan the screen. The cameras are trained on a group of players from both teams. Everyone is fighting.

"Where's Jarrod? Where's Jarrod?" I mutter to myself.

The camera pans over and Jarrod is down on his stomach. My heart sinks.

A replay comes on, and I watch as an opposing player

flies toward Jarrod, both of them behind the net. He hit him helmet to helmet as he skated by. Jarrod's headgear flies off and the other guy's momentum has him pushing Jarrod against the boards. His entire body is lifted up off the ice and thrown into the plexiglass.

My hand goes to my mouth as the cameras go back to the live feed, showing the refs trying to break everyone up. The commentator's keep talking and then there's a quick flash of Jarrod moving as someone leans over him.

"We'll be right back after this commercial break."

"No!" I yell at the TV.

How do I make sure he's okay?

I sit on the edge of the bed, my legs bouncing as I wait for the game to come back on. After what feels like hours, but is probably only a couple minutes, it's back.

"Bivens has been escorted to the locker room where he will be evaluated. In the meantime, we have Johansson stepping in."

I stop paying attention after that. He's being evaluated. That's good, right? They don't elaborate on how serious the injury was, and I don't know if he's being evaluated on site or if he was taken to a hospital.

I quickly reach for my phone and send him a message. I don't expect him to answer any time soon, but I have to let him know I'm thinking about him and hope he can respond at some point.

Elias texts me again and I know without a doubt I won't be able to hang out tonight. There's no way I'll be able to stop thinking and worrying about Jarrod. I send a reply and tell him I've had a family emergency and will be flying out soon. Then I get on my laptop and book a flight.

Forty

JARROD

"You should put that phone down," Doctor Phillips says.

"I will."

"You need to limit TV, phone use, video games, and physical activity. Take this time to rest and relax."

"That's easy for you to say, Doc. My team has to play without me. How can I relax when I'm worrying how they're gonna do?"

"You're not the only goaltender, Bivens. Johansson is perfectly capable. If you don't obey my instructions you won't play as soon as you'd like, so take it easy, okay?"

I groan and put my phone down. "Fine."

"I'll check in with you later. I'll see myself out."

As soon as the door closes, I pick up my phone to see if Devin replied.

I read his initial text late last night, but as I was trying to respond, my phone was snatched from my hand by the doctor. I didn't get to reply until we were already back in California the next day, and he hasn't said anything since.

Maybe he's happy to hear that I'm alive and well and will leave it at that. I mean, I'm mostly well. A minor concussion and some soreness aren't going to kill me.

But now it's been several hours since I sent that text off and he still hasn't responded, and *that* might kill me.

I stare down at our text thread.

> Jarrod. Oh my god, I was just watching the game. I know you can't respond right away, but please let me know you're okay as soon as you can.

> Hey. I'm okay. Just minor injuries. I'm pretty tough, but thanks for worrying about me.

I guess my response didn't invite much conversation. He had a request and I fulfilled it, but I feel like he'd have more to say.

My head throbs a little, so I get up to go to the kitchen for some medicine and then place a DoorDash order, because I definitely don't feel like cooking.

When my phone vibrates, I expect it's just a message from the app telling me my order's been picked up, so when I see Devin's name, I let out a small gasp.

> Thank goodness. I was so worried. Also, sorry for the late reply. My phone died. What's your address?

> Why? You sending me a get well soon package?

> Exactly. Don't worry, I won't release it to the puckies.

I bust out laughing at his message, making my head hurt even more. I sit on the couch and reply back.

> Do you mean puck bunnies?

> I guess?

> Okay. Yes, please don't release it to them. It's 20609 Oaks View Way. San José, CA 95120

> Thanks.

The next time my phone buzzes, I snatch it up, hoping he's continuing to text me, but it's just the DoorDash app letting me know my driver is approaching.

I know I shouldn't get used to texting Devin. We've done good this whole time, only speaking when the universe puts us in the same spot. But just having this quick exchange has brought me joy. I'm not worried or stressed about the games I'm gonna miss or about my own health. I just want to talk to him. He makes me feel better.

My phone rings.

"Hello?"

"Mr. Bivens. You have a visitor," the gate guard says.

"Oh, yeah. Let 'em in, Marshall. Thank you."

Five minutes later, the doorbell rings and I cringe. I should've told them to knock instead. I pull open the door, ready to grab my food and take it to my bed but end up gawking at the person on my porch.

"Devin."

"Surprise," he says with a small smile. "I'm here to personally deliver your get well soon package. Which is honestly just me."

I arch a brow. "Am I living out my porn fantasy?"

I immediately regret the words when they leave my mouth, but to my relief, Devin laughs. "In your fantasy, do you have a concussion that requires no physical activity?"

"Definitely not." I stand back, my smile growing. "Come in. What the hell are you doing here?"

"I'm here to see you, of course."

My phone rings again. "Sorry. One sec. Hello?"

"Mr. Bivens. You have another visitor."

"Oh. Yeah. Send him through. Thanks."

I end the call and close the door. "I thought you were my food. It's coming now, but I ordered a lot, so we can share if you're hungry."

He stands there awkwardly for a second before he moves forward and envelopes me in a hug. His deep inhale is audible as he holds me, and I breathe in the scent of his shampoo, feeling instantly relaxed.

"I was so worried, Jarrod," he says. "I saw it happen. Then again in slow motion. I can still see you lying there on the ice." His voice shakes. "It killed me. I hated not knowing what to do or who to call. I wanted to be there." He pulls away and steps back. "I booked a flight home immediately, then jumped in my car and drove up here. I figured you'd come back home and knew I needed to be on my way."

I take his hands in mine. "I'm fine. I'm okay."

He looks frightened, like he's reliving the moment. He shakes his head. "I hope the guy that hit you got in a lot of trouble."

My lips quirk. "You said you flew home. Where were you?"

"Mississippi."

"What the hell were you doing in Mississippi?" I ask, walking over to the couch.

He sits on the loveseat to my right. "I was filming that movie I told you about."

My eyes bulge. "Oh my god. That's incredible. Congratulations!"

"Thank you," he says with a boyish smile.

"You left there to come to me? Do you need to go back?"

He shakes his head. "It had just wrapped. We were just planning on going to celebrate."

"You're missing celebrating your first movie?"

"Well, my first movie of this kind," he jokes.

"Dev."

"It's fine!" he says. "Honestly. I would rather be here. I wasn't going to be able to have fun after I watched you get hurt like that anyway. I had to make sure you were okay."

I tilt my head. "Why are you so good to me?"

He chews on his lower lip, watching me. "You know why."

My heart hammers in my chest and my pulse pounds in my head with each beat. I feel a little dizzy, and when I get up to move to the loveseat with him, I sway slightly.

"Hey," he says, getting up to guide me to the cushion. "Take it slow."

"I'm fine."

"You have a concussion."

"Just a mild one."

"Yeah, just a mild brain injury," he deadpans.

The bell rings, the loud sound echoing through the house for way too long.

"Fuck," I say, rubbing my head.

"I'll get it." Devin stands and walks to the door, grabbing the food. "Do you want to eat now?"

I shake my head slightly. "I'm feeling really tired now. But I don't want you to go, and I don't want to sleep, because you're here."

Dev puts the food on a table near the door and walks over to me. "I'm not going anywhere. Go to sleep and I'll be here when you wake up."

"Yeah?" I muse, looking up at him.

He smiles and reaches for my hand. "Yeah. Let's go to your room."

I let him pull me up, my lips curving into a grin. "Ooh."

Devin shoots me a serious look. "Don't."

I chuckle. "What?"

"We're just going to take a nap."

"Fine," I say, making my way to the stairs. "I'll let you be the big spoon this time, since I'm injured and all."

Devin laughs, staying behind me as we walk up the steps like he's waiting to catch me if I fall.

Since I'm basically in pajamas already—lounge pants and a T-shirt, I just yank back the duvet and climb in. Devin removes his shoes and crawls in next to me wearing a pair of jeans and a plain tee.

I want to tell him he can get more comfortable, but I figure it's best not to push it.

"You want the TV on?"

He shakes his head. "I'm good."

I turn to my side, facing him as he lays on his back. I take in his long dark lashes, flawless skin, and notice the hair filling out his mustache and beard. His full, pink lips draw my attention the most, and then he angles his head and his ocean eyes pierce through me.

"I thought you were going to sleep."

"I've missed your face."

His pouty lips form a smirk. "Get some rest."

"Your eyes remind me of the water at Black Diamond."

"Turn around," he directs. After a brief hesitation I turn the other way and feel his arm wrap around my waist. "Go to sleep."

"Yes, sir."

I bring my arm up and clutch his fingers, and then I close my eyes and fall asleep.

Forty-One

DEVIN

Thirty minutes after he falls asleep, I slip my hand from his grip and quietly leave the bedroom. I didn't anticipate falling quickly into sleeping in the same bed with him, but I should know by now that when it comes to Jarrod Bivens, nothing happens according to plan.

I never imagined I'd ever see him again, and then we're at the same resort together. I didn't think for a second that anything would happen between us, and then we're kissing. I didn't plan on falling so hard so fast for him, and yet, here we are. I *did* plan on making a clean break. Never speaking to him again. I believed it to be the best idea. We aren't, nor have we ever really been together. It's not in his cards. I should move on, but I can't seem to let him go.

I go back to the living room and grab the food that was delivered and take it to the kitchen. The open floor plan of this house, paired with the floor to ceiling windows, makes it seem even larger than it already is. Driving up, I knew I was in for something spectacular.

His house is high up, tucked into a private area, and from every window there's a view of Silicon Valley.

After putting the food in the fridge, I notice that he has plenty of groceries, so I start pulling things out so I can make something healthy.

Half an hour later, I have cobb salad and turkey clubs prepped and ready for when he's up. I'm checking my messages when I hear his voice.

"Devin? Dev?"

I quickly rush out of the kitchen and toward the stairs. "You okay?"

When I see him, his shoulders drop. "I thought you left."

"I told you I'd be here."

"Yeah, but—" He shakes his head. "Never mind. Whatcha been up to?" He descends the stairs with his hand on the bannister.

"Making myself at home. Hope you don't mind."

"Of course not."

"I wanted to put your food away but saw you actually had a lot of healthier options here, so I put something together."

He has a look of surprise on his face. "You made food for me?"

"And me too. Not completely selfless."

"Yeah, but...you made food for me."

I grin. "It's not a big deal. Let's go eat."

In the kitchen I pull the salad—and the ingredients for the sandwiches which I already laid out on a plate—from the fridge. Jarrod quickly gets the bread and a toaster, and together, we construct our sandwiches and scoop salad into a bowl.

He has stools on the other side of the breakfast bar, so that's where we sit.

"Thanks for cooking."

"It's hardly cooking," I tell him. "But you're welcome."

We eat in relative silence for a while, our knees bumping into each other on occasion. Halfway in, he gets up and walks to the fridge, returning with two Gatorades.

Once we're both done, I take our dishes to the sink.

"I can do that," he offers.

"You have a brain injury. Let me do it."

He snorts before going quiet. My eyes flicker up from the water to peek at him, but he's just staring at the countertop. I wonder if zoning out is a concussion thing.

"I can't believe you're here," he says. "Especially after... you know."

I don't know how to respond to that. I don't necessarily want to bring up our last time together. It was rife with emotions, anger, and frustration spewing from a broken heart.

"Jarrod," I say, placing the last plate on the counter before shutting off the water. "It shouldn't be a surprise that I'm here."

He rests his chin in his palm, finally making eye contact with me. "I don't understand what we're doing."

With a sigh, I dry my hands on a nearby towel and lean against the counter, keeping my position in front of him. I don't want to have this conversation. This, for me, is the part that's so frustrating, because he knows. If it were only up to me, we'd be together. I'd do everything in my power to be with him anytime I could. I want nothing more than to have him be mine, but he's too afraid. He's not thinking about me, or even himself, at least not when it comes to our happiness. He's career-minded, and he's got his teammates to worry about, and while that's admirable, at some point, you have to live for yourself.

I finally say what I've been holding in. "What's the scariest part of this for you?"

"What do you mean?" he asks, sitting up straight.

"Me and you. What are you afraid of?"

"Nothing scares me about us. When we're together, I'm at my happiest. I love everything about our connection and relationship. We're friends and it feels so good to have that foundation underneath everything else. I'm not scared of us."

"If we went out right now and someone took a picture of us together, what's the first thought that would come to your head?"

He shifts. "I guess what people would assume."

"That we're together?"

His hand comes up to rub at the hair on his jaw. "It would be rumor mill stuff. I'd get asked a ton of questions."

"Are you afraid of questions about my job? Because tons of athletes have dated porn stars before. You wouldn't be the first to do it."

He runs a hand through his hair. "I know, and I don't care about your job, but..."

"But I'm a guy. It's fine if athletes are with female porn stars, but not male ones."

"It's not about your job at all," he says on a sigh. "Which might be weird. Maybe I should care more about that, but I'm not going to be the one to tell you to quit something that's made you happy or that's made you money. I'm not telling you what to do when it comes to your career, which is why I don't want you telling me how to handle mine."

I recoil. "I'm not. Not once have I said anything about your career."

He exhales, rubbing his head. "It feels like you want me to just come out and damn the consequences."

Hurt spreads through my body, the pain appearing on my face as I look at him. "That's not what I want. I understand the fear, but I'm afraid, too. I'm afraid of losing you. To time. To distance."

He's quiet for a few minutes, his gaze moving between me and the wall to my right. I watch his eyes bounce around as the thoughts in his head do the same. I never wanted to pressure him to come out. I still don't want to do that. It's unfortunate that the thing I want the most contradicts that. I want him and everything that comes with a healthy relationship, and yet I don't want him to be forced into it. It has to come naturally, but it's really destroying me in the process.

Like with my job, I feel as though I'm ripping myself apart to make other people happy, but with Jarrod I'll endure it, because unlike people I work with, I love him. And I'd rather feel pain than inflict it on him.

I love him.

It's like a lightbulb flicking on. I guess I've known for a while. I've felt it in our times together, but especially in his absences. But right now, the light is blinding me, forcing me to see what maybe I should've seen earlier.

Love isn't always perfect. It's not easy to find or easy to hold onto, but I found it with him, and if being in a secret relationship for a while is what I have to do to hold onto it, maybe I should give it a try. At least then we'll have a little more than we do now.

"Maybe we can give it a go," I say. "In secret."

"What?" he asks, face bewildered.

"I wanted to cut things off with you, because I hoped it would make it easier. And yet, we keep finding ourselves together. I'm always thinking about you and missing you, and doing it this way hasn't made it easier. Maybe we can find more time. Talk on the phone more. At least we'll be a little happier."

He stands up. "Are you serious?"

I nod. "Yeah."

"What about everything you—"

I cut him off. "Never mind that. I've been waiting for you to be ready, but I had years to come to terms with who I am, and it's been eight months for you. You're right. I wasn't concerned enough about what you're dealing with."

What I don't say is that I wanted to stay away from him to keep from falling in love, but it's already happened. I'm in it and there's no getting out.

"No, but you're right, too. I wasn't thinking about what you were going through. I knew I was punishing myself, but I never thought about how far that punishment extended. You deserve more, Devin. I can admit that. You should be with someone who can—"

I hold up a hand, stopping him again as I round the bar. "I should be with you. We should at least try it this way. My way wasn't working out anyway. The world keeps throwing us together. Maybe we should listen."

He steps closer to me. "We have a lot to discuss, but there's something that takes priority. I can't take it anymore."

"What?" I ask.

"Can I please kiss you now?"

My lips twist to the side. "I thought it was going to be something serious."

"This is very serious," he states, grabbing my wrists and tugging me closer.

"Then, ye—"

He doesn't let me finish before his mouth is on mine.

Forty-Two

JARROD

"**F**uck. Your mouth," I breathe, pulling away from his lips just to utter those words.

"Not yet, concussion boy."

I groan and pull him closer, my hands on his neck and the back of his head as my tongue explores his mouth like it's the first time it's been there.

"You're staying the night."

"I can," he says into my neck as I kiss along his jaw.

"It wasn't a question."

"Oh."

"And you'll be in my bed."

"I'm assuming this is also not a question."

"Definitely not." I pull away, taking his hand. "Let's go."

"You just woke up an hour ago."

"It's not like I was asleep long. Plus, it's like eight-thirty. It could be bedtime."

"I am pretty tired. I haven't had much sleep since leaving

Mississippi. I landed at LAX at five in the morning and went home to shower, pack a bag, and sleep for a few hours before I started my drive."

"You're insane," I say with a chuckle, taking him to my room. "But I'm grateful for your insanity."

Once we're inside, I start tugging on the button of his pants.

He smacks my hand. "What're you doing?"

My lips draw up on the right side. "What? You can't sleep in jeans."

"Mmhmm," he murmurs, finishing the job. "Remember there will be no physical activity."

"It's been almost forty-eight hours," I argue.

"So? I'm not gonna be the reason you make yourself worse."

I remove my shirt and watch him do a double take, his tongue swiping at his bottom lip.

"Fine. We'll just spoon."

I remove my pants and take the discarded clothes to the hamper in my bathroom, taking a minute to pee and brush my teeth. When I return, Devin's pulling the covers down, wearing only a pair of boxer briefs.

The groan that leaves my throat catches his attention. Our eyes roam each other's bodies as I make my way to the other side of the bed.

"Can I use your bathroom?"

I nod. "Help yourself."

When he gets back, I'm propped up, one arm behind my head as I watch him approach. His body is fucking perfect, begging me to touch and kiss every inch.

"Just spooning," he says, reading my mind.

"Of course," I say with a smile, sliding under the covers.

Devin gets in and gives me his back. I scoot closer and wrap an arm around his waist. Using my nose, I nuzzle the back of his neck before kissing him behind his ear.

"Jarrod," he warns.

"We're spooning," I reply with a smile. "But you know what they say," I whisper against his neck. "Spooning always leads to forking."

He barks out a laugh. "I hate you."

"No you don't."

Devin wiggles his ass into my crotch. "Shush."

"Don't do that," I say in a low throaty voice.

"Or what? It's already been done."

I thrust forward. "Or you're going to start feeling a lot more."

"Maybe we should put a pillow between us."

"Maybe you should get on top of me."

"You're not supposed to partake in vigorous activities."

I laugh. "Did you memorize that from a Web MD article?"

"Maybe, but it's true."

"If you're on top of me, you'll be doing most of the vigorous work."

He spins around and faces me, our legs intertwining. "Why can't you be good?"

I kiss his lips. "What fun is that?"

"No sex," he says again, his hand skating down my side.

"Okay."

"In any form," he continues, hand dancing along the waistband of my boxers.

"Mmhmm," I say, closing my eyes

"Be good for me tonight," he whispers, his lips touching mine. "And I'll be very good to you tomorrow."

His palm glides over my erection through the material of my boxers, and I suck in a breath.

"Devin."

"Yes?" he muses, his hand traveling up my side again.

"I want you so bad."

"I know, baby," he says softly, his fingers dancing up my spine. "I want you, too."

I thrust into him, making him feel what he's doing to me.

"It's been too long. I've only had your Christmas presents."

He pulls away, and when I open my eyes, I find him staring at me with amusement glittering in his sea green gaze.

"What?" I question.

"You've used my Christmas presents?" He can't keep the smile from his lips.

I roll my eyes. "Were they for decorative use only?"

He props himself up onto his elbow, seemingly wide awake now. "Both?"

My cheeks heat up. "This feels weird suddenly."

"Well, I gave them to you for a reason. Let me guess. You used the mouth first?"

"Obviously. But I was thinking, what if you did one of your ass? Is that in the cards? I'd like one of those, too. You know, for the road."

He laughs. "Have you taken them with you when you travel?"

"Of course!"

"And what about the dildo?" he questions, his fingers

brushing through my happy trail. "What did you do with that?"

Heat floods my body and I look up at the ceiling. "Nothing...at first."

Devin gets excited, his leg wrapping around mine. "Go on."

I groan, turning to my back as I cover my face. "It's gonna sound weird."

He removes my hand from my face, getting up to look into my eyes. "I guarantee nothing you say is going to sound weird to me. I want to know what you did with a replica of my dick. Not because I want to laugh at you, but because it'll turn me on."

"Straddle me first," I say, reaching for his hip.

"We're still not having sex."

"Okay. Lay on me, though."

He listens, moving his body on top of mine before lying down and nuzzling my neck. "Tell me."

"I just wanted to look at it first," I begin. "Touch it."

"Mmhmm."

"I'd stroke it and close my eyes, remembering the nights we had."

"They were good nights," he says quietly.

"Very good," I say, rubbing his back.

"Did you suck it?" he asks, his voice breathy as his hips move slightly.

"Mm," I moan, closing my eyes. "Yes."

He releases a shaky breath, his body unable to remain still. "I'd suck on it while jacking off, wishing you were actually with me to fuck my mouth."

"Jesus, Jarrod," he breathes, his body writhing.

"You wanna hear more?"

"Yes," he begs.

I grab his hips and grind him against my erection. "I'd position the masturbator on the bed and thrust into it, wishing I could hear the sinful sounds you make when you suck me."

"Mmm."

"And I..." I take a second to swallow, grateful that he's not hovering over me right now. Not sure I could say this while looking into his eyes. "And I've tried...using it."

His body goes stiff for a second before he begins placing kisses along my neck. "Yeah?"

"It took a few tries to get comfortable with even just a few inches."

I cringe, feeling my body burn from the inside. I'm sure I sound ridiculous.

"It's best to take it slow," he says, not making me feel awkward, just rolling with it. "Smaller, maybe."

"Yeah, I've since bought some beginner things. I just wanted to try it out, you know?"

I feel him nod. "Of course."

"I wanted to ask..." I trail off, suddenly unsure if I should.

"Go ahead."

"Do you strictly bottom?"

"Not strictly, no."

"Do you have a preference?"

He sits up then, looking down at me as he rocks over my erection. "With you, I'd love everything. If you want me inside of you, you better believe I'm going to make it the best experience for you and love every second. If you want to be inside me, I'm going to love feeling you fill me up." He slides over my cock again. "My preference is you."

Forty-Three

DEVIN

"Interesting," he says, running his hands up my sides, "You're my preference, too."

"Good," I reply with a smile.

"Now, I have a question."

"Okay."

"Did you use my gift?"

"I don't know about *use*," I say with a grin. "I tried it on. It's massive."

He groans. "I'd love to see it on you."

"I have it."

"With you? Now?"

"It's pretty valuable, right? An authentic NHL jersey from the fourth hottest hockey player?"

He digs his fingers into my waist, making me squirm, laughter pouring out of my throat.

Jarrod chuckles, pulling me back down. "It is authentic. Worn in games. I didn't want to just give you one you could buy at a mall."

"I imagine it's quite the gesture for hockey players to give up their jerseys."

"I've never allowed anyone else to wear one of my jerseys, but just imagining you in it makes my cock hard."

"Mm," I groan, rubbing my ass over his cock. "I feel it."

"You better stop teasing me or you're gonna feel a lot more very soon."

I stifle a yawn. "I'm sorry. I'm teasing myself, too."

"Let's go to sleep," he says, rolling over, bringing us to our sides. "The faster we do, the quicker morning comes, and then we both get to come."

I laugh. "Okay. Goodnight, Jarrod."

"Goodnight, Devin."

He kisses my forehead, and I mewl like a kitten, a smile on my lips as I drift off to sleep.

I WAKE to Jarrod placing kisses along my torso, his large body hidden under the covers.

I moan, stretching my legs.

His head pops free when he pulls the covers back. "Oh. Did I wake you?"

"Am I supposed to pretend to be asleep? You into somnophilia?"

"Not sure I know what that is."

I chuckle and push his head back down. "Okay, then continue."

He gives me a crooked grin before pulling the duvet back

over his head. His fingers slide into my boxer briefs, tugging them down.

"Good morning," he says when my cock slaps against my stomach. "I missed you."

"Please stop talking to my dick," I say with a laugh.

Jarrod shuts me up when his tongue licks up the shaft before his lips close around the head. He takes it in one hand.

"Is this better?" he asks, stroking me.

"Y-yes," I say shakily. "Keep going."

"Fuck," he curses, his hand moving up and down my shaft while his tongue dances around my tip. "I love the dildo, but there's nothing like the real thing."

"Suck me," I beg. "Please. I want to be in your mouth."

He groans, throwing the covers off him completely, his eyes meeting mine. "Say it again."

My pulse spikes as I stare into his eyes. "Please, Jarrod. I want to be in your mouth. Suck me. Please."

Jarrod slowly takes me between his lips, his eyes never leaving mine. I try to keep eye contact because he looks so fucking sexy down there, telling me what to say, but my eyes close on their own volition as the pleasure hits.

He slurps and sucks, taking me deep as his free hand fondles my balls, massaging them in the way I like.

"Baby," I moan, running my fingers through his hair. "You're so good."

After a couple more minutes of driving me crazy with his mouth, he eases away and plants kisses lower and lower until his tongue slides over my hole.

"Oh fuck," I cry.

"I can't wait to be back in here," he says huskily before continuing to tongue me down.

"Oh god," I whimper, my body Jell-O in his hands. "I want you so bad."

He drops me back to the bed and crawls over my body. I realize then that he's completely naked, his dripping tip grazing over my stomach.

"How bad?" he questions, his mouth kissing me from the corner of my lips to my earlobe. "Tell me how bad you want me."

"Desperately," I say, my legs wrapping around him. "More than anything, because you're everything I need."

He looks at me, something in his eyes I can't quite decipher. His mouth descends and lands on my lips in a soft yet passionate kiss.

"Let me worship you now," I say when he pulls away.

His lips quirk before he lies down on his back, his muscular body spread out for me to devour. I get up and straddle him, taking my time kissing his neck, throat, and chest while I move over his erection, feeling it slide between my cheeks.

I travel lower, licking along every cut and crevice of his abs and that beautiful fucking V. The sex lines. God, I love his sex lines.

"Your body is incredible," I say, my nose brushing against his close-cropped pubic hair.

"It's yours," he says quietly. "Do whatever you want to me."

His words hit me and make my stomach flip and my heart soar. I swallow down the words I want to say, that I just want this forever, to love him for the rest of our years, and instead focus on the moment.

I take his shaft in my hand, kissing and licking my way around it before I suck him into my mouth and lower my head. His cock slides over my tongue, knocking at the back of my throat.

"Fuck," he groans, stretching the word out for a few seconds. "Yes."

Once his dick is nice and wet, and I've reduced him to heavy breaths and strings of cuss words, I come up for air.

"Lube?"

He reaches under the pillow and hands it to me, a crooked grin on his face. "I got prepared earlier."

I take it from him with a smile and uncap it, squirting the liquid onto my fingers. "Do you trust me?"

He nods. "Of course."

"Tell me when to stop."

"I'll never do that," he says with a cocky smirk.

My fingers dance over his hole, smearing the lube before I pour even more on both of us.

I start with one finger, gently pushing in while I take his dick back into my mouth.

"Holy fuck. God. Oh my." He gathers the covers at his sides as he rambles.

I moan around him as I continue to slide in deeper.

"How does that feel?" I ask, watching his face flush as he squeezes his eyes closed.

"Good," he says through gritted teeth. "Good. Yes. Oh god."

I stick with just one finger for a while, penetrating him with slow and gentle movements while I suck on his tip.

"I'm gonna try one more," I say, grabbing the lube with my other hand.

"Okay."

With two fingers, I slide inside him, watching the pleasure on his face.

"God."

"I love how tight you are. You're gonna strangle my dick, aren't you?"

"Oh fuck," he cries.

I curl my fingers up when I get deep inside. "But for now, I want your come in my mouth."

"But I..." He sucks in a breath. "But I want you to come."

"I will," I say. "But I'm about to make you explode."

When I press on his prostate, he gasps, his back arching and his mouth opening into the perfect O.

"Oh my god, what...oh fuck."

I keep my fingers moving, knowing when to press on that special spot as I stroke him with my other hand.

"Baby," I croon. "Look how wet you are for me."

He opens his eyes, staring down at his dick in my hand. His precum drips down his head, and when I squeeze at the top, the stream falls to his stomach.

"Holy shit," he breathes. "Keep going. Please. Fuck me."

Those words hit me in the chest, making my heart thump hard against my ribs. God, I can't wait to fuck him. To have him so needy and desperate. But right now, I want to keep things relatively gentle, still concerned about his head injury.

I move my fingers a little faster and deeper, focusing on that prostate as my hand slides up and down his dick, using his precum as lubricant.

"Tell me how it feels," I breathe.

He moans. "It's so good. You make me feel so fucking good, Devin. I'm so close. It's so intense. Oh my god."

"Yes, baby. I want that cum. I want it down my throat."

"Fuck!" I wrap my lips around his cock, waiting for his release. "I'm about to...I'm gonna..."

His cum shoots out of him, filling my mouth and sliding down my tongue. I moan, loving the taste of him.

Jarrod roars into the room, his screams of pleasure loud enough to echo through the entire Silicon Valley. His body jerks as he expends every last drop into my mouth.

I swallow. "Mm."

Gently, I pull my fingers from his ass, sucking on him a bit longer.

"Devin," he breathes. "Oh my god."

I move toward his head, brushing the hair from his sweat-slicked forehead. "Now you get to taste me."

"Yes," he says with excitement, his tongue darting out to lick the underside of my head.

I stroke my shaft, already ready to explode. "Open your mouth," I command. "Tongue out."

"Yes, sir," he teases, obeying.

With my shaft in hand, I slap my tip against his tongue a few times, sliding it across his wet mouth.

"Angle your head this way," I say, gently turning him to face me.

I thrust into his mouth, doing my best not to go too hard or too deep. I keep my tip in his mouth while I stroke.

"Give it to me," he whispers. "Fucking drown me in it."

"Jesus," I breathe, his words pushing me to the edge. "I'm about to come."

"Let me taste you."

My cum shoots mostly into his mouth, some landing in a stream across his cheek.

"Oh fuck," I grunt.

He swallows quickly, his tongue swiping at his lips before he parts them again, waiting for more. God, he's gonna be the death of me.

"Yes," he croons. "So good."

I release my spent cock, reaching out to wipe the cum from his face. He grabs my wrist and guides my fingers to his mouth where he sucks the liquid from the tips.

My teeth sink into my bottom lip before I lower myself to lie next to him and press a kiss against his mouth.

"Thanks for waking me up."

He grins. "You're welcome."

Forty-Four

JARROD

After I've showered and thrown on some more clothes to lounge around the house in, I head to the kitchen, wanting to return the favor Devin did for me by preparing me a meal. He's just getting in the shower himself, so I should have at least twenty minutes to figure something out.

Five minutes into pulling out my ingredients, there's a knock on my door. When I pull it open, I find Cory's smiling face on the other side.

"Hey, man. You're still alive."

Fear scratches at my throat, making my words come out choppy. "Uh, yeah. Wh-what're you doing here?" I clear my throat, hating that panic sits heavy in my chest.

"Making sure you're alive. Obviously," he says, walking right in.

Cory lives in the same gated community, so I don't get a heads up when he decides to come over.

"You making breakfast?" he asks, sniffing the air. "And whose car's out there?"

"You really shouldn't be harassing me with all these questions. You're gonna hurt my already injured brain."

He snorts. "Right. The doctor's coming over again today, right? When're you coming back to practice?"

"Whenever the doctor says I can," I reply, my eyes flashing to the stairs.

"They'll probably start getting you back to light conditioning in the next day or two. We can't wait to have you back, man."

"Yeah, well, I can't wait to be back. But I'm kinda feeling tired. I might head back to bed for a bit."

He gives me a weird look. "You just woke up and started making breakfast. You're tired already? Maybe the concussion is more than mild."

"No, no. I'm good. I feel fine, but just tired, I guess. I don't know."

He sits on my couch. "So, whose car's out there?"

"Why are you so nosy?"

"Because I'm your best friend."

"Well, as your best friend, I'm telling you to get out of my house, and you'll do it because we're friends, and you'll just harass me about this later."

His lips curl up on the sides. "It's a girl. Dude, what the fuck? You're not supposed to be fucking already. Are you faking it so you can have time off to get your dick wet?"

"You're so annoying," I say, walking over to him and gesturing for him to get up. "Let's go."

"Maybe I should meet this one."

"Maybe not."

"Ah," he says, standing up. "So there *is* a girl."

"Cory, please," I say, getting desperate. More afraid.

"All right, all right," he says, walking slowly toward the door. "Please just tell me it's not another puck bunny."

"Oh, you're one to talk."

He spins around and then his eyes travel upward and over my shoulder. Then I hear, "I forgot my bag in the car."

My spine stiffens and Cory's mouth drops slightly. I spin around and find Devin descending the stairs in only a towel.

I swallow and watch the moment he lifts his gaze and notices someone else is here.

"Oh." He stops in place. "Sorry, I..." He doesn't finish.

Terror squeezes my lungs and sweat starts trickling down my spine.

"Is that your friend from Vegas?" Cory asks.

I turn and face him. "Yeah. Devin."

"Right," he says, eyes bouncing between us. "Hey, man."

Devin shifts awkwardly. "Hey."

"You live around here?"

I find myself watching Devin with my stomach in knots. "I'm down in the LA area actually. I just was up here for," His eyes flicker to me. "Business, and then thought maybe I'd stop by to see how this guy was doing."

My head angles back at Cory who lifts his chin. "Oh okay. Yeah, he took quite the hit."

"I'm pretty tough," I say with an awkward chuckle.

We all stand in place, and I wonder if it's only me that feels uncomfortable.

"Well, I guess I'll go," Cory says, giving me a strange look.

"Okay," I reply cheerily. Too cheerily. "I'll talk to you later."

"Mmhmm," he murmurs, pulling open the door.

As soon as he's gone and I shut the door, I sag against it

with an exhale. When I look up, I see Devin looking at me with pain in his eyes.

"I didn't know anyone was here," he offers, coming down the steps.

"I know."

"Are you okay?"

I stand up straight and sigh, running a hand through my hair. "It's not like this looks suspicious, right? Guys can have friends stay over, and it's not like I haven't been around guys in towels or some state of undress. It's not weird, right?"

His lips pinch together as he studies me. "Right."

My phone buzzes in my pants pocket and I pull it out and read the message.

> So, let me know when you have some time to talk. Like, one-on-one.

"Fuck!"

"What's wrong?" he asks, making his way toward the front door.

"Cory texted me. He can't even be a block away. He probably sent this from the stop sign."

I feel myself panicking, sweat prickling under my arms as my heart lodges itself in my throat.

"What did he say?"

"He wants to talk one-on-one."

Devin watches me, his face blank. "It could be about something different."

"It's not."

"He can't know. It's not like we were caught in a compromising position."

"Yeah, but..."

I don't say anything else, my brain working overtime to come up with possible topics he might want to talk about. Or if he happens to actually question me about this, what I could even say.

The door closes, getting my attention, and I realize Devin left to go to his car. When he gets back, he's holding a small duffle bag. He doesn't say anything, just gives me a forced, tight smile before walking upstairs.

I can't even think about making breakfast, because my mind won't stop whirring.

> Okay, is everything cool?

I stare at the phone, waiting for Cory to respond, to put me out of my misery. But I never see the bubbles pop up.

The sound of Devin's bag hitting the floor steals my attention.

"I'm gonna go," he says.

"What?"

"Yeah, I should head back home. You obviously need to talk to your friend, and I'm sure you'll be back to work soon, so—"

"I don't want you to go."

His head falls to the side. "I'd like to stay too, but—"

"Then stay."

He sighs. "Jarrod, you're already freaking out over your friend *maybe* being curious about what's going on. What happens if someone else comes over? Do I hide?"

I stand up. "No. I don't want you to hide. I just..."

"It's okay," he says, once again placating me.

"Will you still text me? Are we still gonna try to do this in secret?"

When the words leave my tongue, I'm left with a bitter taste in my mouth and I cringe.

"In secret," he repeats. "Yes, I'll text you when I'm home."

He comes forward and gives me a hug, trying to step away quickly.

"Hey," I say, holding his face between my hands. "Please don't be upset with me."

"I'm not upset with you," he says, his hands going to my waist. "I'm...I don't know." He shrugs. "I'm fine. I will be in touch."

I yank him in for another hug before I kiss him repeatedly, not ready to be away from his lips.

"Drive safe."

He grins. "I will."

I walk him to the door and grab his hand, squeezing it three times. He does it back, giving me a wink, and then I watch him walk to his car.

Forty-Five

DEVIN

I don't blame him. In fact, I try to put myself in his position. By putting yourself in the shoes of someone else, you gain a better perspective and are able to empathize more. I never had to deal with coming out on this level. He's a known figure in a masculine sport where it's not common for people to be gay or bisexual and be out. He's afraid. That one I understand.

I was afraid before I came out. I think that's a common and normal response, though I don't think we should have to feel that fear. We should be able to like, love, kiss, and fuck whoever we want regardless of gender. We shouldn't have to fear what people will think, say, or do when they find out. I hate that this is the way it is, but I get it.

However, like I've always been, I'm afraid of the hurt and pain this could cause. That it *is* causing. I don't think I'm being selfish by feeling hurt, even though I understand his reasoning. Nobody wants to be hidden or kept a secret. Everyone deserves to be loved outside of the shadows and locked doors. My pain and frustration doesn't mean I don't get where he's coming from, but I feel it nonetheless.

I made the decision to try. We can text and FaceTime, and maybe even meet up when time allows, but it doesn't prevent me from thinking this could end up destroying us both. The emotions and feelings between us are strong. Personally, I've never experienced a relationship like this, and we're hardly using labels and terms such as *relationship* and *boyfriend*. I just know this is something special, which is why it sucks that it can't be more than a secret. It's going to hurt like hell if it doesn't turn out well, but I'd be an idiot to not try. I'm mad that I missed eight months thinking I was protecting us both.

To be fair, I wasn't in love yet. I thought I was preventing that, only for it to happen anyway.

So when I get home, I'll text him and everything will be okay.

Forty-Six

JARROD

After the team physician leaves, I go over a million possible things I can tell Cory when we talk. He never replied to my question about whether everything was good or not, so it's left me feeling even more anxious.

I send him a message.

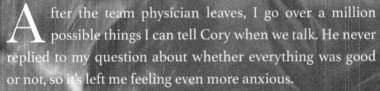

I'm free now if you are.

Come over.

His response was immediate, and now I'm left with a racing heart and a stomach full of knots. I grab my keys, put on my tennis shoes, and head out the door. Ten minutes later, I'm pulling into his driveway.

I decide to play it cool. Normal.

When he opens the door, I greet him with a wide smile. "Can't believe you're making me come to you. I don't even know if I should be driving."

"Please. It's not that far. You're only going twenty-five the whole way."

I relax a little when I hear his usual kind of response.

He makes his way to the kitchen. "Drink?"

"I'm good," I reply, making myself comfortable on his couch.

When he joins me, he's carrying a water bottle in one hand and a banana in the other. He sits on the couch across from me.

"So, what's up?" I ask, hoping my skin doesn't flush.

Cory uncaps the water and takes a drink. He smacks his lips. "We're friends and I've never been one to beat around the bush, so I'm just gonna spew out the words and you respond however is fitting."

I swallow. "Okay."

"Is something going on with you and that Devin guy?"

Though I knew it was coming, my eyes bulge when the words leave his mouth. It feels wrong to deny it. To deny Devin and what he means to me. My first thought is to maybe laugh it off. Ask him what the hell he's talking about. But I'm like a deer in headlights, frozen in place, my gaze unwavering. I don't know how much time passes while I sit in silence, but it feels like forever.

"I suppose that's answer enough," he says.

I sit up, dropping my leg to the floor and give a tiny shake of my head. "What makes you think that?" I ask.

He tosses the water bottle between his hands. "It was the way you acted when I showed up. Cagey. Nervous. I brought up a girl being there and you didn't just say, *No, it's my friend who came into town.* You led me to believe it was someone you were sleeping with. Then I saw him on the stairs and you both froze. It's not like if I was there and someone came over to find me walking around in my boxers. We wouldn't think twice."

"I don't—"

"And then once I left, I thought back to that night in Vegas. You could've hooked up with that waitress, but you didn't. After you joined us again once Devin left, you were a little different. Uninterested in keeping your own birthday celebration going. So, I don't know."

Part of me is furious that he'd question me like this, putting me on the spot to either come out or lie. The other part is ready to get it over with. Just tell him and see how it feels. Cory's my closest friend, and the one I feel like would accept this easier than most.

With a sigh, I say, "Yes, there's something going on between us."

Even though he questioned me, he looks shocked at my answer. His eyes widen and he stops tossing the water bottle between his hands.

"What? Really?"

I blow out a long breath. "Look, I don't even know how to explain it."

"Jarrod," he says with a disbelieving laugh. "I don't even...I'm so confused. When? How?"

"You think *you're* confused," I say.

"So, you're bi? Have you always known?"

I shake my head. "No. I don't even know. I mean, it's just him."

His brows furrow. "What do you mean?"

I sigh. "It started in June."

"June?" he exclaims.

"Yeah. When I was at Black Diamond. He was there, too. We hadn't seen each other in over ten years, but it was like no time had passed at all. We were just spending time together. Eating, snorkeling, hiking, all that stuff. Just like regular friends. Though I knew instantly that he was an attractive dude, at some point, I started thinking and feeling differently about him. I've never experienced that before with a guy."

"Damn. Not even me?" he jokes, and it takes some weight off my shoulders.

I snort. "No. Sorry."

He puts the bottle on the table next to him and leans forward. "So, what now? Y'all have been together this whole time?"

I shake my head. "No. He actually broke it off before we left the island. He said it would be too hard. The distance, the secrecy."

Cory nods along. "You're not ready to tell people."

"I don't feel like I should have to say anything."

"So, in Vegas? Just a coincidence?"

"Yeah. Then I saw him on Christmas Eve. I invited him to spend it with my family because he wasn't going to be with his."

Cory's eyes double in size. "Wow. Christmas with the family."

"As a friend."

"Hmm. And now?"

A smile begins to form on my lips. "He saw me get hurt. He flew home and drove straight here."

"Damn," Cory says, eyebrows reaching for his hairline. "That's...something. Is he just waiting at your place now?"

I rub a hand over my forehead and lean back. "No. He left. He saw that I was freaking out about the possibility of you knowing. It's not really a point of contention, because he hasn't pressured me about it all, but it sits between us. We're both aware of the situation. Me not being out and being afraid to be seen with him has him feeling a certain way."

"Well, yeah."

"You think I'm wrong?"

"I think you're dealing with a lot, but the man flew back into town and drove up to see if you were okay. He obviously cares a lot about you."

"I feel the same way, but I didn't want the press to cover this and not care at all about our season. If it comes out, they'll have a field day. They won't care about how well we're playing."

"So? Fuck the media. Whether they focus on us or not isn't going to affect the games we win or lose."

I begin to feel a fissure of relief that at least Cory doesn't care, but then I remember there's one more thing.

"Uh, well, there's something else," I say, rubbing the back of my neck.

"What?"

"He's kind of a well-known gay porn star."

I bite down on my lip as I watch Cory's reaction. His jaw drops and he just stares at me.

"What?"

"You heard me."

"No. What? Are you kidding me?"

"I'm not. He actually has his own production company and everything. Think Jenna Jameson but for men."

"Ho-ly shit," he says, breaking up the first word. "Well, yeah. That's gonna add a little spice to the story."

"I wanted to make sure our team had the best season considering how fucked it ended last season. Coming out and dealing with all that will overshadow what we do as a team."

He shakes his head. "You're too nice, man. If I had met a porn star, I'd be out on the streets with her, making sure everyone took a picture. Are you kidding?"

"That's because it would be more acceptable."

Cory makes a face. "Yeah, I guess you're right."

"So, you're okay with this?" I question.

He looks at me like I just grew another head. "Why wouldn't I be?"

I shrug. "I don't know."

"It's shocking as hell, that's for sure, but ultimately it doesn't affect me."

"It will if I come out and they start questioning all of you on what it's like to have a queer goalie on the team."

"Man, fuck that. I wish they'd ask me some stupid shit like that. You're the best fucking goalie there is. Who you're fucking isn't going to change that."

I grin. "Well, I don't know. We haven't been talking since we left the island, minus the couple of times we ran into each other, but now we're gonna start trying. In secret."

"And he's okay with that?"

I scrape my teeth along my bottom lip. "Probably not thrilled, but it was his idea. We can text and call and try to make time for visits."

Cory laughs. "Oh, dude. He's in love with you."

"I'm not sure about that."

"Okay, we won't mention him dropping everything to come see you, but now he's willing to be your little secret when he has no reason to hide. Why else would he do that? Why would he put himself back in the closet?"

I shake my head, my brows furrowed. "I don't know."

"Because that's where you are. He's going where you are so he can be with you."

After several seconds, I say, "And I'm letting him."

Cory sighs. "I get it. I'll never have to worry about the media saying anything about me except critiques on a bad game. I couldn't imagine everyone being in my personal business and throwing their own opinions into the mix. I understand your hesitation."

"Well, we got a couple more months of regular season," I say.

"Then the playoffs, which you know we're making it to."

"So possibly four months. It's not that long. I can come out during the offseason and let the frenzy die down before next season."

He shrugs. "I guess."

With a sigh, I say, "I don't know. Just gonna take it one day at a time."

Cory sits back and grabs his banana, peeling it. Before he puts it in his mouth, he looks up at me. "Is this gonna turn you on?"

I throw a pillow at him. "Fuck off."

He smacks it to the floor. "You know I love you."

I shake my head and feel a lot lighter now that Cory knows and isn't being weird about it. Just his normal annoying self.

Forty-Seven

DEVIN

My phone rings as I'm getting gas two hours from home. It's a FaceTime call from Jarrod.

"Hey," I say, answering with a smile.

"You're stunning."

My cheeks redden. "Thanks. Am I the fourth hottest porn star?"

"Number one for sure."

I laugh and lean against the car. "You're my number one, too. That article was way off."

"I appreciate that," he says with a chuckle. "But uh…I wanted to tell you something."

"Oh?"

"I told Cory. He knows everything."

"Oh." My brows raise. "And how did that go?"

"Good. Kind of unremarkable," he says with a laugh, lifting the hat off his head and putting it on backwards. "I think I psyched myself into expecting the worst reaction. He asked plain and simple if something was going on with us."

"And you just said yes?" My heart thumps faster.

"Yeah. I asked why he thought that and he explained I kind of gave myself away, so I told him the truth. About Black Diamond. About everything."

I swallow, putting the nozzle back into the pump. "And he was cool?"

"Extremely."

"That's good. I'm happy for you," I say, getting back into my car.

"I feel a little relieved. Less worried."

I nod. "It's a good feeling. I'm glad you have an accepting friend."

"I'm glad I have you."

I rest my cheek on my fist as I prop my elbow near the window, my smile unstoppable.

"I..." I stop myself. "I'm glad I have you, too."

He grins. "I guess I'll let you go so you can get home safely. Text me when you're there."

"I will."

"Bye."

"Bye."

We stare at each other for a few seconds before we both start laughing, eventually ending the call around the same time.

For the remaining drive to my house, my smile hardly leaves my face.

Fifty-Eight

JARROD

March-May

> How much do you love the LA area?

> Why?

> I hear San José is pretty nice.

> Oh really?

SHIP   HOCKEY CHAMPI***

> Nice game. Loved seeing some of the warmups.

> Hope you mean you loved watching me.

> I like the stretches.

> I like stretching you.

Oh my.

***

So what did your agent want when he interrupted our phone sex?

He really had bad timing, but the director I worked with for Absolution reached out about another movie within the next year.

Wow, that's awesome. When's Absolution coming out?

Probably not for another six months.

I can't wait to see it.

I can't wait to see you.

Do you think you'd want to come to some of the finals?

I get to watch the stretches in person? Hell yeah.

Behave.

Yes, sir.

***

So about San José being the best city to live in...

Is it?

Well, I'm here.

That's true.

***

I miss your ass.

I miss your mouth.

I can't wait to fuck you.

Fuck. I can't wait either.

Have you been doing what I said?

Yes.

What a good boy.

You know I love it when you praise me.

***

Just want to say I'm yours and only yours.

God, I'm crazy about you. I think we really need to talk soon. In person.

Okay.

***

I get to see you next week!

I can't wait. I miss you so much.

Miss you more.

Should I get a hotel room or...

Are you serious? No. You're staying with me.

I just wasn't sure if you'd have anyone over.

You're staying with me.

***

See you in an hour. Getting gas.

I'll be the one in the yard with balloons.

Forty-Nine

DEVIN

May

When I pull up to his driveway, I bark out a laugh because he really is in the yard with balloons. Not only that, there's a sign staked into the ground that says *It's about fucking time*.

I ignore my bag in the backseat and rush over to him, crashing into his body.

He squeezes me, and I push my face into his neck and inhale, my body relaxing in his arms like it knows this is where I'm supposed to be, like we're finally home.

"It's been too long," he says.

"I know."

"Come inside. We have some time to make up for."

As soon as the door closes, we're pawing at each other, grabbing at the material that keeps us from being skin-to-skin. The balloons float into the air above us as Jarrod removes my shirt, and then I start yanking on his shorts.

We stumble into the living room, unable to keep from kissing or touching as we shed what's left of our clothing. Jarrod pushes me onto the couch, making me fall to the cushion before he drops to his knees and devours my cock.

"Oh fuck," I exclaim with a quivering breath, my hand sliding through his soft hair.

Jarrod moans and murmurs around me, his hands climbing up my torso as his mouth does all the work.

"I missed this," he says as he takes the time to now kiss along my shaft. His eyes lift, meeting mine. "I missed you."

My hand caresses his cheek. "I missed us."

His tongue slides out, licking my balls as he continues to watch me.

"God," I say on an exhale.

Jarrod's lips quirk. "I'm the one worshiping you."

"Then let's switch places," I say, moving to stand up.

He gets to his feet before dropping down onto the couch. I make my way between his legs and don't bother with any teasing. I'm too horny. Too desperate. I swallow his length, taking every inch into my mouth until he's coated with saliva.

The blowjob is sloppy and wet, wanton and needy. I moan and whimper because I'm so turned on and yet desperate for more.

When I pull away, I quickly get into his lap, balancing on his thighs as I bring our cocks together in my hand.

"Oh fuck yes," he groans, watching me stroke the both of us.

He takes my other hand and brings it to his mouth, licking my palm before placing it around our shafts. His large hands remain on mine, helping with the up and down movements.

"Holy shit," I say, watching him. "You're so perfect."

Jarrod bites his lip and shakes his head slightly. "We are."

"Baby," I pant, my gaze moving to where our dicks rub against each other. "I'm gonna come."

"I'm close. You feel too good."

"I can't wait to have you inside me later."

"Fuck," he grunts, moving his hips. "I can't wait either."

I watch him and wait for him to look at me. "And then I can't wait to be inside you."

"Oh god," he cries, his eyes closing. "I'm coming."

I watch the first jet of cum shoot from his tip, landing on our hands.

"Oh yes. Come for me. Oh god," I exclaim, my orgasm hitting me hard.

My cum flies into the air, landing on his stomach before the rest drips over my cockhead and mixes with his, sliding down our shafts.

"Holy shit," he says through heavy breaths.

"Oh fuck, baby. Oh my god," I cry, my breathing shallow.

"We're a fucking mess," he says as we release our cocks, hands covered in cum.

"Worth it."

"Always," he says with a smile, leaning forward to kiss me.

We get up and try to keep any fluids from dropping to the floor as we make our way to the bathroom. Once we clean up and get our clothes back on, he pulls me in for another hug.

"I don't think we should wait three months ever again."

"You've been pretty busy," I say, my fingers lightly running up his back. "You've only been here like half that time anyway."

He pulls away just a bit, still holding my hands. "If you lived here..."

I tilt my head. He's been bringing this possibility up, and at first I thought it was just this cute thing to say, but I'm beginning to think he truly wants me to live here. And I understand why. Our commute isn't extremely long, but for someone who spends a lot of time traveling, it would be better to live within the same city limits to expand on our time together when possible.

However, we're still very much a secret, and I'm not sure how long the secrecy will last and when or if Jarrod will be willing to be out in public with me in a way couples usually are.

"You know I'd love being closer to you," I say.

He groans. "I feel like there's a *but* coming on."

My lips twist. "It's a very big change," I start, not wanting to cause a fight by bringing up the main thing that's keeping us from being fully together.

"It is," he says with a nod.

"Quite the step to take."

He gives me another nod, his eyes widening slightly as a lightbulb goes off. "For something that doesn't have a name," he states. "I get it."

"Let's not talk about it right now," I say, tugging him to the kitchen. "I think you owe me a meal."

"I do," he says with a smile. "You're gonna need all the energy you can get."

Fifty

JARROD

As we're warming up on the ice, I look up to where I know Devin is sitting and catch his eye. He waggles his brows and does the tiniest wave like he's cooling down his face while he watches. I roll my eyes and laugh before going back to stretching my legs.

Cory skates up next to me before dropping down to stretch. "I see Devin's here."

"Yeah," I say, forcing myself not to look at him again.

"That's kind of a big deal, right?"

"Lots of people will be here tonight."

"Don't be stupid on purpose. He's here for you. Supporting you. You told me he doesn't even watch sports and now he's surrounded by fanatics."

"I do love that he's here," I say, failing to keep the smile from my face.

"Then we better fucking win," Cory says with his own grin.

"Damn right."

It's the first game of the Stanley Cup Finals, and my boyfriend is here watching me. *Boyfriend?* Somehow it sounds right and yet not nearly significant enough.

We score first, but it's quickly followed by a Dallas goal. In the second period, we're the only ones that score, but just once. At the start of the third period, one of the Dallas defensemen checks one of our guys into the boards which starts a fight. Cory almost gets the puck into their net, but it bounces off the crossbar and flies in the opposite direction.

Everyone heads toward me, one of the Stars taking a shot from half past the center red line, mid-stride. I move out to stop the puck, sending it back to my guys. They fly to the other end of the rink and shoot it into the net. The crowd roars its excitement, and my eyes find Devin standing with the rest of them, yelling and cheering.

We get through almost the whole period before one of our guys fouls an opposing player, allowing him to get a penalty shot.

Great. No pressure.

The player who's taking the shot is a guy I know. Not personally, but his game and the way he likes to play. Stratsford is good, but with Devin watching, there's no way I'm letting this guy get this puck in.

The puck is dropped on center ice and Stratsford begins skating up to it. Once the puck is in his possession and he's making his way closer, I push past the crease, positioning myself to better defend.

He skates straight at me, and I move just slightly to the right. He'll see the marginally larger opening on the left and think it's his best shot.

Stratsford attempts to deke me, but I know that's his

move. He feints to the right, hoping I'll move more in that direction before he switches quickly to his left and takes aim. My body goes left immediately and as soon as the puck leaves his stick, I'm already in position, blocking it from getting close.

The arena roars to a deafening level. We only have a minute and eleven seconds left. All we have to do is keep them from scoring.

Instead, Cory goes down there and sinks one into the net within forty seconds which nearly solidifies our win. There's no way they can outscore us in twenty-one seconds.

Game one is ours.

The arena is jam packed with screaming fans, but I only care about one. I find him immediately, skating toward the glass. I lift my stick in a partial wave and he grins from ear to ear, his arms up as he yells his excitement. His happiness radiates off of him, filling me with an intense kind of joy.

It feels like it takes forever to be free to go home, but as soon as I'm done talking to who needs to be talked to, showering, and getting dressed, I rush out to find Devin, ready to celebrate with him.

"Congratulations!" he yells, his smile still just as wide and bright as it was an hour ago.

"Thank you."

There are a few people around, so we don't embrace, but it's killing me not to. Sure, friends hug, but it's hard to hold Devin in a platonic way. If I do it, it's going to be obvious I care about him.

"Ready?" I question, giving him a look.

He nods. "Yes."

At home, as soon as we cross the threshold of the doorway, we drop everything we're holding and he jumps into my arms.

"That was incredible to watch," he says, already breathless. "You're so good at what you do. It was thrilling."

I nibble at his throat as I walk to the stairs. "I'm about to show you just how good I am at *everything* I do."

"Mmm," he moans. "Put me down and let's run. It'll be faster."

We race up the stairs, barging through my door and landing on the bed.

I pounce on top of him, kissing and licking his neck as I grind against him. Through heavy breathing and short kisses, we undress.

"I want you inside me," he begs. "Now. Fast. Hard. I want it all."

My teeth bite into my lip. "I like you like this."

"I'm so fucking horny for you," he breathes, grabbing my neck and pulling me down for a kiss. "I need you."

I rock into him, my cock sliding against his. "Say it again."

"I need you, Jarrod. Please."

"Anything you want, baby."

I get up just long enough to grab the lube. I quickly coat my fingers and smear some around his hole before I slide in up to the knuckle.

He hisses. "Yes."

As I move inside him, I use my other hand to stroke his length. After a minute, Devin bears down, greedily fucking himself on my finger.

"Want more, sweetheart?" I ask.

"Yes. Yes," he whimpers

I slide in another finger, scissoring them slightly to help stretch him. We had sex yesterday, so I try not to hurt him, but he's desperate for it.

Once I've taken at least the minimal amount of time to prep him, I pull my fingers out and cover my cock with lube, dripping more into his ass.

"Fuck me, Jarrod. Fuck me hard."

I growl, positioning my tip at his hole, ready to fucking destroy him. I'm so turned on by the sight of him, especially when he's so needy like this. So horny and ready for me. My adrenaline has been high since the win and now I'm ready to ravage him.

After a couple inches slide in, he sucks in a breath and I push all the way in.

"Oh fuck!" he calls out. "Yes. God."

My hips thrust back and forth, stretching his tight channel and filling him up the way he likes. I hold his knees up and apart, watching my cock disappear into his ass.

"Fuck, you take me so good."

"Yes," he cries. "I love the way you feel inside me. You're so thick."

I drop his legs and lower myself over him, kissing him with furious passion as I continue to move in and out.

"I'm fucking crazy about you, you know that?"

He nods, pressing his lips against mine again. "Me too. Fuck. I...I..." He stops himself from saying anything else, succumbing to moans and grunts.

"You like the way I fuck you?"

"Yes," he calls out desperately. "I love it."

"Me too, baby. Now get up. Turn around."

I pull out and watch him get situated on his hands and

knees. With another small squirt of lube, I push inside him again.

"Fuck," he grunts.

My hands slide up his back, gripping onto his shoulders as I move in and out of him with deep, hard strokes.

"I love the way you take me," I say, my hand curving around his neck, pulling him up.

He moans, his back touching my chest. "Maybe I was made for you."

I kiss along his jaw, my free hand reaching for his erection. "I know you were."

"God," he groans. "The way you touch me. I love it."

"Tell me you're mine," I growl.

"I am. I'm yours," he says instantly. "All of me."

"I'm yours, too," I say into his ear. "Always."

I release my hold on him and he drops back to his hands. All the emotion sizzling inside of me—the deep feelings of adoration and love that I can't bring myself to express come out in my physical desire. I touch every part of his body, complimenting every single inch while I make sure he feels just how much my body responds to his.

When I feel myself getting closer to orgasm, I pull out and get him on his back once more, needing to see his face when we come.

"Stroke yourself, baby," I tell him. "I'm so close. Let's come together."

He nods, his hand moving up and down his shaft. His face is always so beautiful but when he's blissed out like this, my heart squeezes when he looks at me. He's vulnerable and open, his pretty pink lips parted, his eyes hooded and on me in a way that makes me feel warm. I've never felt so desired until I met Devin. I've never been this happy in a relationship in my life. I love him so much it hurts. It hurts to not tell him. It hurts to not be open and honest. But now's not the time, and he deserves for it to be perfect.

"Oh god," I moan. "I'm coming, baby. I'm coming."

"Yes, yes," he chants, his hand moving faster.

I slip my arm under his neck, hovering over him as I slam my hips forward, my lower stomach grazing over his balls as he continues to stroke himself.

"Give it to me," he breathes, his tongue snaking out to lick my bottom lip.

My eyes close and my head drops as my orgasm pours out of me and into him.

"Oh my. Fuck. Shit. Yes," I say through grunts.

"I'm coming," he cries, digging his head further into the pillow.

I ease away enough to watch his hand move and witness his cum shoot out of him and onto his stomach.

"Yes, baby."

"Oh my god, oh my god," he cries. "So good."

After we've both stopped shaking and our breathing is somewhat regular, I cradle his cheek in one palm, staring into his eyes. I want to say it. The words are dying to come out, fighting over each other to leave my lips. I can't. Not now. He can't think they're sex-induced words. The declaration needs to come with something more than a mess of cum between us.

I lean down and kiss him gently before resting my forehead against his.

Fifty-One

DEVIN

I'm there to witness the Bobcats win game two of the Stanley Cup Finals, and it was just as thrilling as the first time, if not more so. It went into overtime and came down to the last minute. Watching Jarrod on the ice is insane. I'm so proud of him and amazed at his skill and talent while also remaining constantly afraid he's going to get hurt.

As I wait for him, I make my way outside to make a call and send a couple emails. A few guys walk past me, and I see through my peripherals that one does a double-take. When I glance up and give him a friendly, close-lipped smile, our eyes meet before I'm looking back at my phone.

"I'll catch up."

I lift my head and watch him standing a few feet away, slipping his hands into his pockets.

"Hey," he greets.

"Hey."

"I saw you inside. I was a few rows back."

"Oh okay," I reply, a little confused and only slightly uncomfortable. "It was a good game."

He nods. "Yeah. Did you come alone?"

I look around, noticing there's still plenty of people making their way to their cars, but nobody's really hanging around near the steps of the arena. They're yards away.

"Yeah. Kind of," I amend. "I'm waiting on someone."

"Oh." He looks off to the side, watching where his friends are going. "Um, this is kind of awkward, but I know who you are."

My brows lift. "Oh?"

He nods, looking at me briefly before turning his gaze elsewhere. "Dickie, right?"

I grin. "Right."

"My friends don't really know. I mean, they *really* don't know. They wouldn't know who you are, but, well..."

"I get it," I tell him.

"Anyway, it's probably weird to say I'm a fan." His cheeks redden and I can tell he's embarrassed.

I laugh. "It's not. I'm glad I have fans."

He chuckles. "Right. Well, besides that, I've read and watched some of the interviews you've given."

I watch over his shoulder as a black SUV rolls up, the windows tinted so dark there's no way to see inside. It's Jarrod. He doesn't like to drive to and from the games, so he hires a driver for game days.

"Oh okay."

My phone buzzes, but I think it would be rude to start reading messages while this guy is talking, so I don't look at it.

"In one of the interviews you talked about what it was

like coming out versus what it was like to tell your friends what you did for a living and how coming out was easier for you."

"Right," I say with a nod. "Easier, but not easy."

My phone buzzes again, but I don't look at it. It's probably Jarrod, but I have a feeling this guy just needs someone to talk to about this, because he doesn't have anyone else.

"Were you afraid you'd lose friends?"

As he asks, I watch the back door of the SUV open, Jarrod stepping out. He's wearing a baseball cap and a hoodie, trying his best to disguise himself, but it's hard when you're as big as he is.

He walks up the stairs, but I hold up a finger low at my side, telling him to give me a second. He stops and cocks his head slightly before leaning against the guardrail on the steps.

"It's going to sound pathetic," I say, answering this guy's question, "but I didn't have many friends when I came out. I waited until I was done with high school, even though I was convinced people knew already anyway. I left my parents' house and started over somewhere else. So I was able to make the decision to be open and be myself before meeting anyone new. I understand that's not helpful."

He chuckles. "No, it's fine. I'm transferring to a different college soon, so I can maybe use that opportunity to have my own new start."

"Of course, but I'll tell you what, if your friends decide to end a friendship over who you like, they were never friends, you understand? People should respect you regardless of your sexual identity. You will always be you. Being afraid is normal, but don't let it prevent you from living openly and embracing who you are."

He nods, his smile growing. "I understand. Um, well, thanks for talking to me, and sorry for harassing you."

"I'm glad you did," I say with a grin. "I wish you the best."

"Would it be okay if we take a picture? I may not show it to anyone anytime soon, but..." He shrugs.

I laugh. "Of course."

He pulls his phone out, and I glance over at Jarrod who's watching us with a small grin on his lips.

We pose for a selfie and then he smiles at me again. "Thanks. I really appreciate it."

"It's no problem."

He happens to turn around and then does a double-take when he sees Jarrod lingering six feet behind him.

"Oh shit."

"What's wrong?"

He looks again and Jarrod stands up straight, maybe realizing he's been recognized.

"That's Jarrod Bivens," he says in a whispered tone. "The goalie for the Bobcats. How do you not know?"

I pull my lips in to keep from laughing. "Oh."

Jarrod meets my eyes and communicates through quick glances and eyebrow movements. I wave him over.

"Try not to bring too much attention, okay?"

The guy looks at me with wide eyes. "What?"

"I know him. We're friends from school."

"Hey," Jarrod says when he walks up.

"Oh my god."

I laugh. I can't help it. "Jarrod, this is..." I trail off, realizing he never told me his name.

"TJ. Well, Timothy James, but TJ. Holy shit is this happening?"

"Hey, TJ," Jarrod says, shaking his hand.

"Can I get a photo of you, too?"

My eyes scan the area to see if anyone's paying attention. A few people on the other side of the stairs are kind of looking in this direction, but it should be okay.

"I'll take one of you two real quick, but then we have to go."

"Okay, yeah. Cool. Thanks."

He thrusts his phone at me and goes to stand next to Jarrod, looking up at him in awe. I snap a few before stepping forward and giving him his phone back."

"Remember what I said," I tell him.

"Okay. Yeah. Thanks. Both of you. Oh my god."

"Let's go," I say to Jarrod as I notice the people on the other side of the stairs getting more interested.

We rush down the steps and climb into the backseat, laughing.

"Well, that was interesting."

"Sorry I didn't look at your texts. He was talking to me about—"

"I know. I heard when I came up. It was nice of you to talk to him and give him that advice."

I nod. "Yeah."

Jarrod watches me with a somewhat sad expression. I know the message I gave TJ probably hit close to him as well. I haven't questioned him on his timeline of coming out or if he's got certain people he's afraid won't accept him afterwards. I know he's dealing with it, though.

"Next two games are in Dallas," he says. "I'll be leaving early in the morning and won't be back for five or six days."

I nod. "I hope you win them both."

He grins. "I won't get my hopes up, but that's the plan." He waits a few seconds. "I was thinking you could just stay at my place. In the event that we have a game five, it'll be here, and I'd like you to be there again."

"I could go home and be back when you are."

He leans in closer, his eyes flickering to the driver when he puts his hand on my thigh. "I like the idea of you being at my place," he says quietly. "Unless, of course, you're needed home for work."

"I'll stay at your house," I say, butterflies taking flight in my stomach.

He smiles and squeezes my thigh, and I wish I could throw myself on him, or at the very least, lean over and give him a kiss.

Fifty-Two

JARROD

We lost our first game in Dallas by two, but by game four we got our edge back and won by three. A shutout.

After lots of pressure from Cory and some other guys from the team, we all find ourselves out at a restaurant around eleven o'clock. Most of us are exhausted, but I agreed to eat before I go back to the hotel and pass out.

Almost immediately, I knew coming was the wrong decision. The restaurant is packed, and though we have a private room, a couple of the guys keep opening up the door and going to the bar. It gets people's attention.

Toward the end of our meal, fucking Popov brings two girls into the room, pissing nearly everyone off. A few guys get up and leave right away, but I wait for Cory to return from the bathroom before I go.

"What's going on?" he asks, looking around.

"Popov invited some girls in here, pissed everyone off, so they're leaving."

"Dumbass," Cory says, looking over my shoulder where Pop has his arms draped over both girls' shoulders. "That girl is looking at McKinney anyway."

"Puck bunnies." I sigh. "Anyway, I'm going to the hotel."

"Yeah, I don't blame you."

"The other guys left money on the table, so someone needs to wait for the check."

"I'll do it," Cory says. "Go ahead and leave."

I hand him a few bills and pat him on the shoulder. "Talk to ya later."

Unfortunately, as I'm leaving the restaurant, Popov and the girls follow me out. I do my best to ignore them as I attempt to walk the block and a half to the hotel, but halfway there, one of the girls puts her hand on my shoulder.

"Hey, you're the goalie, right?"

I shoot Popov a glare and flatten my lips into a stiff smile. "Yep. That's me."

Flashes start going off from the cars across the street and I quicken my pace as I hear the girls giggle behind me.

Once I'm finally inside the safety of my room, I breathe a sigh of relief. It's late, I'm tired, and now annoyed, so I strip down to my boxers and send Devin a goodnight text before I fall into unconsciousness.

I wake up with the sun and quickly get my shit together and head out the door. We're all taken to the plane where most of us fall back asleep. I read Devin's text when I first woke up and decided not to reply back until it was a decent hour.

As we're taxiing, I feel someone nudge my arm.

"Hm?" I murmur, opening my eyes and pulling out one of my earbuds.

"Dude, what the fuck happened last night?" Cory asks, shoving his phone at me.

"What? Nothing happened."

"That's not what everyone is saying."

"What?" I repeat, blinking my eyes a few times before I focus on his screen.

Photos of me, Popov, and the two girls from last night are splashed across internet gossip pages with headlines like, *Bobcats players, Jarrod Bivens and Andrei Popov score twice in one night,* and *Will Bivens let this puck (bunny) in or will she be just another girl left on ice?*

"This is bullshit," I say. "I wasn't even with them. And these headlines are dumb as fuck."

"These photos look pretty damning. They've zoomed in on just you and the one girl with her hand on you. Looks like y'all are laughing and having a good time together."

"I barely smiled."

Cory shrugs. "It's all about the angle, and she looks like she's having a blast."

"I bet they fucking called the photographers out there themselves."

"It wouldn't be the first time it's happened," he says.

I toss him his phone and shake my head. "Great."

He leans in and lowers his voice. "What do you think Devin will make of this?"

"I just gotta hope he'll listen to me."

"Listening is one thing, believing is another."

I DON'T TRY to get in touch with Devin, wanting to talk to him in person first, hoping beyond hope he hasn't gotten wind of the articles and fled to his place already.

When I pull up to my house, I don't see his car, but it could be in the garage, so I try not to panic. I unlock the door and walk in, dropping my bag to the floor.

"Dev?"

Nothing.

I walk through the lower level and don't see any sign of him.

"Devin?"

Walking up the stairs, my heart begins to thump rapidly, afraid he's left.

"Dev!"

He's not up here. He must've seen the photos and assumed the worst.

Dejected, I trot down the stairs, but halfway down, the click of a door closing hits my ears.

"Dev?"

He pops around the corner, gazing up at me. "Hey."

"Oh my god," I exclaim, running down the remaining steps and rushing toward him.

Devin chuckles before I slam into him, forcing a grunt from his throat. "God, I thought you were a hockey player, not a football player."

"You're here."

He wraps his arms around me. "Of course I am. I was out back."

I squeeze him tighter before kissing his lips. "I missed you."

"Yeah?" he questions. "How much?"

"A sad, pathetic amount."

He laughs. "Same."

I pull away. "I need to tell you something."

Devin turns his head slightly. "Uh-oh."

I shake my head. "Come here. Come sit with me."

With his hand in mine, I walk him to the couch and pull him onto my lap. He smiles, but it wavers.

"What's going on?"

"After the game last night, several of us went out to eat. It was at a restaurant maybe two blocks from the hotel. Anyway, Popov was getting the attention of some of the other guests and ended up bringing a couple girls into our private room. It annoyed everyone and we all started to split. I left alone, but Pop and the girls followed shortly after."

I pause and look at him watching me with patient curiosity. When I don't finish the story right away, he says, "Okay."

"Well, halfway to the hotel, one of the girls with him reached out for me and asked if I was the goalie." I shrug and roll my eyes. "She knew, but you know, whatever. Anyway, I turned and said yes, then kept on walking. There were photographers around and they snapped photos of us leaving the restaurant and walking to the hotel. The girls went inside with Popov, but I wasn't aware of that. I remained several steps ahead and went straight to my room."

Devin's brows dip in the center as he begins chewing on his lower lip. "Okay, so..."

"So, the photos are all over the internet today. There's articles and speculation. Stupid headlines and rumors."

He slowly nods his head like he's just trying to take it all in. "I see."

"I wasn't with them, Dev. Nothing happened. I don't

know those girls' names or anything. Besides answering that one question, I didn't speak to them at all, but it could look bad."

"Can I look it up?" he asks.

"Sure."

He gets up off my lap and finds his phone in the kitchen before coming back to sit next to me. I don't watch as he searches, but the silence seems to stretch forever.

"Um," he starts. "Not sure if you've seen this, because you didn't mention it."

"What?" I ask, my head snapping in his direction.

"The girl already gave a statement to CNE."

Celebrity News & Entertainment. It's the sewage of celebrity gossip.

"What did she say?"

"She's saying you four all had a fun night together. Paints a picture of you all being in the same hotel room and spending all night partying and getting to know each other."

"What the fuck?" I exclaim, typing into my own phone.

My night with Jarrod was a dream come true.

"She's a fucking liar. Her night with me? I was asleep fifteen minutes after getting in my room. I texted you and fell asleep!"

Devin nods. "I know."

Anger brews in my stomach, frustration bubbling in my veins. "You believe me?" I ask.

He gets closer and puts his arm around me. "I believe you."

"Fuck." It's said more out of relief than anger. I drop my phone and pull him into my lap, resting my head on his chest. "I'm sorry."

"You don't have to apologize to me."

"I do."

He doesn't question why, maybe he knows.

I've been saying I wanted to avoid the press talking about me and overshadowing my season, and yet, here I am in this stupid story which seems to be growing by the minute. It was just photos outside on the street and now she's making up stories. I'll have to call my agent and my attorney to keep this from growing into anything larger. Next thing I know she'll say she's pregnant.

After a few minutes, he runs his hands through my hair and lifts my head. "You could be a Stanley Cup winner in two days' time. Let's focus on that."

I smile at him. "What if we lose?"

"Then you'll have another game to play."

"What if we lose the rest of them?"

"You won't, but if you do, I will l—" He stops, swallowing his words. "I will still think you're the greatest player to ever grace the ice."

I snort. "That's because you like me."

"I'll think you're the hottest player on ice because I like you."

My lips draw up on the side. "I'm taking you to bed now."

"Yes, please."

Fifty-Three

DEVIN

Game five of the finals and the arena is thrumming with excitement. There's a sea of black, gold, and white jerseys filling every single seat. Everyone is hoping for a win for their home team, and I'm simply cheering for one person. I want this for him. I've never wanted something so much for someone else before, and I'd be heartbroken if they lost the series, simply because he'd be heartbroken.

Jarrod got me tickets right behind the glass and near the center, so I have a perfect view, especially when he skates in front of me, stopping to give me a smile.

My heart flutters in my chest. God, that man.

He does a double-take when he sees what I'm wearing. I watch as his eyes scan the white and gold jersey with the bobcat in the center. On the arms is the number thirty-one. I didn't tell him I'd be wearing his jersey tonight, and since he left before me, this is a surprise for him.

His eyes widen and he gets close to the glass. "That's my jersey." I barely hear him, but I know that's what he says.

I shake my head. "It's mine."

His eyes darken and he mouths, "You're mine."

Warmth floods my entire body, melting my insides and nearly turning me into a puddle. I bite my lip before I realize I shouldn't. I try not to look at him like I'm in love with him and want to break through the glass to fuck him right on the ice, but...

The first period ends without either team scoring. The second period starts with Dallas scoring one, but by the end, the Bobcats get one of their own in. In the third period, neither team is able to get a puck in until the last three minutes, but unfortunately the Bobcats' goal is immediately responded to with one from Dallas.

When nobody scores again, we go into overtime.

Dallas makes numerous attempts, but Jarrod is on his game and blocks every single one. However, the other goalie does the same, keeping us from scoring as well.

Halfway into the second overtime, a fight breaks out and everyone, including me, is screaming and/or banging on the glass.

I watch the clock tick down the remaining sixty seconds, my eyes moving back to the ice where I see our guys heading toward the opposing net. My stomach is in knots as I watch the puck being passed back and forth, getting closer and closer. Forty seconds left.

I don't pay attention to names or numbers on the jerseys. I just keep my eyes trained on the puck and watch as it gets smacked and slides across the ice. Closer. Closer. The goalie drops low and the puck goes between his legs before he's all the way down.

"Did it go in?" I say to myself.

The alarm blares, alerting everyone of a goal. I bang on the glass with the neighboring fans, screaming and yelling.

They won. They won.

"They fucking won!" I yell, turning to some random guy beside me who's just as excited.

The noise is deafening. People are yelling. Some are crying. There are flags being waved and signs being held up in the air. On the ice, helmets and sticks are scattered around and the guys are hugging and celebrating.

It feels like forever before the arena begins clearing out, but I spot some of the players' families on the ice with them, cameras in their faces as they're interviewed about how they feel about the win.

I'm watching with a wide grin as Jarrod and Cory have their arms wrapped around each other's shoulders, talking and laughing while one of their teammates is being interviewed.

Jarrod's eyes scan the room until they land on me. I moved from my original spot, but when he sees me, his grin widens and he heads toward me while waving me forward.

I make my way to the door that leads to the ice. There's so many people milling about, but when I get there, Jarrod's there reaching out to pull me through.

I can't keep the smile from my face. "I'm so happy for you."

He hugs me and I wrap my arms around him and close my eyes.

"I'm so glad you're here," he says.

"Me too."

"I told you I'd get you into a jersey."

I laugh. "I can't wait until you get me out of it."

He growls, giving me a final squeeze before releasing me.

Cory comes over. "We're next."

Jarrod nods.

"Congratulations," I tell him.

He smiles wide. "Thank you. Nice jersey."

My cheeks feel warm. "Thanks."

"I'll be back," Jarrod says. "Stay there."

I nod. "Okay."

They go only about ten feet away to talk to a woman with a microphone. She speaks with Cory first and Jarrod keeps looking my way, his white teeth on constant display as he smiles at me. I start worrying he's being too obvious, and I glance around to see if anyone is paying attention. Luckily everyone is pretty preoccupied.

When she addresses him, he gives her his full attention and I listen in.

"So, Jarrod, tell us how you're feeling at this moment. Last year ended not so great, but now you're a Stanley Cup champion. What are you thinking?"

He exhales, pure joy on his face. "God, so many things. I'm so grateful. I'm happy to be able to prove myself, to show everyone that even if you mess up, you can pick yourself up and keep going. I'm happy my teammates had my back and so thankful to be on the best team with the best players." He shakes his head, like he doesn't know what else to say. "I'm so happy. That's it. I'm just soaking it all in."

"I know you and Cory are pretty close off the ice, too, so I'm sure you guys will be celebrating later, right?" she asks with a laugh.

"Oh, we'll celebrate. I'm not sure when the celebrations are gonna stop, to be honest."

"Where are Mom and Dad?" She asks Jarrod the question like she knows them, and I guess it is her job to know details about the players.

"My mom had a medical procedure a few days ago," he says. "My dad is taking care of her, but I guarantee they're both at home watching through tears right now." He looks at the camera. "Stop crying. I'm gonna call soon."

The interviewer laughs. "Yes, make sure you call them. Do either of you have plans for the offseason?"

Cory talks into the mic first. "After we're done celebrating here for like, a week straight? What do you think?" he says to Jarrod with a laugh. "I'll probably head home and visit family for a while, and of course," he states, looking straight into the camera, "I'm going to Disneyland!"

Everyone laughs, and then Jarrod says, "Well, yeah, like he said, we're gonna be celebrating first and foremost, and then after that I'm hoping I can convince my guy to sneak off to a private island with me."

He looks at me then and winks and my jaw hits the floor. The interviewer follows his gaze briefly before saying, "Oh. Okay, well, I hope you two enjoy your time off."

I don't understand what's happening. My brain is short circuiting as I watch Jarrod make his way toward me, the camera following his movements. My eyes find Cory who looks nearly as shocked as I feel and then Jarrod is in front of me, trapping me between his arms and against the boards.

"So, what do you say?" he asks. "Wanna head back to Black Diamond with me? Or are you annoyed by me already?"

I grin, my lips stretching across my face as my heart

hammers against my ribs. "I think my brain is malfunctioning. What are you doing?"

He leans in close, our noses almost touching. "I'm loving you."

Before I can register the words, he presses his lips against mine in a quick but meaningful kiss. All around us people are gasping and then the sound of dozens of cameras taking photos fill the air.

When he pulls away, there's a lump in my throat and I can barely see his handsome face through my unshed tears.

"Are you concussed?" I ask through a laugh that sounds like a sob.

He laughs. "I'm so happy, Devin. I've never been happier than in this moment, and it's not just because of the win, but it's because I have you, too. I didn't want to celebrate without you. I didn't want to wait until we were alone to hug and kiss you. You're my everything."

My eyes bounce around, noticing people are still watching. "Well."

He grabs my hand. "Come on. Let's celebrate now and worry about the rest later."

I join him on the ice and he takes me toward some of his teammates and their families. They all clap each other on the back again, some of them taking notice of him holding my hand, but nobody questions it. He doesn't tell them anything, and he doesn't have to.

Fifty-Four

JARROD

I didn't plan it. I was caught up in this dreamlike moment, having just won the Stanley Cup after a heartbreaking loss last season, and I was extremely happy. Devin was there, watching me with joy on his face that mimicked what I felt. He was so happy for me. Everyone around me was celebrating with wives and girlfriends, sisters and dads. It makes sense to share such a huge thing with the people you love.

My mom underwent LASIK surgery, so it's not like she could be here, and my dad needed to be home with her. My sister is a very busy doctor and mother of two, but she was hoping we'd lose this one so she could try to be here for the next game. But Devin is here and that's all I need.

A few of the guys gave me questioning looks when I brought Devin over, but nothing was said. I'm sure that'll come, but right now, nobody cares about anything else other than the fact that we just won the Stanley Cup.

The team eventually makes it to the locker room so we can shower and get changed, do more press interviews, and finally be released. My phone is lit up with notifications, and I'm thinking I should've maybe given my family a heads up, but it's too late for that now. Gina knows, but she's probably fielding calls from Mom and Dad and doesn't know what to say. I'll have to respond later.

For the first several minutes in the locker room, everything is normal. Lots of hugs, celebratory cheers, champagne being popped and sprayed everywhere, and an all around good time. Coach comes in and gives us a speech.

Before he walks off, he looks at me, his stride never stopping. "Come speak with me."

My eyes slide over and find Cory watching. He shrugs and I get up and find Coach Bennett.

"Coach."

He turns around. "Is there anything you need to tell me?"

I put my hands in my pockets. "No, I don't think so."

His lips downturn. "Bivens."

I stare back at him. "Did any of the other guys make the announcement you're looking for?"

"There's never been a need for an announcement before."

"And there isn't one now."

He sighs, squeezing the bridge of his nose. "I'm not judging you, Bivens. But I need to know what to say to protect you."

"Plausible deniability, Coach," I say with a grin.

"I will have to speak with the team. We have to make sure there will be no discrimination or hate speech. I have to know what I'm dealing with here."

"I'm in love. Plain and simple."

He dips his chin once. "I'll be in touch."

I drop my head back and inhale deeply through my nose before I spin around and head back toward the guys. I suppose something needs to be said, but I refuse to give people details I've never been given. I don't think it's necessary for anyone to discuss their personal life with people who are in no way affected by it.

"Hey, hey, hey," I yell, my hands in the air to get everyone's attention. Once it quiets down, I say, "Some of you may be confused or wondering about who was out there with me, and there may be questions and rumors in the future, but I think all that needs to be said is I'm in love. I hope to be given the same respect I've always shown all of you and the relationships you have. I haven't changed. I've grown. I love you all and I can't wait to celebrate this win with you."

There's a bit of a silence before Cory starts clapping and runs up to wrap his arm around my neck. "I love you, man. And I will beat the shit out of any of you that has anything to say," he says, switching his tone up and pointing at the group. "This is our fucking goalie. We always protect the goalie. We protect each other."

I pat him on the back, thankful for his friendship. "I'm gonna get out of here. I'll see you guys at the parade."

"We're gonna party at my house in a couple days," Cory says.

I nod and grab my things. I have more celebrating to do.

IT'S REALLY LATE when Devin and I get home, but I'm still energized. The high of this night may never end.

Once inside, I grab him and push him against the door, tugging on the jersey. "I really like the way this looks on you."

He smiles. "I guess I can wear anything."

I bite my lip. "Definitely." I lean in and kiss him, my hands traveling under the jersey to touch his skin. "How narcissistic would it be to bend you over and fuck you while you wear this? Staring at my own name?"

He chuckles. "Pretty narcissistic, but I'm okay with that." He kisses me once more before saying, "Maybe we should talk first?"

"Definitely."

I take his hand and walk to the kitchen. "I'm gonna snack while we talk."

Devin laughs. "Of course."

I pull out a Tupperware dish of vegetable pasta bake that we had the other night and pop it into the microwave.

"I like how your snack is a full meal," he says with an amused grin as he hops onto the counter.

"Shush. I'll share with you."

"So, tonight was crazy. In more ways than one."

I lift my brows. "Mm. I'd say so."

"Do you want to talk about what happened? Besides the win, of course."

"Right. Besides that little thing," I say with a chuckle.

"No, it's incredible. Babe, I'm beyond excited for you. It was amazing to watch, and I'm so glad I was there to witness it."

I step between his legs, a smile on my face. "I didn't think you were downplaying it," I say, kissing him. "But we do have important things to discuss."

He nods, swallowing. "You came out. Very publicly."

"I didn't think of it as coming out. I didn't think about it at all, I guess. I saw you and wanted to kiss you. I wanted to be with you and hug you, and I didn't care if people were around. You are my entire world, Dev. And if there's gonna be stories out there about me, I want them to be true. I want them to be about you. I want everyone to know who I'm with and who I love."

He drapes his arms around my shoulders. "I love you so much. You know that, right? I've loved you for a long time."

I close my eyes and breathe. I've known. Or at the very least assumed. But it's nice to finally hear the words.

"I love you. I love you in a way I didn't think possible, in a way I've never experienced before. I think about you anytime we're not together. I want to share everything with you—the good, the bad, the hard, and easy. I want life with you, whatever it entails."

Devin smashes his mouth into mine, kissing me with all the love in his heart, and I do the same.

After several minutes, we break apart.

"You're the best thing to ever happen to me," he says. "Honestly, if I lost everything else in my life, I'd be happy as long as I still had you. You're what I've been seeking without even knowing. When I left you at the airport, I said, *thank you for reminding me what's important*. Do you remember?"

I nod. "Yeah. I wasn't sure what you meant."

"For a long time, especially when I was younger, I was living out of spite. I needed to prove my parents wrong while pissing them off in the process. Then I went through a phase of giving people what they wanted so they'd like me or spend time with me. I thought that was normal. I believed

376

ISABEL LUCERO

their lies when they were just with me for what I could provide. Right before I went to Black Diamond, I was struggling with figuring out what I wanted. From life. From relationships. From work. Then I ran into you." He smiles, squeezing my hands. "And everything was easy. I didn't care about work or previous hardships. I lived in the moment, for once. I fully enjoyed myself. And then once we got past you finding out about my work, and you didn't judge or push me away, and you still wanted me, I couldn't wrap my head around it. I struggled to believe someone could want me considering my job. You were perfect. You were the serenity I'd been looking for. It was never a place. It was you. I found my home in you."

His words sink deep into my heart, burrowing there to stay forever. "So, why didn't you want to stay in touch?"

"I was afraid. I wasn't in love with you then. I think my feelings were starting to grow at the end of the trip and it made me afraid to go any further. I was protecting myself. Everything I said was true. I thought it would prevent heartache. And I also hadn't convinced myself that you weren't embarrassed by my job. I had to do something else. I wanted to be someone you'd be proud of if we ever were together again. I wanted you to be able to say I was in a movie and be able to name it and have people know it."

I shake my head. "I don't care about that, babe. I don't. I've said it before but I need you to know, I don't care about the porn. I don't care if people know about the videos or the toys. You're a big fucking deal," I say with a laugh, squeezing his biceps. "My man? A fucking legend in the porn game? Damn straight." I pause. "Well, not really." Devin laughs. "And I get to be with you? *Pft.* People are gonna be jealous, and I don't care what they'll say. You have your own production company. You're a director. You acted in your first non-pornographic movie, and I know it's not gonna be the last one. I am proud of you."

"Really?"

"Yes. It was never that. I just wasn't ready. Maybe my thought process was misguided, but I was afraid. It wasn't until recently that I realized it's okay to be afraid, because I have you. I can handle the other shit, as long as I have you. And you're worth the fear. You're worth the questions and the stories. I shouldn't have kept you a secret for so long. I'm really sorry about that, but I promise that from now forward, I will love you in public as much as I do behind closed doors."

"You weren't misguided. We were both afraid for our own reasons."

"I love you." I hug him and kiss his neck. "I love you. I love you. I love you. I have to say it for all the times I didn't."

He wraps his legs around me. "I love you, I love you, I love you."

"Will you go back to Black Diamond with me?"

"Of course," he says immediately.

"We have some stuff to do around here in the next week, but after that we're free to leave."

"Think we can get one of our bungalows?"

"I hope so." My phone buzzes from my pocket. "Oh shit."

"What is it?" he asks.

"My family's been trying to get in touch with me. And my agent."

Devin looks nervous. "What do you think they'll say?"

I shrug and look at my phone. "My agent wants to

schedule a meeting, and Gina says I better call her in the morning. My parents went to sleep and she's going to bed now too, but I guess they were harassing her earlier. I'll deal with that in the morning." I pull him off the counter, holding him in my arms. "And I'll deal with you now."

"What about your food?"

"You're more important than food."

"Wow. That's big coming from you."

I playfully bite into his neck as I walk through the kitchen. "Shush or I'll be forced to eat you."

"Mm."

Fifty-Five

DEVIN

I n the bedroom, Jarrod sets me down on the bed and deliberately takes his time removing my shoes, socks, and pants. He teases my cock through my underwear before removing them completely. He doesn't touch the jersey.

He undresses, his eyes hardly ever leaving mine, and then he crawls between my legs. I part them wider to allow him more space and he continues up my body until he's planting kisses on my lips, cheeks, and chin.

Without words, he travels back down, taking my dick into his mouth. He's gentle and slow, enjoying every second while driving me crazy.

"Turn over," he says huskily.

I bite my lip and do as he says, pushing my ass in the air. His hands grab my cheeks and spreads them, and then his tongue glides over my hole.

"Oh god," I moan into the covers.

He buries his face in my ass, licking and penetrating me

with his tongue. Jarrod moans and grunts like it's being done to him, and I truly can't wait to repay the favor.

After a while, he moves away to grab lube, and then his slick fingers are pushing into me as he strokes my heavy cock that sways below me.

"God, baby. Your ass is so perfect."

I moan, thrusting my ass back at him, fucking myself on his fingers.

"You ready for me?" he asks.

"Yes. Please."

I hear the lid to the lube opening again before the squishy sound of him stroking himself with the liquid before he pushes his tip into my hole. Once he's all the way in, he shoves the jersey up higher and holds my waist while he thrusts.

"Fuck, you feel so good," he moans.

"It's yours," I tell him. "I'm yours."

"Forever?" he asks with a deep thrust.

"Ah! Yes. Forever."

He moves in and out of me at the perfect pace and angle, hitting my prostate. I look down and notice my cock leaking onto the covers.

"Baby, that's it. It's so good."

"You like that?"

"Yes! My cock is dripping all over the place."

"Mmm. I want it in my mouth. Don't come yet."

"But..."

He pulls out, spreading me apart. "Fuck," he grunts, dragging the word out. "The way your ass gapes for me." He dips his cockhead back in before pulling away again.

"Jarrod," I beg.

"I want to fill your ass with my cum."

"Yes, do it," I cry.

"And then I want to watch it drip out of you."

"Fuck." I arch my back even more.

He keeps sliding inside me with long, slow strokes, grunting and moaning with each one. "God, this is incredible."

My fists clutch the covers with each forceful push in, my cock throbbing between my legs.

Jarrod pulls out and pushes my back down until my face is pressed against the mattress, my ass in the air. Stroking himself with one hand, he pushes the fingers of his other hand into my ass, making sure I stay full. After a minute, he pulls out and squeezes the flesh of my cheek before coming down with a smack.

"Oh god," I cry out in surprise.

Jarrod's slowly becoming more aggressive with me, and I love it. I love that he's growing more comfortable in our sex life.

The bed shifts and I feel his tip at my entrance. "I'm gonna come inside you. I'm gonna watch it drip into your hole."

"Oh yes. Fuck yes. Come inside me."

Jarrod strokes himself, the sounds of his movements and breathing letting me know he's getting closer.

"Oh god," he roars. "Oh god, oh fuck."

The warmth of his cum lands on the top of my ass before he adjusts his aim and the rest drips down my crease and inside me.

"Yes," I say, drawing the word out.

"Fuck," he says with a quivering breath. "Oh my god." His tone is reverential.

With his hand on my hip he guides me back, slowly pushing inside me once more. When he pulls out, I feel his cum drip out of me, and then his finger wipes it up and pushes it back inside before he slides inside me again.

He revels in the visual and sensation, continuing to make appreciative noises and giving me words of praise while I mewl and whimper, desperate to come.

"Turn over, baby," he says, giving my ass another smack.

I move quickly to get to my back, instantly reaching for my cock. He stops the movement and places my hand back at my side before grabbing it himself.

"So messy."

I nod frantically. "Yes. I'm a mess for you."

His teeth graze across his bottom lip. "I guess I should clean you up," he says, licking his lips.

"Yes, please."

Jarrod opens his mouth and takes me across his tongue, swirling it around my shaft to taste my arousal. My eyes roll back before I squeeze them close, my toes curling as he sucks me deep, his hand gently massaging my balls.

I plant my feet on the mattress and start thrusting my hips, fucking his mouth in a frenzied attempt to come faster.

"Mm," he moans around my length.

In a quick movement, he's rolling onto his back, pulling me on top of him. After just some minor adjusting, I'm straddling his chest, my knees above his shoulders as I thrust my cock between his lips.

"Oh god," I moan. "Yeah."

Jarrod gags and I pull away, but he brings me back,

keeping his hands on my waist and holding the jersey out of the way. I continue my movements, making sure I give him sporadic moments to suck in a breath of air, while also trying not to choke him. With a hand on the headboard, my hips undulate, loving the way he slurps and sucks me.

"I'm gonna come, baby," I say. "I'm gonna come down your throat."

Jarrod attempts to nod, moaning his approval. It's not long before my orgasm hits, pouring out of me and into his mouth.

"Fuck, fuck, oh fuck," I chant, squeezing the headboard between my fingers as my body convulses.

As soon as I can manage to move, I climb off his face and flop down next to him, attempting to catch my breath.

"Holy shit," he exclaims, wiping his lips. "It's been too long since you've fucked my mouth like that."

"Kind of different from a dildo, huh?" I ask with a chuckle.

He playfully elbows me. "Slightly."

I turn to face him and run my fingers through his hair. "I love you."

"I love *you*."

Fifty-Six

JARROD

"Y ou ready?" Devin asks.

"Yep. I think," I say, dialing my mom's number.

Devin remains on the couch in the living room as I begin pacing around the entire lower level of the house. Mom answers on the third ring.

"Jarrod." She says my name like she's out of breath. "What is going on?"

"Hey, Mom," I say, giving Devin a nervous smile. "Did you watch the game last night?"

Devin twists his lips at me and I shrug.

"Honey, of course we were watching, and we're so happy for you, but what...who...was that the kid that was here for Christmas? Are you? What's going on? Hold on, let me get your father."

I walk to the front door before making my way behind the couch, letting my fingers trail across Devin's neck before I'm heading toward the kitchen.

"Okay, we're both on the line. Now, what is going on?"

With a deep inhale, I find myself heading back to the living room. "Well, I'm sorry I didn't say anything before. I wasn't really planning on doing that."

"Are you...gay?" Mom asks quietly.

"No." I stop walking and turn to face Devin who's watching me with worry on his face. "I'm just in love with a man."

Devin smiles just as Mom gasps. "In love?"

"Son, I think we're just a little caught off guard here," my dad says. "You've never mentioned this or had any other relationships...with men."

"That's right. I've never had a relationship with a man. Not until Devin."

"So, what does this mean?" Mom questions.

"It means just that, Mom. I'm in love with a man I'm in a relationship with. If you need a label, then you can call me bisexual. I just like to think that I've found the person I'm supposed to be with."

I can hear my mom sniffle on the other end of the phone. "Were you together on Christmas?" Mom asks.

"No. Not really. We started a relationship last June, and then we broke it off and went our separate ways. It's complicated, Mom, but we're together now. Officially."

"And publicly. Are you ready for that?" Dad asks.

"Yes."

Mom sniffles again. "Can you invite him over again? I'd like to get to know him as your boyfriend and not as a long lost friend."

My heart swells and tears burn my eyes. "Yes. Of course. We'd love that."

"We love you, J," my dad says. "Always. No matter what."

A tear slips down my cheek. "Thank you. I love you guys, too. I'm sorry I didn't tell you earlier. I was afraid and—"

"It's okay," Mom says softly. "We love you, too. Call us later and we'll plan a get together."

"Okay."

Once the call ends, I take a deep breath and Devin gets up and heads over. "So? All good?"

I pull him into a hug. "All good."

He breathes a sigh of relief as well. "Good."

"They want to meet you as my boyfriend."

Dev pulls back, wide eyes on me. "Now I need to bring flowers, right? What does your dad like? Liquor?"

I laugh. "Don't start freaking out. They already like you."

"Yeah, but now they know I'm fucking you."

With my arm around his shoulder, I walk toward the couch. "Mm. Are you?"

He hits me. "You know what I mean."

"It's going to be fine." I drop to the couch and pull him with me. "We have a busy few weeks ahead of us. Do you need to go home at all?"

"I should. At least to check on things. I can do most of my work from anywhere. I have people in place to handle day-to-day tasks."

"Okay. We'll figure it out."

"Okay."

And we do. We go to Cory's for a team party and nobody acts any differently around me. They meet Devin and everyone gets along. Some of the guys make a point to get to know a little more about him than his name, and then we drink and celebrate until nearly four in the morning.

We had the celebratory parade and since there's more media around, there were definitely questions being thrown at me, but I was still able to enjoy myself with my teammates.

At one point, Devin went home to take care of his house and get things in order since he'll be with me for a while, and while I was out with Cory, trying to get something to eat, we were bombarded with cameramen both taking photos and recording videos.

"Jarrod, where's the new boyfriend? Are you two serious? Have you always been gay? How do you feel about him being a porn star? Are you jealous? Cory, how do you feel about him being on the team? Do you think it's gonna change anything?"

We ignored them and even though they attempted to follow us, Cory was able to get away and get us home safe.

I've been trying to stay inside a little more, and my agent is suggesting I give some sort of statement or interview, but I'm not trying to make my relationship a side-show. I don't understand why people need to hear from me. They know the facts. The internet sleuths have discovered exactly who Devin is and what he does and who his parents are. They're making up stories and coming up with theories on how we met, but I also read an article where someone actually knew we went to school together, and it freaks me out how people find out this information.

Once I have nothing else to do in the immediate future, I get in the car and drive down to my parents. Devin's going to meet me here so we can have dinner together, and then we're going to head back to our piece of serenity in Black Diamond.

I can't wait to be back with him. Everything is easier to deal with when we're together, and now I have a very important question to ask him.

Fifty-Seven

DEVIN

The nerves I feel driving up to his parents' house are tenfold what I felt last time I was here. I fear tension and awkwardness, and maybe even uncomfortable questions. At the same time, I'm happy that this is happening.

I've recently talked to my own parents, who actually reached out to me once news spread of mine and Jarrod's relationship. To my surprise, they didn't bring up my job, but instead questioned if I was doing okay and wished the best for Jarrod and me.

I ended up telling them about the movie I filmed, which was met with excitement, followed shortly by saying they could help me get another opportunity. I explained that I only want this if I do it on my own, and I think they've finally accepted that. I will always be a porn star. That'll never change, but I can try to crossover and reach new audiences.

At some point, maybe after Black Diamond, I'll take Jarrod to meet them, but right now I have to focus on his parents.

I pull the flower bouquet and box of rare cigars from my backseat and approach the front door. Jarrod pops out with a smile on his face, laughing when he sees the gifts. "You didn't."

"What? Leave me alone."

He kisses my cheek. "I love you. They're fine. I promise."

I take a breath and walk inside, following Jarrod to the sitting room. His parents both stand up when I walk in, a smile on his mom's face and easy contentment on his dad's.

"Mom, Dad," Jarrod says, "This is my *boyfriend*, Devin."

His mom comes forward first, tears brimming in her eyes already. She hugs me and I awkwardly try to return it while holding flowers and cigars. Luckily, Jarrod takes them from me with a chuckle while I hug his mom.

"I wish I would've known before. I wouldn't have brought up his exes or potential girlfriends."

She pulls away and I chuckle. "Oh. It's fine, we weren't..." I look at Jarrod. "Well, it was complicated."

She nods. "I heard. Well, I'm so glad you're here."

"Mom, Devin brought these for you."

"Oh," she says, her hands flying up. "Thank you. These are gorgeous."

"And Jarrod mentioned you like having a cigar from time to time, so I found this for you," I say, gesturing to the box in Jarrod's hands.

Mr. Bivens steps up and takes the box, looking it over. "Oh wow. These are quite nice. Thank you, Devin. You didn't have to." He ends it with a hand on my shoulder.

"Dinner will be ready soon," Mrs. Bivens says on her way out the door. "I'm going to put these in water." She jerks her head at her husband, telling him to follow her.

"See?" Jarrod says once they're gone. "It's fine."

I blow out a breath. "Yeah."

Dinner goes better than I could've imagined. Both of his parents are not only comfortable around us, but seem genuinely happy for their son. We talk about Jarrod winning the Stanley Cup, a bit more about our first trip to Black Diamond and all the PG stuff we did, and how we're going back soon. I told them about the movie I filmed and how I hope to do more. Apparently, Jarrod kept the details of my main job pretty vague when speaking with them before, saying only that I work in the adult film industry. I think that says enough, but nobody wants to talk to their parents about porn in any regard. They're going to get word via the internet and TV, if they haven't already, but they never questioned me about it or made me feel like they judged me. His mom even extended another Christmas invitation.

After another hug, we left and drove to my house, and now I'm showing him around for the first time.

"This is a really nice place," he says, looking at the tiled fireplace against the black accent wall.

"I like it," I say. "It was my first big purchase. I lived in a couple of apartments before buying this."

He goes to the bifold doors and looks into the backyard. "Nice pool too."

"Yeah, I have the same doors in the dining room that open right to it."

Jarrod's eyes take in the room again. "It's very you."

"What's that mean?" I ask with a grin.

"Sleek and elegant."

"I'm sleek?" My grin grows.

He nods. "Definitely." His gaze travels around again. "It has everything you need. I almost hate to ask you to leave it."

My heart squeezes and I sit in the corner of the sectional. "Almost?"

Jarrod moves closer, coming to sit in front of me. "I can't leave San José, but I also can't live six hours away from you. I know it's a big step. I know I brought it up before and you seemed hesitant."

"I was only hesitant because of where we were at that time."

"And now?" he asks, hope in his tone.

"Now, you're out and people know we're together, and we've finally confessed our feelings."

His lips quirk. "*Finally*. When did you know you loved me?"

I chew on my bottom lip. "I knew and accepted it after seeing you in Vegas. I had spent months away from you, and it didn't help quell the pain. It intensified after our brief encounter. My heart wanted to stay with you and I ripped it in half when I walked away."

"I knew during our separation, too," he says. "At Christmas, I was in dreamland. I wanted to believe I could convince you to be with me, even though I knew I wasn't ready to give you what you deserved. I've never felt heartache like I did that night." He looks down, running his fingers over my knee. "I'm so grateful that you waited for me."

I cover his hand and squeeze it. "I love you."

His lips curl up. "I love you, too. I know my house isn't as nice as this one—"

"It's bigger," I offer.

"But we can buy a new one. Our own. Together."

My eyes bulge. "You want to buy a house with me?"

"Well, we can rent first if you want." His cheeks burn red. "But I want us to live together. I don't know how many more hockey years I have in me, but there's gonna be at least a few more, and while I'm still playing I'm going to be gone a lot, and I want every second I'm home to be with you."

I stare at him for a while, thinking everything over. "Are you sure? The media is still going crazy over us being together. What if it gets to be too much?"

"It won't," he says quickly. "I'm done putting other people first. I'll never forgive myself for putting you on the back burner. You bring me happiness, Dev. You *are* my happiness. You come first and I no longer care what people have to say or think. It's me and you against the world."

My eyes burn with unshed tears. "Okay."

His face lights up. "Okay?"

I nod. "Okay. We'll find a place together. I can't imagine being without you again. I fell hard and I fell fast, but this feels right. It feels worthy of big steps."

He lunges forward and snatches me into him, pulling me on top of his body as he lies back on the couch. "This is going to be amazing."

Fifty-Eight

JARROD

"Welcome to Black Diamond Resort and Spa. Is this your first time?" the woman at the counter asks us.

We share a look. "No, we've been here before."

"I see you've requested bungalows six or eight, and I'm happy to let you know that eight is available, so your bags have been delivered already. Matteo will drive you down to the pier. Enjoy your stay with us."

"We will," I say.

"Thanks," Devin adds as we walk toward our golf cart.

Once inside, we look around the room before coming face-to-face with matching smiles.

"We made it back," I say.

"We did." He pushes up on his toes to meet my lips in a kiss. "What do we do first?"

"Eat."

He laughs. "Of course. Let's freshen up and then head out. Wanna visit our good friend, Holden later?"

I chuckle. "I won't mind seeing him, but he better not try to flirt with you."

"Can you blame him?"

I spank his ass as he walks to the bathroom, and then once he's done, I take my bag with me and change my clothes.

Twenty minutes later, we're sitting down at Bamboo Terrace with a view of the water.

"Should we tell them it's our anniversary? Maybe we'll get champagne and cookies again."

"Technically, it's not far from the truth," he says. "But when would our official anniversary be? The night of the Stanley Cup win?"

I think about it for a little bit. "I want it to be when we first had sex here. From that moment on I was yours. There was never a chance for anyone else."

"Am I that good?" he teases, before putting his hand on my thigh and squeezing. "I agree. We started here. Even with the breaks and distance, you had my heart."

"Happy anniversary."

"Happy anniversary," he replies with a smile.

"Oh, you're celebrating an anniversary?" the waitress asks when she stops at the table. "Congratulations. We'll send over some goodies."

I nudge Devin in the side. "Thank you."

We place our order and when it's delivered, so is a bottle of champagne. At the end of the meal, we get a large plate with a piece of five-layer chocolate cake. Written across the top of the plate in syrup is *Happy Anniversary.*

"Well, this might be my favorite dessert," Devin says, digging into the cake with his fork. I watch as he puts the food in his mouth, moaning around the chocolate. His eyes slide to my face. "What?"

With my cheek resting on my fist, I just smile back at him. "Nothing. I just love looking at you."

He finishes swallowing and gets another forkful, bringing it to my mouth. "It's good, right?"

I finish chewing and nod. "It is."

"Why are you still smiling?" he asks with his own grin.

"Thinking about some stuff."

"What kind of stuff?" he asks, digging into the cake again.

"How I'm hoping you'll fuck me tonight."

My stomach flips at the words, but Devin's hand freezes halfway to his mouth, his head slowly turning to face me. "Oh." He puts the fork down, rubbing his hands over his pants. "You're ready?"

"Remember that plug you bought me?" I ask. He nods and I lean forward, my lips at his ears. "I'm wearing it now."

"Fuck."

My tongue licks at his earlobe before I gently bite on it. "That's the hope."

"At dinner?" he questions, bringing his chin close to his chest as he gives me a flirty look. "Such a slut."

I bite into my bottom lip. "So, treat me like one."

"Oh god." He looks around, fidgeting in his seat as he fans himself. "I'm getting hot."

With my arm around his shoulder I pull him into me, my mouth at his ear again. "I'm ready to feel you inside me. I want it. I want you. In all the ways I can have you."

Devin's green eyes find mine. "Then I'm going to take you."

"LIE DOWN. I'm in charge now."

My teeth sink into my lip as I watch him undress. "Yes, sir."

His eyes flash to mine, darkening. He strips to his boxer-briefs before digging into his bag and bringing back some lube and other small toys. My pulse spikes when I see everything laid out next to me. It's not like I haven't been experimenting. Devin explained everything I should start with and try before we got to this point, and I have. But having Dev be in charge of the toys sends a thrill up my spine.

He removes my clothes from the waist down, instructing me to remove my shirt and to lie back down.

Naked, with the plug in my ass, I thrum with anticipation.

Devin crawls over my body, kissing my neck. "I've been dying to slip inside you," he whispers. "To fuck you. Own you."

I shiver. "Yes. Yes, please."

He slowly kisses across my chest, sucking a nipple into his mouth. "Keep begging."

"Devin," I plead, thrusting my hips. "I want you inside me."

"Hmm."

He moves lower, kissing over my abs and across my right hip. I shift, wanting him to take me in his mouth.

"Please."

"You really are a slut, aren't you? Already so desperate."

I nod. "Please taste me."

He barely lets his tongue graze the underside of my head. "Like that?"

"More," I grunt.

Devin flattens his tongue and licks up the shaft. "Like that?"

"Fuck. Dev, please. Take me to your throat." His fingers dance over my balls before finding the base of the plug. "Oh shit."

"Mm." He gently tugs on it, pulling it out a fraction of an inch before pushing it back in. "Spread your legs wider for me."

I listen and he grabs the lube and pours some on me before he starts to pull it out. "Fuck, baby. Your hole looks so good."

My eyes close as I moan. "I want more."

"You're gonna get it." He discards the plug and grabs something longer. "This is a little bigger, but not too thick. It'll vibrate inside you."

"Oh shit."

He looks amused as he covers it with lube and slides it inside me, turning it on. "You're gonna love it."

I tighten my grip on the covers as I suck in a gasp. "Holy god."

Devin chuckles before wrapping his lips around my cock. He uses his insane mouth skills while remembering to reach down and move the vibrator inside me from time to time. My toes curl and my body ignites with each sensation.

After several minutes, he moves away, grabbing the vibe from my ass and turning it off before removing it. Coating his fingers, he begins slipping them in my ass, one at a time until he's at three.

"God, you're gonna feel so good."

"I don't know how long I'm gonna last," I admit, squeezing my eyes closed. "I'm already on the edge."

"You already ready to bust for me, baby?"

"Fuck yes."

He removes his finger. "Not yet."

On his knees, he pours lube on his shaft, covering his length before he places his left hand on my thigh, pushing it up higher and farther to the side. His tip pushes at my hole and I gasp, tightening my body.

"Relax," he says in a soft voice. "Breathe."

I take a couple deep inhales through my nose. "Okay."

He pushes in a little more, breaching the ring of muscle. A slight burning sensation has me hissing, but then he goes in deeper.

"Oh fuck," I cry.

Devin releases a sexy moan. "Oh god. Baby, you're doing so good."

Every inch is glorious torture. I've never understood how pain could feel good at the same time, but I get it now.

"Dev," I say on a breath. "You're so big. Holy fuck."

"You're taking it so good. God, the way your ass is stretched around me," he says, pulling out slightly. "Fuck."

He pours more lube on his shaft before pushing in again, sliding in a bit easier. We both groan together, and as he buries himself deep, I clench around him.

"God, your hole is so needy."

I reach for him and he drops lower, bringing us chest to chest as his hips move.

"I feel so full."

"I'm deep inside you, baby. "

I whimper, clinging to him tightly. "Ah. Feels incredible."

The more he moves, the more my body relaxes. My cock is so hard between us, his stomach giving it just enough friction to drive me crazy.

"Were you waiting for this dick all day?"

I nod. "Yes."

"Do you want more of this? More switching?"

"Please," I beg. "Devin. Oh my god."

He moves a little faster, his strokes deeper. "Tell me how much you love it."

"I love it so much," I say quickly. "I love the way you stretch and fill me."

"Mm," he moans. "Such a filthy fucking boy. I love it. I love how much you want me."

"I do. I want you so much."

"You want my come?"

He eases back, holding my knees apart as he thrusts inside me.

"Yes. Please."

"You want it deep inside you?"

"Yes."

"Ask nicely."

"Please, Dev. Please come inside me."

A low rumble in his chest sends goosebumps down my arms. "Good. Fucking. Boy." He punctuates each word with a thrust. "But first." He stops.

"Dev," I whine.

"You'll enjoy this. Because you're such a slut for me."

He leans over and grabs something I didn't notice earlier.

It's the masturbator sleeve made from his mouth. He pours some lube inside it and then puts a little on my dick, giving it a couple strokes.

"Now you can fuck my mouth while I fuck your ass."

Devin brings the masturbator down over my length, moving it slowly up and down while keeping the same pace inside me.

"Holy shit, Dev," I say through quivering breaths. "Oh my god. This is fucking mind-blowing."

"Take it," he says, "Fuck it while I fuck you. Make yourself come."

I reach down and take it in my hands, the hard exterior easy to grasp while the soft inside grips my cock.

My body buzzes with electricity, and with every pump of his hips, I feel like I might ignite. He pushes my legs up higher and his cock begins knocking at my prostate. Fireworks go off behind my eyes when I squeeze them shut, euphoria flooding my veins.

"Dev." His name is a hoarse whisper on my lips.

He somehow manages to go even deeper, his pubic bone grinding against my cheeks as he buries himself to the hilt, rotating in just the way to get his cock to continuously rub against my prostate.

"Come for me, baby," he grunts. "I want to see the mess you make."

"Oh fuck," I cry, my muscles aching as I stroke faster. "Fuck, fuck, fuck. I'm coming. Oh god, I'm..."

The words die on my lips, replaced by an animalistic roar as I pull the masturbator from my cock and toss it aside. My cum shoots out of me and lands on my chest and stomach in thick ropes. I reach for my shaft with my right hand, squeezing the length as more cum drips from my slit.

"Holy shit. Oh my fuck..." I suck in a breath, the sound shaky. "God. Please."

I don't even know what I'm saying. I'm done for. My brain has imploded, my heart is working overtime to keep me alive, and my lungs expand with each deep breath I pull in.

"God, you're so fucking sexy," Devin says, his hips working slowly. "Your ass is clenching around me so tight, baby."

I gaze up at him, cum dripping down my body as sweat glistens across my skin. I'm a mess, but he looks at me like I'm the most beautiful thing he's ever seen.

"I wanna feel it," I say, my voice rough like gravel. "Come inside me, Dev. Give me every drop."

"Fuck," he curses, moving faster, his fingers bruising my skin with his grip. After another minute, his full lips part and his eyes droop. "I'm about to come."

"Mm. Yes."

His cock twitches in my ass, and then he falls over me, his hands on either side of my body as he thrusts. He yells, stilling deep inside me as I feel him pulse.

"Oh god," I moan, wrapping my arms around his back. "Yes, baby. I fucking love it."

He moves some more, giving me a few more thrusts before he pushes in deep and stops, his cock twitching some more.

"Baby." He breathes heavily. "Holy shit. That." Another inhale. "Was intense. Oh." His body jerks before he has a full-body shiver.

I clench around him and we both groan.

After a minute, he pushes up and slowly pulls out.

I wince, hissing between my teeth.

"You okay?" he asks.

"Oh yeah," I say on a breath. "Just can't walk. Or move. Can barely breathe."

He chuckles and gets up, disappearing into the bathroom for a minute before returning with a warm rag. He wipes up the cum from my body before folding the cloth and gently placing it between my cheeks.

"While you use the bathroom, I'm going to run a bath."

It takes a minute before I gather the courage to get up, everything sore and sensitive. I know I'm walking funny as I make my way to the toilet, but Devin doesn't say anything.

When I come back out, Devin's already inside the tub, the water still running, and bubbles taking over. The soaking jacuzzi tub is set just inside a doorway that leads out to the back deck, and he's opened the door so we can look out at the water.

"Well, this is nice," I say, my foot cutting through the bubbles. "It's a good thing this is oversized."

Once I'm inside, Devin stands, bubbles coating his body, and then he sits between my legs, his back to my chest. "It's the perfect fit."

I put an arm over his shoulder, gently wrapping it across his collarbone. Leaning down, I kiss his cheek. "We're a perfect fit."

He angles his head and looks at me. "I love you so much."

"I love you. Always."

We settle in and look out over the turquoise water. The sun is disappearing below the horizon, painting the sky a beautiful mixture of orange, pink, and purple. And while this day is coming to an end, I smile, because I know I have many more to look forward to with the love of my life.

Epilogue

DEVIN

Two years later

June 8th has become our official anniversary date. It's fitting that the numbers correlate with our bungalow numbers from that very first trip. Six and eight. We've been back to Black Diamond on that date every year since our first chance encounter. The length of stay varies, depending on what we have going on, but we always make it back to where it all started.

In the last two years, Jarrod has won another Stanley Cup with his team, and I've grown my production company even more. Besides our own Straitlay subscription-based website, we've acquired two more porn sites, and opened up a sex shop in LA.

Absolution came out and was a hit at Cannes, gaining speed and growing to a level none of us anticipated. The movie was nominated for a few awards, and both Elias and myself got rave reviews for our acting and were nominated by the Los Angeles Film Critics Association for best lead and supporting performances.

That opened more doors for me, so I've since filmed two more, one being mid-budget like *Absolution*, and the other was more of a blockbuster. It was directed by legendary director, Richard Davies, and already has Hollywood abuzz. It doesn't come out for another six months, but it's very exciting.

My parents are overjoyed, but I continue to have to remind them that their connections aren't needed nor wanted. They will always have to deal with the fact that I chose to do porn, but they can't deny that I turned it into a very successful empire. Something they didn't think possible. While I'm branching out into mainstream movies, I still love the adult industry. I'm heavily involved in it in many aspects. While I don't star in triple X movies, I continue to do photos and videos for OnlyFans. Jarrod likes being the man behind the camera and isn't at all bothered that people continue to want to watch me. I think he likes it, knowing that I belong to him.

In repairing my relationship with my parents, they've been able to form one with Jarrod. They liked him immediately, and now they've grown to love him.

Jarrod's parents feel like second parents to me. They're warm and loving people. I've gotten really close with his sister, and we sometimes text without even involving Jarrod in the conversation. Though he pretends to pout about losing his sister to his fiancé or his fiancé to his sister, I've watched him smile when she and I are talking. He loves that we're all so close.

It took seven months to sell my house, but while it was

on the market, Jarrod and I spent a lot of time looking for the perfect place for us. We found a contemporary masterpiece in Los Altos with fifteen foot ceilings that manage to make Jarrod look small. While it's a modern house with some opulent design choices, it feels cozy and warm. Jarrod and I brought some of our own furniture into the new home while also buying new pieces to fill up all the rooms.

It's our first time living with a partner, and while I was sort of afraid it would be a big adjustment, it wasn't. We get along so well, and we're the best of friends. We have so much fun together, even if we're just lounging on the couch and laughing at a TV show. I've never been so comfortable. Living with him has been a dream.

The media frenzy lasted a little while, especially when the new season started back up, but toward the end, it was old news. We still get people taking photos of us, but it's something that rolls off our backs. It's not like they're hurling insults at us, they just want to know how we're doing and what's the next step.

Which means, when we land back in California, I can expect a spike in the news again, because this year, it's not just us at Black Diamond. Our closest friends and family are joining us, and with a guest list of about thirty, Jarrod and I will get married on the beach.

He asked me to marry him seven months ago. It was November 15th and we had both just come back into town. He had been in New York, and I was filming in Vancouver, but he had two days off and then a home game, and I was coming back to spend some time with him before I was due in Canada a few days later.

We enjoyed a nice meal we ordered from one of our

favorite restaurants, then poured some wine and sat in front of the TV to watch a movie. Toward the end, he got up to get more wine and came back with a ring.

"I have a secret. I could live in this world without anything else as long as I have your arms to lie in at night. I want to get lost in your eyes for the rest of my days, because I know I'll always find love in their depths. I'm not sure how I lived without you. You've taught me so much about myself and what it is to truly be in love. I refuse to be without you, Devin. Please marry me. Please spend your life with me. I promise to try to be the best husband— to give you everything you deserve."

I still remember his speech to this day. I was so caught off guard. I probably stared at him for thirty seconds with my mouth agape. I told him to give me a second, and then I disappeared into the room and came back with a ring.

"I have a secret too. I was going to propose tomorrow."

It was his turn to be frozen in silence, staring at the box in my hand.

"My life is only whole because of you. My heart knows the beat of yours, and though I could live without you, I don't want to. I choose not to and will choose you every day for the rest of my life. To be without you, would be to live a partial life. To be partially happy. To be incomplete. And I want to be whole. I choose unbridled and unapologetic joy for us from now until we grow old together. I want you to be my forever."

With tears in both our eyes, we exchanged rings and made love on the rug in the middle of the living room. It will remain one of my favorite nights.

Today will likely show it up.

Going the traditional route, Jarrod and I spent last night apart. It was not something either one of us wanted to do, but we appeased our parents by agreeing. However, as the clock ticks down, my anticipation rises. It is a little more exciting this way, and I can't wait to see him.

"Are you doing okay?" my mom asks as I stare at myself in the mirror.

I nod, smiling at her in the reflection. Her brown hair is half pulled back, and her skin, thanks to a little cosmetic work, does not reflect her age. She's stunning. She's always been gorgeous. Her bronze skin shines, and her teal-colored dress looks perfect on her.

"I'm perfect. Happy. Excited. Nervous, but I don't know why. I know he's gonna be there."

Mom laughs with me. "It's all normal. I'm so happy for you, baby."

I turn around and give her a hug. "I'm glad you and Dad are here."

"We've had a rough road, us three, but I'm thankful you've given us a chance to be in your life again."

"Of course," I say, pulling away. "Don't start crying yet."

She sniffles and grabs a Kleenex. Dad walks in wearing his pressed khakis and light blue button up. We're going with appropriate beach attire, so no need for suits and gowns.

"Almost time," he says, clapping his hands together once. "You look great, son."

"Thanks, Dad."

With another look in the mirror, I check my appearance again. I have an embroidered, white, chiffon button up. Jarrod was a big fan of the black one I wore our first time here, so I had that in mind when I got this one. The embroidery is floral, done in white thread, which I thought fitting for the wedding, and it's not extremely see-through, so it won't be tacky. That paired with my beige pants makes the perfect beach wedding outfit, I think.

We leave the bungalow and get driven to a private section of the beach where I can see our guests already sitting in their chairs facing the floral arch.

Jarrod and I have our own canopy tents with curtains hanging around all sides so we don't see each other until we're supposed to.

"All right. We're gonna go grab our seats," Mom says. "See you soon."

I nod, too nervous to say words. My dad claps me on the shoulder and gives me a smile.

A couple minutes later, Gina walks in wearing a dress that matches the water. "Oh my god, you look amazing," she squeals, wrapping her arms around me.

"Thank you. You do too. How's Jarrod?"

She grins. "Can't stop pacing. He's like a caged tiger, but he's excited."

I exhale and smile. "Okay. Good."

"I'm gonna go sit. Good luck," she says, squeezing me again. "I love you."

"Love you."

At exactly four-thirty, I leave the canopy and walk along the beach, headed toward my future. The sun will set an hour from now, but we'll have enough sunlight to get through the ceremony before we're ready to party all evening.

I see Jarrod walking toward me, both of us getting closer to the arch where our officiant awaits. His smile is beaming, and I have to force myself to keep from running and jumping into his arms.

He's wearing white pants and a tan linen shirt, and he looks good enough to eat. Music plays softly from a speaker nearby, stopping when we get to our spots.

We immediately clasp hands and only have eyes for each other, our smiles never wavering.

"Hi," he says quietly.

"Hi."

"We're about to be married."

I bite on my lip, my cheeks hurting from smiling so wide. "I know."

"I love you so much."

My eyes slide to the officiant as she patiently waits for us to be done. "I love you, too."

"Okay, stop talking so we can become official."

I laugh and he gives me a wink. Together, we squeeze each other's hands three times and shortly after, become husbands.

Epilogue

PART TWO

JARROD

We've been dancing and partying for the last three hours, enjoying time with our family and friends as we celebrate the next chapter in our lives. As I stand near the table with the tropical fruit spread, biting into a piece of cantaloupe, I watch Devin dance with my sister on the makeshift dance floor we had set up on the beach.

"You look happy over here," Cory says, snatching a strawberry from the table.

"I am. I can't believe I got so lucky. Look at him."

Cory smiles. "It's good that your family loves him, too."

Connor and CeCe run up to my sister, and Devin reaches down to pick CeCe up and puts her on his hip as he spins around. She squeals with delight as Gina does the same with Connor.

My mom and dad dance nearby, watching the same scene with a smile on their faces. Devin's parents stand off to the side with their arms around each other, having their own romantic moment under the warm string lights.

The song switches to something upbeat that gets several partially drunk NHL players to the dance floor. Cory rushes in to join the line dance, and though it looks like a mess for the first thirty seconds, everyone is laughing and having a good time. That's really all that matters.

Devin makes his way to his parents, who he speaks with for a few seconds, before they embrace. As I chew on another piece of fruit, I watch my new in-laws come toward me.

"We're gonna turn in for the night," Sofia says with a smile. "We're so happy for you two. I'm glad he found you. You've been so good to him."

I give her a hug. "His happiness is all that I want."

When we part, she gives me a nod, a hint of sadness in her eyes. I know they struggled for a long time, and while they should've only been concerned with his happiness, they cared more about their reputation and their own dreams for him. I know now they've realized their mistakes, but that kind of pain lingers. I'm just glad we're all able to try to start over.

I shake his dad's hand. "I really appreciate you guys coming out here."

"Of course," William says with a nod. "We hope to see you for Christmas."

I smile. "We'll be there."

They disappear into the night, making their way to their bungalow, and I latch eyes with Devin across the dance floor.

With a signal to the DJ, I make my way toward my husband, interlocking my fingers with his and pulling him away from our guests.

"Hey, husband," he says with a flirty smile.

"Hello, beautiful."

"Where are you taking me?"

"I just want a moment alone with the love of my life."

He rests his head on my shoulder as we walk through the sand. I'm sure to stop close enough to the dance floor so we can hear the music, but far away enough that we have some privacy.

I face him, wrapping my arms around his waist as he locks his wrists behind my neck.

"Thank you for marrying me today."

Devin's lips curl into a smile. "Anytime, handsome." He kisses me, his hand on the side of my neck. "Life with you is going to be incredible. I can't wait to find out what all we do and experience."

Etta James' "At Last" starts playing on the speakers and we sway to the music.

"I love you so much, Devin. I'm beyond grateful for everything you brought into my life."

He moves in closer, resting his head on my shoulder, his lips touching my neck when he says, "I love you, Jarrod. More than I'll ever be able to fully express. You're my dream come true."

We fall into silence, our bodies moving to the music, and I softly sing the last couple of lines of the song to him.

He is mine. At last.

ACKNOWLEDGMENTS

Well, you made it to the end, and for that, I'm grateful! Thank you, dear reader, for taking a chance on this book. I hope you enjoyed it, and if so, I'd love if you'd leave an honest review.

As mentioned before, I enjoyed writing this book so much. It was easy and fun, and felt right from the very beginning. It's not always like that, but this book was a dream for me. I fell in love and I fell fast.

Huge thanks to my husband, WS Greer, for being my sounding board, listening ear, first editor, and all around favorite person. I wouldn't want to do this without you. I love you so much and I'm so grateful for everything you do.

I have to thank two cover designers this time. The original, black and blue diamond cover was designed by Kerry Heavens, and the beach cover was designed by Robin Harper—my go-to designer who never fails to impress me. Thank you, ladies!

Thank you to Tori Ellis, my editor, for helping me polish this baby up! I appreciate your work so much.

Jasmine, my PA—thank you for all your work! Sorry I'm a mess who doesn't like to have messenger notifications on. You make my life a bit easier and I'm grateful.

To my beta readers, Lauren, Heather, and Melissa, I'm so

appreciative of your help and opinions. The story is better because of you.

Massive thanks to The Author Agency for working with me this time around. I'm so pleased with your hard work and dedication. Thank you so much!

I can't end this without thanking all the authors in this shared world. I've really enjoyed gaining friendships, and getting to know you all a little more. Thank you for everything during this process. I've learned so much. I'm here for you anytime you need anything.

Readers and influencers, I can't thank you all enough for the time you take to read, review, make edits, post images, create videos, and so much more. You're the real heroes!

If you want an extra scene from Devin and Jarrod, as well as some NSFW art work, plus other extras and exclusives, please consider subscribing to my joint Patreon with my husband. You can find us at http://patreon.com/TheAuthorCouple

Until next time.

ABOUT THE AUTHOR

Isabel Lucero is a bestselling author, finding joy in giving readers books for every mood.

Though born in a small town in New Mexico, Isabel currently lives in Delaware with her family. When not completely lost in the world of her next WIP, she can be found reading, or in the nearest Target buying things she doesn't need.

Isabel loves connecting with her readers and fans of books in general. You can find her on Facebook, Patreon, Instagram, and TikTok

ALSO BY ISABEL LUCERO

WAR

Resurrecting Phoenix

Think Again

Darkness Within

Dysfunctional

The Prince of Darkness

The Kingston Brothers Series

On the Rocks

Truth or Dare

Against the Rules

Risking it All

South River University Series

Stealing Ronan

Tasting Innocence

Breaking Free

Tempting Him

Made in the USA
Las Vegas, NV
26 April 2024